TRAINS
& BOATS
& PLANES

Killen McNeill was born in 1953 in Co. Derry, Northern Ireland. He read German at the University of Ulster and moved to Germany in 1975, where he still lives.

TRAINS
& BOATS
& PLANES

KILLEN MCNEILL

POCKET BOOKS

TownHouse

First published in Great Britain and Ireland by Pocket/TownHouse, 2001
An imprint of Simon & Schuster UK Ltd and TownHouse and
CountryHouse Ltd, Dublin

Simon & Schuster is a Viacom Company

1 3 5 7 9 10 8 6 4 2

Simon & Schuster UK Ltd
Africa House
64–78 Kingsway
London WC2B 6AH

Simon & Schuster Australia
Sydney

TownHouse and CountryHouse Ltd
Trinity House
Charleston Road
Ranelagh
Dublin 6
Ireland

A CIP catalogue record for this book is available from the British Library

ISBN 1-903650-04-6

Typeset by SX Composing DTP, Rayleigh, Essex
Printed and bound in Great Britain by Omnia Books Limited, Glasgow

For Brigitte

"PEOPLE JUST COULDN'T keep their eyes off her. Everywhere we went they'd stop and stare." Harry turns to nod at this and sees Monsieur Bruckmann's face looming unexpectedly close. He's got one of those beards with the hair on the cheeks and upper lip shaved away, and the way his lips bulge when he purses them, as he is doing now, is somehow repellent. Like naked snails copulating.

Harry turns away again. The queue they are in shuffles forward a few steps. Harry isn't quite sure what they are doing in it. Monsieur Bruckmann seems to take it for granted that Harry knows all about the cathedral, and has been doing a voice-over on the guide's explanation with a narrative of his own. As far as Harry can see they're circumventing a pulpit. From all corners of the gloomy Byzantine interior come commentaries in French, German and Italian, and in front of the altar a woman is speaking English through a microphone. It's all a great sea of noise that washes to the recesses of the cathedral and eddies back in booms and sighs.

"It made me feel so proud, do you understand? I was a young man then, of course."

Harry nods with a backward tip of his head without turning round. This is what he's been listening to since Bruckmann picked him up at the airport two hours ago. His tragic love affair with British cars of the sixties and seventies, in particular the unabridged history of his Triumph Spitfire's many breakdowns.

There should be an organisation for them. Like Alcoholics Anonymous.

Harry looks at his watch. Ten past five. If he doesn't get out of here soon the shops will have shut. He breathes deeply.

The people in front of him are reaching into the lattice-work of the stone staircase that leads up the pulpit. Touching something. Encouraging whispers and bantering murmurs come from the swelling throng of those who have broken ranks after completing the ritual and are now watching the others go through it. Maybe it's some kind of holy relic they're touching. Some saint's bones or teeth. Or worse. Like that children's birthday party game they used to play. Brian was a great hand at it. You were blindfolded and led by the hand into the mummy's tomb. "This is the mummy's coffin," Brian would say, and let you feel the table top. "This is his wrapping." The tablecloth. "And this is the mummy's eye," and he'd dab your finger into a mound of jelly. Screams all round. A girl they did it to once fainted on to the birthday cake.

Funny thinking of Brian today. I haven't seen him for thirty years.

"You wouldn't believe the money I paid on pick-up trucks."

Now Harry sees a puppy, carved of stone, peeking out floppy-eared from the side of the staircase. Relieved, he pats its head. You can probably wish for something. To get out of here. To see Marie again. Too late.

"My friends got so used to seeing it standing about broken-down they'd stop and check I was just parking. All I was left with were the photos. A whole album full. If you'd stayed at my place I could have shown you them."

"Next time," says Harry. "If the exchange comes off." *God forbid.*

A man's mobile phone bleeps and he moves away to the exit.

"That reminds me," says Harry, "I promised I'd ring home as soon as I got into the hotel, but then we were in a rush to look at the school. I'd better go."

"You haven't heard about the big end in Bourge-en-Bresse yet."

"No, really," says Harry. "I've got to run. My wife's the worrying type."

Outside Harry affirms that he'll be able to find the way back to the hotel and to the school in the morning, shakes the Frenchman's hand firmly and sets off purposefully across the square in front of the cathedral.

It's bustling with tourists and huge African vendors festooned with belts, bracelets and beads, and with layers of leather hats stacked on their heads. Harry walks on down the slope leading away from the cathedral, zigzagging his way without hesitation through the souvenir stands that jut into the street. Imagining himself pursued by Monsieur Bruckmann's gaze, he passes storks with long dangly red legs and beaks, glasses containing the cathedral, which must snow when you turn them upside down, miniature long-necked bottles of Alsatian wine as key-rings, and prints of Strasbourg by that artist who painted the whole of France in rain.

At the bottom of the street he turns to the right and walks in the direction of his hotel, stopping as soon as the house on the corner has blocked off the view from the cathedral. Twenty past five. Time enough. Marie's shop will still be open. If it's still there.

Right. Now for it. Bash on, crash on, get the job done.

But he hesitates, looking round. He has been certain he'll find the way all right, but there's something wrong here. There should be a real park in front of him. With trees and benches, the yellow leaves from the maple trees scudding dryly along the paths, like in his memory. But not this underground car park squatting in a Tarmac whorl like some huge sea creature in its retreat. Of course they cut the trees down for the car park. Yes, this is the way. Thirty years ago the old man pointed me across the square. "Straight down that street in the middle," he said, "you can't miss it."

Harry is poised on the kerb like a swimmer hesitant to take the plunge. Can he really be going to see Marie again, after all this time?

There's only one way to find out.

He moves forward, walking fast, shoulders hunched against the cold.

He sees the shop from quite a distance away. It's on the right of the square with the smaller church in the middle, just as he remembers it, even down to the lettering "Fischer et fils", gold Gothic script on a black backboard. He slows and comes to a stop just outside the pool of light its window casts on the pavement.

No more easy options. No telling himself he did his best, the shop wasn't there. It's either go in or not. But what will he say? He has put so much thinking into this, he has a whole array of phrases off pat, a different scenario for every conceivable mood, but now he isn't sure what mood he's in. He stands there, getting his breath back, as the sun's last rays slip up the chimney stacks and off into the night, and the square settles into blackness around the orange glow of the street-lamps.

Maybe there's some inspiration, some clue to Marie to be had from the shop. The window display looks exclusive, piles of thickly folded sweaters, pliantly draped ties, and Donegal tweed blazers and costumes on black dummies, set against a background of driftwood and pebbles. It's all indirectly lit from below so that the expensive fibres rise shimmering from the weave in tiny golden forests. The impression is of a beach party of the landed gentry. Harry recognises the message. Too expensive for you and your Marks & Spencer's anorak, that's what it's saying.

Quarter to six.

What will she look like? He has only the vaguest memory of her face, an impression of wide-apart eyes and pronounced cheekbones. There had never been any photographs of that summer.

What if she doesn't recognise me? Doesn't remember me even after I say who I am? The palms of his hands are sweating. He rubs them on his trousers.

Bash on, crash on, and get the job done. He moves to the door and opens it.

Tinkle.

God, two women to choose from.

"Mesdames."

"Monsieur."

A small one with a close, dark, impish haircut and a taller one with long hair standing behind her, looking up from something they've been reading on the counter. Both too young.

"Puis-je vous aider?"

A woman coming from the back of the shop. Blonde, for God's sake. Marie was a brunette. Wasn't she? The eyes are wide apart and they have a sceptical expression as they take in his appearance. Not her usual kind of customer. She clasps her hands together.

"Marie?"

"Nous nous connaissons?"

"Je suis Harry."

It comes out Harree, the way she used to say it, in spite of her excellent English.

"Harry?" She stares at him and makes a little intake of breath. "Harry Moore?"

He smiles. He sees panic rising in her eyes, but doesn't know how to help. All his carefully thought-out phrases are wrong. The only thing he can do is stand here and look like an idiot. It's like the school play when the actors forget their lines and the *souffleuse* has lost the place. Only now Harry is on the stage. He reaches out his hand, and she shakes it slowly. It's all right, is what he's trying to communicate through the palm of his hand and his smile. *Don't be afraid. I don't want anything.*

"Harry, what a surprise."

"Nous pouvons parler français. Je suis professeur de français."

"No, no . . . give me a moment. I haven't spoken English in years. Not since Grandma died." She's using the foreign language as a lifebelt, he sees, gathering herself as she grasps at it.

"Sorry to barge in on you like this." He could apologise for not phoning beforehand, but he knows she knows he couldn't have. This is the only way.

"It's all right."

"I wasn't sure you'd remember me."

"You've changed."

"You haven't."

And then she smiles, and her features shift and click into place. Of course it's her. Those dimples at the side of her mouth. He had completely forgotten them.

"It would be nice to have a chat. I'm here for three days. We could arrange something if it's not convenient now."

She looks at her watch. There's a nice curve to her arm above the wrist. "We close soon . . ." She bites at her lower lip, makes a half-turn, looks back at Harry. "I'll finish now." Her mind made up, she marches briskly to the back of the shop, giving instructions to the two girls about closing up. In charge again.

A shiver runs through Harry's body and he shakes it out with a twitch of his shoulders and a toss of his head. That's the hardest part over.

The girls behind the counter are whispering to each other, casting interested glances his way. He pokes at a row of scarves. Jesus, the prices. You could buy a coat for that at Marks & Spencer's. Marie is taking her time about reappearing. Maybe she's having second thoughts. But here she is, in a red woollen coat and tweed scarf, pushing her hair out at the nape of her neck. She heads straight for the door. Harry opens it for her. "*Salut*," she says to the girls and steps out. He follows her. She goes off to the left in the direction he has come from, and turns to wait as soon as they are out of sight of the shop, her eyes gleaming in the darkness.

Keep the thing nice and casual, breathe slowly.

"What are you doing in Strasbourg, Harry?"

"I'm staying here for a couple of days. I'm a French teacher and I'm trying to get a school exchange organised with a *lycée* here."

"How long have you been here?"

"My plane got in early this afternoon." No sense in saying that he'd dashed straight out. "I was looking at the shops and then I thought I might as well try and find yours. I never thought it would actually be there." He gives a little laugh.

"You gave me a shock."

"Sorry."

She's watching him closely, appraisingly. Worried, even. Maybe she thinks she has to invite him into her house.

"Is there somewhere we can go for a cup of coffee? Some café, or restaurant?"

"Good idea."

They walk on side by side.

"A French teacher," she says. "Fancy that."

"Yeah, considering my French used to be so bad. Second worst in my class. Now I'm head of department at my old school. My old teacher nearly had a fit when I applied."

"Do you often come to France?"

"Yes. Mostly to the Loire and Périgord, though. This is the first time I've been to Strasbourg. Since then."

"Ah, yes."

"It was funny. It has seemed like a dream for years, but then when I came to your shop and saw it it seemed like yesterday."

She nods.

"We were very young," says Harry.

"Children."

They walk on for a bit in silence.

"Do you still live in that village?" says Harry, as if its name hadn't been burned into his mind.

"Obernai. No, I have a flat in Strasbourg now. With my daughter."

"Oh."

"I don't really know the restaurants around here," Marie says. "My daughter and I seldom go out. But I think we can go in here." They are back at the square Harry crossed before, approaching a well-lit restaurant called Zum Stadtwappe and, under that, Aux Armes de Strasbourg, in the Alsatian way.

Inside he helps her out of her coat at the coat-stand. Her hair feels silky. It's dyed, of course. Or do you say coloured? He follows her to a place by the window, thinking about what she's said. A daughter. But no mention of a husband. Divorced, with any luck.

The waiter brings them the menu and they study it. Harry holds his up a bit so he can look at her over the top. She obviously takes good care of herself. Not too thin either, like a lot of women think they have to be when they get on a bit. What age will she be? Forty-six. A year younger than him. Well made-up. Nice, the way the dark eyebrows contrast with the blonde hair. She looks up, catches him watching her and looks back at her menu.

When the waiter comes she orders a glass of Silvaner and Harry does the same. Then she lifts her handbag from the back of her chair on to her lap, opens it and rummages inside, her elbows pushing at the air. Some women pick at their handbags with small jerks, like birds at a worm, but there's something pleasing about Marie's movements, something unselfconscious and generous.

Harry remembers the first time he saw her with a handbag. It was in the hospital in Letterkenny that day she came to see him. The last time before she left Ireland. The last time he had seen her, in fact, until today.

She offers him a cigarette from the packet she's taken from her handbag.

"No, thanks."

"Didn't you used to?"

"We all did. But I've never smoked since then."

"Oh." She lights up.

Their wine arrives. They clink their glasses.

"I can't believe I'm sitting here with you," Harry says. "I've imagined it so many times. Do you know the last time we saw each other was thirty years ago? In the hospital in Letterkenny? You left for the ferry with your parents straight after that."

"It was a horrible journey."

Harry nods. Why was it horrible? Because you were missing me?

"I hitch-hiked all the way through France to see you that autumn," he says. "Do you remember?"

She is giving her wine-glass small twists, to and fro. "I'd rather not talk about that time, if you don't mind," she says, not looking at him.

"But it's all so long ago. Surely it's all water under the bridge now."

"Still."

This throws Harry off. What should they talk about, if not that summer? That is what he wants to know, what she thinks about it all. Whether it was true what his later calculations had worked out, that they'd only been together for four weeks. Whether it had seemed like ages to her, too.

Whether she'd really loved him.

But he's been too eager, too pressing. He'll have to take it slower.

"All right," he says. "Tell me about yourself."

"What do you want to hear?"

That you never loved anybody else after me, that you never forgot me.

"Are you married?" he asks.

"Divorced."

"How old is your daughter?"

"Eighteen."

"Is there a boyfriend?"

"Not that I know of."

"I mean you. If you don't mind my asking."

"No. Annie has a way of putting off any suitors. She and her father are very close, he has her at weekends and so on. What about you? How long have you been married?"

"Let me see. I went to university in Canterbury in 1969, met Jenny in my last year. That was 1973, we married when she finished five years later. 1978. Twenty years ago." Whoops. That sounds like a missed celebration. What is twenty anyway? Surely not one of the important ones.

"Happily married?"

"I'd say so, yes. As happy as people are. You know. We have our ups and downs, of course." Harry wonders whether to tell Marie about Helen. Would she think more of him, or less?

"What made you become a teacher?"

"Inertia. It's what happens to you in Britain if you never get off the educational conveyor-belt."

"And why French?"

Can't you guess? All those letters I wrote to you in French and you never got. Did your parents ever give them to you? What did you make of them? "A process of elimination," he says. "Did you go straight into the shop after finishing school? I mean, you didn't study or anything?"

She sips at her wine and inhales deeply from her cigarette without answering. Maybe he's hit on a sore point. "Mind you, a university education isn't all it's cracked up to be," he goes on. "If you'd seen some of the idiots I studied with. If you'd seen me."

"No, I didn't study," she says at length. "Is your wife a teacher too?"

"Yes, at the local girls' school." With Helen, worse luck.

"Any children?"

"No."

"Didn't you want any?"

"No."

"Maybe you're right. Children can be very wearing. You always think they'll be over the worst in a couple of years, but they never are. The problems only change. No sleep at nights, illnesses, school, puberty, unsuitable friends, boyfriends, sex, jobs. I think nobody under twenty-five really knows what they want."

Harry nods. *I knew what I wanted all right. You.*

"Did you see the display in my window? What did you think of it?"

"Great."

"Annie did it. She's really talented at creating fashion, too. And at prices people can afford. I've already made some of her designs, and people have actually bought them, and can wear them here in Strasbourg without getting arrested by the police. Art provokes, the critics say, I don't know whether that's true or not, but I do know that if something provokes that doesn't automatically make it art, like some of these crazy new British couturiers seem to think." Marie has come alive, rolling her eyes at the ceiling over people's craziness, gesturing in the air palms upwards, frowning, shaking her head, smiling ruefully. A passionate woman in the prime of her life. What is she like in bed? Harry wonders. Different from then, whatever that was like. He can't really remember, apart from an image of kissing her closed eyes.

"Annie's not like that. She's got her head . . ."

"Well screwed on."

"Exactly. It would be great if she'd come into the business, but I have to be very careful about how I approach her. When I try to praise her she thinks it's only her silly mother who loves her."

"I'm sure she loves you too," Harry says, and clears his throat.

"She's stubborn and independent, it must be her great grand-mother's blood."

"Did she know your grandmother?"

"Not really. Grandma died when Annie was only two. She doesn't remember her at all. Just as well, because Grandma spent her last years in a constant bad temper. She just couldn't bear not being in charge of things."

Served her right, the interfering old bitch. He sees the old woman's trembling chin, the white bristles twitching on it, her eyes wide open in panic and rage as he struggled to stop her wheelchair from keeling over and spilling her out on to the floor, her mouth working so close he can feel her spittle on his cheek.

Marie moves her hands under the table. She's looking at her watch. *Oh, God.* Their glasses are almost half empty, just above the widest bulge, the point after which the level starts to fall faster and faster, and you notice the ugly smudge marks.

Half an hour? A quarter?

"Do you have to go?" he asks.

"I'll just give Annie a ring." Marie pushes the chair back and leaves the table.

Harry looks out past the space she's left to the window. The reflection of the restaurant's interior is superimposed on the scene outside; the cosy inside, the chequered tablecloths, the students' tables with their clouds of smoke, the workmen in their blue overalls, the single man at the table in the middle mixing egg yoke into his raw mincemeat with absolute concentration, as if looking for augurs, the yellow walls and the old enamel beer signs; all floating above the square. A fog has come up, tinged orange by the street-lamps, fudging the outlines of the statues and the lanterns.

It'll be even colder outside now.

He can see his own reflection too. He lifts his head to stretch his double chin. Van the Man, the pupils call him, referring to his similarity to Van Morrison. In looks, not talent.

What will he do if Marie goes now? Will she want to see him again before he leaves? Or will it be an exchange of addresses and vague promises?

He sees her coming back in the window. She's weaving her way through the tables, nodding thanks to the people who pull in their chairs. The solitary eater looks up from his plate as she passes, and follows her legs and behind with his eyes.

Eat your heart out, she's with me.

She is smiling at Harry from the window.

"It's all right," she says, as she slips in behind the table. "Annie's going out for the evening anyway. Why don't we have something to eat? I'm ravenous."

"Surely you could have found an exchange school in some more convenient part of France? Somewhere closer?"

That was exactly what Harry's headmaster had said too. Repeatedly. The wee fart.

"Nowhere's close to Northern Ireland," he says. "The flight's only twenty minutes longer than to Paris. And besides, these exchanges depend on the depth of involvement of the people concerned at both ends. My French colleague and I get on very well together. That's what counts."

"I suppose you're staying with him?"

"Well, no, actually. I've got a room in a small hotel. But he met me at the airport. I like to keep my freedom of movement," Harry says, and sips at his glass. Pinot noir, his reprieve. Almost run out again.

They've had a delicious meal, small liver dumplings on salad, trout fried in almonds, and Munster cheese with caraway seeds to finish. Marie has talked about her business, about how well it's going, and Harry has told her about meeting Monsieur Bruckmann and his long-suffering wife in the Périgord when he was on holiday with Jenny two years ago, about the plans for the exchange, and how his hopes for promotion hinge on them. He hasn't told her what a pain in the arse Bruckmann is, nor that his only saving grace is living in Strasbourg.

"What are you doing tomorrow?" Marie asks.

"I have to sit in on some English lessons in the morning. But I'm free in the afternoon. In the evening too, for that matter."

The evening invitation to the Bruckmanns' can soon be got out of.

"What would you say to a drive in the country? I could show you the mountains and the vineyards. What do you think?"

"Great." Harry grins, then sees his nutcracker impression in the window and tries to fight it down, but Marie is smiling too. Her hand is curled around the stem of her glass. He'd love to reach across and cup it. Maybe she sees that in his eyes, because she's shaking her head slightly at him, but still smiling, as though she's seen through his game.

"Marie." Harry leans forward. He sees the sudden anxiety in her eyes but he goes on. "Couldn't we talk about what happened? It's so long ago. And it was nobody's fault. Nobody was to blame."

She's looking through her handbag again. "Maybe," she says. "Where will we meet? I'd better go now."

They arrange to meet at the Place Kléber at four o'clock. Marie calls the waiter over.

"Let me get this," Harry says.

"It's out of the question. You are my guest." While she's checking the bill she says, without looking up, "Do you ever see that other boy, man, I suppose, what was his name?"

Harry can feel his heart stumble, and then race on like a hurdler. Brian. She must mean Brian. "Brian?"

"Yes. Do you ever see him?"

"No. The last I heard of him he was a real-estate broker."

"Ah, yes, that sounds like him all right. And what about Marjorie?"

"She's living in England. She married a minister, would you believe, and now she's got lots of children."

"Surely not that one . . ."

"God, no."

Harry waits to hear what she says next, but she seems to concentrate on finishing her cigarette. He doesn't speak either, not wanting to change the subject, but afraid of making the next move himself.

Then she's putting out the cigarette, and they're getting up to go. He follows her out through the restaurant, seeing the men's looks lingering on her, watching her hair bounce at the nape of her neck. He helps her into her coat. He can smell her musty-sweet perfume and feel her shoulders move beneath his hands.

She waits for him outside. "See you tomorrow, Harry," she says.

"Shouldn't I walk you home?"

"There's no need. It's perfectly safe."

Her face is turned up to him. He bends towards her left cheek. He can see the tiny folds at the corner of her mouth. Right cheek. Her mouth is slightly open. What would she do if he kissed it? Left cheek again. He stays there for an instant, feeling the coolness of her skin against his. Then he straightens up.

"Goodnight, Marie."

"Goodnight, Harry."

She is off, tossing back her hair, footsteps clacking down the street.

He remembers seeing her figure like this many times before, a long time ago, for years after that summer in 1968, moving away from him, slipping into a shop or on to a bus. He used to run after her. It was always somebody else.

"Marie!" he calls. She stops and turns back.

"Did you ever go back to Ireland?"

"Never." She stands looking back for a minute, then waves and disappears round a corner.

★

Harry walks back through the quiet streets. He can feel the cool night air washing round the edges of the big grin on his face, but he doesn't care. If he'd known how easy it would be to see Marie again he'd have done it years ago, he thinks. All that unnecessary worry and her such a fine, capable woman.

He wonders if there's any chance of sleeping with her while he's here. Her daughter might be a problem. Maybe Marie would stay overnight in his hotel room.

And suddenly he's thinking of the Secret Strand, and laughing to himself, so that a startled couple give him a wide berth. He and Marie found it one day that summer in Donegal. They were out on the bikes one morning on Horn Head when, instead of going on up the road to the mossy heights above the Horn, they turned left down an untarred lane towards the lower, more arable end. It wound over Horn Head's back towards its far side, tenuously connecting a few scattered farmhouses, and after a while it became rutted and overgrown, and they had to push their bikes. It petered out finally at a deserted farmhouse, whose door hung open on one hinge to ankle-deep mud throughout. There was a field of thistles behind it sloping down to a belt of rocks and the heaving sea, and out in the Atlantic lay the flat dagger of Tory Island. They propped their bikes against the farmhouse, climbed over a wobbly stile, crossed the field to picnic on the rocks, and then they came upon the beach by accident, a perfect half-moon of sand enclosed by a circle of rocks with only one channel through the rocks to the sea, hidden from the mainland by two dunes with a sandy path between them, invisible unless you were almost upon it. Perhaps only the farmer knew of its existence, and he'd abandoned his old abode to the cows. There wasn't a soul in sight. They could have been the last people in the world. That was where they made love for the first time, and afterwards walked out through the channel to watch the sea gather itself for the change of tide. Then Tory Island had disappeared in a veil of grey, and they saw the curtain of rain approach them across Tory Sound like the Spirit moving on the face of the waters.

"Christ, we're in for a soaking," Harry said, as a blustery wind came up, and they started back, Marie struggling to put up her umbrella in the gusts of wind until it was blown inside out. The rain, driving in from the sea, pelted their backs until they were soaked through, and then it moved on landwards towards Muckish.

By the time they reached Dunbreaghy on the bikes they had dried out again. They wanted to go back to the Secret Strand another day, but they never did. About a year later Harry started to dream about coming upon it suddenly, always in the most unlikely places, down a dismal back entry in Kilmartin, or behind some huge industrial complex like the oil refineries near Londonderry, and each time he came upon it in his dream a part of him was surprised and a part of him had known it was there all the time, waiting just round the corner. The first years Harry woke up with a feeling of desolation; as he dreamed it less and less he learned to make it into a happy dream and he would wake up with a feeling of content at the continuing possibility of the place.

He hasn't had the dream in years; remembering it now seems a good omen. He takes his time, stopping to look at the shops and restaurants he rushed past this afternoon, no longer feeling the cold. A restaurant by the name of Zuem hailiche Graab. The holy grave indeed. Very cheerful. Should have a roll-away stone for a door. Something stirs in a corner of his memory, just out of perception, the ripples in a pond after a fish has jumped. Has he been in this place before?

A window of Alsatian delicacies. Marzipan walnuts, chestnuts, snails. *Tartes de fruits* like still-life paintings. *Filets de porc du pruneaux*, roulades filled with mushrooms, parsley, herbs, eggs and cream. It's always the same. You think we're catching up at home, what with everybody turning out the quiches Lorraines and *boeuf bourguignons* as if their mothers had never cooked anything else, and the hotel tables set as if they'd never seen an upturned teacup. But there's no catching up with the French, they're always ahead, it's like with age.

Look at that. Five different kinds of *foie gras de Strasbourg*.

But none for Jenny, thank you. The poor geese, getting those spoons stuck down their throats, perverse.

And what about the poor hens? The poor pigs?

Another fight.

She'd been very quiet all the way to the airport this morning. Waiting for him to ask what was wrong, as usual. But Harry hadn't. Why should he always be the one?

In his cramped, overheated room he sits on the bed, studying the instructions for telephoning on the yellowed card. When he gets through he hears his telephone beeping in its niche under the stairs, jangling out across the old coloured tiles. High time he did some redecorating at home. Jenny will be getting up, switching off the TV. Unless she's out. When had he said he'd ring? When are her painting classes? Seem to vary a lot lately.

"Hello." As always her English accent is more pronounced on the phone.

"It's me."

"I thought you were going to ring this afternoon. I've been waiting all day."

There's a familiar wound-up something in her voice. Harry can almost see the set of her jaw. He goes on the alert. One of their sparring sessions is in the offing.

"I've been on the go since I got in. Run off my feet. Why, is there anything wrong?"

"You know I hate waiting."

"Nobody said you had to wait. I'd have got you in some time. And the flight was fine, thank you."

Silence.

"What's the matter?"

Silence. Then: "I'm so sick of it. You're all the same."

All? "Who all?"

"Nothing."

"I'll ring back when you're in a better temper. We can fight when I get back home, it's cheaper."

Silence. Harry is about to put down the phone when he hears a whispered aside. "Is somebody there?"

"Only William."

Who the fuck is William? "Baldy Willie? What's he want?" Baldy Willie McNutt is Harry's headmaster, detested by the whole staff for his unaccountably bloated self-esteem and two-faced manoeuvrings. It has taken a considerable effort on Harry's part to get over his aversion to the smug wee toad to push the exchange thing through.

"Nothing," said Jenny. A simmering at the back of her voice, like a pressure cooker.

"Why doesn't he go home and do nothing?"

"Ask him yourself." All kinds of hisses and rumbles. Jenny comes back again. "Apparently he doesn't want to speak to you. In fact he's completely disinclined." There is a yelp that could be a laugh or a scream.

"What's going on?"

"Nothing much. Only we've been having an affair and I've just finished it. This very minute. Because the little shit says he can't leave his wife yet. And he's been saying that for a year. And now I've had enough. Isn't that a fair summary, William? Whoops, there he goes. *That's right, run away home to your wife. Where did you tell her you were going this time, you bastard? The Masonic Lodge? A meeting of church elders? Get away out of my sight!"*

"Jenny?"

There is a great outflux of air from her nostrils that washes into the mouthpiece like a far-off sea.

"Is this all still because of Helen?" he asks.

"He's gone."

"I thought we'd got over that."

Another breaking wave of air.

"I know I haven't been very attentive lately . . ."

"It is not always because of things you do or do not do, Harry Moore." She is enunciating every word as if she's reading a difficult text, or drunk. "It is because of me this time."

"I never noticed a thing."

"No, well, that doesn't surprise me. You're not one of the world's greatest noticers."

"Why him?"

"I don't know. Love, or passion, or something."

Harry sucks in air between his teeth. "*With that wee bald sweaty fart? They were serving things in sauerkraut tonight that looked like him. Passion, for fuck's sake.*" There is a thump at the wall, right in front of Harry's face. He has got to his feet at some time during this exchange. He thumps the wall back. A purr spills out from the handset, and seems to fill the whole room. He dials again and listens to the beeps, willing Jenny to lift the phone. She must be standing right beside it. He dials again. Engaged.

Harry flops down on the bed and reads the telephone instructions again. He dials.

"Enquêtes internationales?"

"Je voudrais bien un numéro en L'Irlande du Nord."

"Quelle nom?"

Harry spells it and the number comes through in a computerised voice. He dials.

"McNutt." A woman's voice.

"This is Harry Moore, Mrs McNutt. I'm ringing from Strasbourg."

"Oh, Mr Moore, how nice of you to call, yes, indeed, how are things going? We were talking about you earlier on. How was the flight?" Her voice has that pressed quality that comes from having to come through a mouth that has been cranked up into a great big false smile. Doubtless her nose is crinkled too.

"This isn't the time to exchange pleasantries, Mrs McNutt. Your husband is having an affair with my wife."

"Pardon?" Harry can imagine her smile melting, like one of Dali's clocks.

"Your husband is having an affair with my wife."

"This is Ballyraine 40276."

"*And this is Harry Moore ringing from Strasbourg where your husband, William McNutt, otherwise known as Baldy Willie, has induced me to go, ostensibly to organise a school exchange but in fact so that he can get into* my *bed with* my *wife.*"

The handset is purring in his ear again.

1 Northern Ireland, 1968

LAST DAY OF school before the summer holidays: last journey
home on the bus; bedlam unleashed; hysteria unbound,
schoolbags, caps, scarves and hats flying up and down the aisle.
The screams of provoked girls, the whinnies and croaks of
pubescent boys; a mêlée of pulling, punching, wrenching,
throwing, catching dervishes. And in the eye of the hurricane on
the sideways-facing seats at the back of the bus ignoring the
mayhem around them, sits aloof Mildred Hazlitt and opposite
her the still, slouched figure of Harry Moore, head tilted
backwards, to all appearances asleep. Through the slits of his eyes
he's ogling the whites of Mildred's crossed thighs above her
black uniform stockings as her skirt sways to the motion of the
bus. Sitting as she is on the left side, her right leg crossed over
the left, she sways to the right and her skirt moulds to her thigh
when the bus accelerates, but when it brakes she leans to the left,
her skirt billows out, and a tantalising triangle of white above her
stockings comes into view.

Harry pretending to be asleep, Mildred pretending not to
notice him ogling; everybody happy.

And then the bus brakes sharply. A clutch of boys who have
been scuffling in the aisle fall in a heap and Mildred, with a tiny
shriek, grabs the stanchion beside her seat and sticks out her legs
for support. Safely jammed in between two big-boned farmers'

sons Harry forgets his sleeping guise and gapes wide-eyed up her skirt.

"Seen enough?" she hisses at him, tugging furiously at her skirt, then, "I know the type. All eyes and no hands." Harry tries frantically not to care but the prickling in his cheeks turns into a burning that rapidly spreads over his face, his whole head, even his scalp and the tops of his ears. Within seconds he has the familiar feeling of radiating heat all around him. A one-eyed squint down his nose confirms his impression of inhabiting a beetroot. And that fat fucker Big Archy is swaying his way across to Harry, rubbing his hands together in front of Harry's face, as if it was a brazier in winter, then putting on his sunglasses.

"Jesus, boys, that would blind ye. The fuckin' Red Army." The whole bus in stitches.

The Red Army. Ha-ha-ha. Harry's face, hovering between two silvery patches in the old mirror above the chest of drawers in his bedroom, looks back at him with the surprised expression of the early Irish saint in his history book. It's the way his eyes slant upwards to the bridge of his nose. And his open mouth. He shuts it. Come out and show yourself, I know you're in there somewhere.

From the fair hill outside comes a sudden, panicky clatter of hoofs on wood, moos, a burst of farmers' shouts and the lashes of their sticks. Cows being loaded on to lorries. It's the fair day in Kilmartin.

The back door opens downstairs and his mother shouts: "Full shop!"

Fuck. He mouths the word to his reflection. It's starting all over again. First day of the holidays and not a moment's peace. He trudges downstairs and out of the back door, crosses the yard, unlatches the door to the shop store, and goes in, blinking to adjust to the darkness. His parents are saving electricity again and the lights are off, casting the shop in gloom. It's the display of cornflake boxes, too, the window's too small for it, Harry said they should use Heinz beans tins but they didn't listen to him. As per usual.

He switches on the lights as he comes out of the store and four heads turns to him. His mother's fresh perm, beyond that a blue rinse, a battered tweed hat, and a cloth cap swathed in cigarette smoke. Full shop indeed. It's only that old twit Wallace, under the tweed hat, holding everything up.

"Where's Dad?" he asks.

"He had to go out," his mother says. That means he's up the street, talking to a crony. He always does that when their holidays in Donegal draw near, just to keep Harry and his mother on their toes. Just because he can't get away for the whole six weeks, like them.

"Would you finish Mr Wallace's order, Harry?" his mother says, and flashes a big smile at him. She's in that mood she gets in before Donegal. It makes her look younger, even good-looking. Guileless, and eager, like the young, broad-cheeked farming girl on her old photographs. Gullible was what his father said. So how come we always end up doing what she wants?

"A quartah pound of ham," old Wallace says. Jesus, that English accent. And him born and bred in Kilmartin. Harry fetches the string-tied roll from the cool room, careful not to let in any bluebottles. They buzz about in there, waiting for the ham to come back so they can lay their eggs in the little ledges between the whorls. You end up guillotining maggots if you don't watch out.

The slices from the machine crumple on to the butter paper.

"Five ounces all right, Mr Wallace?"

"Yes, yes."

"Anything else, Mr Wallace?"

Mr Wallace shuffles up to the counter, groping in the depths of his raincoat. "The magazines," he says, laying a pile of curving periodicals on the counter, with a sidelong glance at Mrs Moore.

"Thank you very much, Mr Wallace, very kind of you," says Harry's mother, flashing him the same smile she gave Harry. Mr Wallace brings these magazines every month – *The Field*, *Town and Country* and *Tatler*. He's a relative of the Coopers, the owners of the local linen mill, who live out the road in the big manor house. The nearest thing to quality Kilmartin has. They speak with great English accents and send their children to boarding-schools across the water. But why the old man sees in his mother a kindred soul who would read his English magazines is a mystery to Harry. She isn't from Kilmartin, that's true, but she isn't from England either. She throws the magazines away unread.

"That's eleven and fourpence, Mr Wallace," says Harry, finishing the sum his mother has started.

The old man fixes Harry with his watery yellow eyes. He leans across the counter. Harry knows what's coming.

"My discount." His moustache bristles, flecked with snuff. "Doctor's son." His father has been dead for twenty years. And left him with a pile of money.

"I've already deducted it, Mr Wallace," Harry lies. "Ten per cent."

Mr Wallace nods and fishes out an ancient, bulging wallet that looks like a dead rat from his raincoat pocket. He starts to count the coins on to the counter.

"How is Liam?" Harry's mother asks Mrs McCloskey, the owner of the blue rinse. She's their Catholic neighbour from across the street.

"Och, och," says Mrs McCloskey, putting the things in her

basket. "He's writing away at his whaddyyecallit, his PhD, but would he lift a finger to write to his own mother?" She shakes her head.

"What'll that make of him, now?" Harry's mother asks.

"A doctor. Of philosophy."

"He'll hardly be coming back to Kilmartin with that."

"He will not, the same boy."

"Fancy that, now. Dr McCloskey. We'll have to be thinking about sending Harry to university soon, too. It would be great if he could go on and study. The first in the family. Isn't that right, Harry?" Harry grunts, pretending to be engrossed in Mr Wallace's mounting pile of coins. Any minute now she'll start on about how nice it would be to have somebody in the family going on for the ministry. He'll look a right fool if he's made a ballocks of his O levels. It's the euphoria about going to Donegal. It always gets his mother like this.

"Mind where you send him, Mrs Moore. I always said Queen's was as good a place as any. But he wouldn't listen. No place here was good enough for his lordship. The last thing we heard was he's coming home for Christmas, unless something better comes up. His words."

Mrs McCloskey and Mr Wallace leave the shop at the same time. The farmer takes a last drag from his cigarette, the butt so short in his big paw that it looks like he's whistling. Then he drops it on the floorboards and screws it out with a hobnailed boot.

A car horn parps out in the street. A black Rover has drawn up and the driver's window is being lowered. Harry's mother primps her hair. "It's Mrs Cooper. I'll get it."

"Why can't she come into the shop like everybody else?"

But she's already bustling out of the door. Good humour for the world and its wife today. Harry serves the farmer with a fresh packet of Gallaher's Greens. His mother reappears. "Here's Mrs Cooper's order. Make it up like a good boy."

A good boy, indeed. Harry slouches about the shop, fetching the things on the list headed "William Cooper & Sons Linen Merchants" – water biscuits, a corner of Kraft cheese spread, a tin of pears and half a dozen red apples. Hardly worth the bother.

His mother is out on the street again, talking in through the car window to Mrs Cooper. Every Friday afternoon Mrs Cooper sweeps into Kilmartin and makes her honking progress up the town's one long street, summoning shopkeepers out to her Rover, its engine running. Moore's is the first stop, then McVicker's the butcher, McAtamney's hardware, then Quigg's, another grocery, and Burnside's newspaper shop. Spreading her custom around, she calls it. Thin as the butter at the Church of Ireland socials, Harry's dad says.

Putting half a dozen apples in a brown bag Harry sees a shadow fall across the shop window. He looks up from his crouch and sees the fat figure of Big Archy looking in at him over the cornflake boxes. Archy, with his back to Harry's mother, tugs the golden top of a packet of Benson & Hedges out of his trousers and jerks his head conspiratorially down the street towards the Orange Hall where they sometimes go for fags. Harry shakes his head, pointing to the apples, then revolves it to include the whole shop. Big Archy grins and gives him his gunslinger's version of the fingers, that slight contraction of the upper digits from hip level, more hinted at than performed. It makes you feel you aren't worth the bother of the full fingers. Upper lip curved in a sneer, Big Archy continues his way in the rolling slouch he's copied from John Wayne. *Fucker.*

With worsened temper Harry carries out the cardboard box, with the purchases shifting about its bottom, to Mrs Cooper's car, where his mother is still standing, talking in through the window. Not wishing to interrupt the conversation he waits, looking up the street. The town has that muddled, fair day look about it. Groups of farmers stand about, chatting, their big, battered cars parked two deep, sideways, anywhere.

His mother is framing the window of Mrs Cooper's Rover with her hands, head almost inside. At teatime she'll be all full of how nice and just like the rest of them Mrs Cooper is.

"And we're off to Donegal tomorrow. For six whole weeks," his mother is saying. Harry sees the fake eyebrows stencilled above the real, shaved ones rise in annoyance on Mrs Cooper's white powdered brow and her fingers tap the steering-wheel. Doesn't his mother notice?

"I'll just put the groceries in the back," Harry says, hoping his intrusion will put an end to the scene. But his mother goes on talking as he sets the box on the soft, dark leather of the back seat.

"We take a house up above the harbour," she's saying, "with my sister Flo and her husband Alec from Ballymena. We grew up near there, Flo and I, in Ardbane, the family home. It had belonged to my father's family, the Hutchinsons, for three hundred years."

Mrs Cooper fetches out her hand mirror and inspects her makeup with pursed lips and eyebrows still raised. Then she says, "Yes, well, it won't quite be Mallorca, will it, dear?" and puts the car into gear. Mumbling farewells Mrs Moore withdraws from the window. As she stands up Harry turns away so she won't think he's seen her hurt, blushing face.

Oh, God, at her age, does it never end?

After locking up the shop they have a quick salad for tea. They eat in silence in the small kitchen because Harry's mother, who normally tries to get a conversation going, is sunk in thought, looking out vacantly at the small patch of earth under the shadow of the backyard wall where the flowers she tried to grow in spring are slowly withering. Harry's dad, a small, red-faced man, is sitting at the head of the kitchen table, staring into space. He clears his throat. "Had a look round Stewart's today," he says.

Harry pricks up his ears.

"Oh, yes?" says his mother.

"Said he might have something coming in for us."

"New?" Harry asks, although he knows the answer.

"New to us. A year old."

"A Corsair?"

His dad shakes his head dismissively. "A sensible car." His brother, Harry's uncle Alec, has a Corsair.

Please, God, not an Anglia.

"A Cortina," says Mr Moore.

Could be worse.

"What do you say, Eileen?" his dad asks.

"I'm sure it's very nice."

"We've been taking the A45 up for nine years now. It's time we had a change."

A thought strikes Harry. "They have bucket seats, don't they?" he asks.

"What about it?"

"Oh, nothing. You were talking about buying a Vauxhall Victor, that's all. I thought you said it was the better car."

His mother is eyeing him strangely. He puts on his most vacuous face and hums into the cup of tea he's holding, not looking at her. He'll be getting his driving-licence next year. A Vauxhall Victor has a bench front seat and the gear-stick on the steering-column. Ideal for courting.

"Aye," says his father, "but you have to take what you get."

★

Harry's in his room again, finishing his packing. On his bed is a big cardboard banana-box from the shop on which he has marked "HARRY" with a thick felt-tip. In the box are his scratchy striped hipsters and the wide plastic belt he wears with them, the black polo-neck sweater, the black blazer for Sundays, the blue-and-red striped blazer from his crap school, Ballyraine Academy for Boys, the grey flannels, the grey and white school shirts, his best blue one, two V-necked pullovers, orange cords, the desert boots for wearing with the hipsters, the black school shoes, the brown ones for Sundays. The sandals. The wellington boots, one tucked into the other. Assorted socks and underpants, inside trousers, his mother calls them. A striped tie for Sundays, the psychedelic one for the hooleys.

On top of the clothes are the other things. Rubber Pirelli diving-mask, table-tennis bat, orange nylon swimming-trunks, windcheater, James Bond paperbacks with their spines broken at the dirty bits, Alistair MacLean ones with no dirty bits and the pages falling out anyway, *The Lord of the Rings*, *Dune*, money saved during the year – seven pounds eleven shillings and eightpence in the new wallet, present from Auntie Flo and Uncle Alec, transistor radio with new batteries, that should be the lot. He lifts the Alistair MacLean paperbacks out again. He's never read any of them more than once, anyway.

Still in his drawer, and going to stay there, are his khaki shorts. He can't believe he wore them last year. And, shimmering greenly at the back of his wardrobe, the item that has brought his packing to a stop. His corduroy jacket. He hasn't tried it on for a while. Maybe . . . He reaches in, slips it off its hanger and puts it on. He squares his shoulders, pulls at the lapels and inhales deeply as he turns to face the mirror, then expels the air in sudden disappointment. The jacket has swallowed him up, like a magic cap. Lost in space. The shoulders take a sharp dive downwards from a point about their middle where his own cease to support them and the lapels flap in front like an open tent. His mum bought it for him, his first grown-up jacket, after he first took communion two years ago.

"You'll grow into it," she told him, tugging and brushing with pursed lips. She took the sleeves in and let them out again last year; the holes and the extra fold across the cord are witness to that, marking off the darker shade of green that used to be inside the sleeve. His arms have lengthened but his shoulders haven't broadened. He shuffles them like a Hollywood gangster but to no avail. Maybe it'll do for a hooley, he thinks. When it's dark. With the psychedelic tie and the hipsters. But there's nothing more embarrassing than the way a girl's hand bends your right jacket shoulder back to meet your real one when you're dancing with her. You think about it so much you can't think of anything else to talk about. And you're sure the girl can't either.

Fuck. He throws it on the bed. The light reflected from the lamp ripples along its folds. It had been very expensive. His mum had probably thought he'd never need another. Be buried in it, like a pharaoh. She'll be all disappointed if he doesn't take it. *Many's the boy would be happy to have it.* He throws it in on top of the box.

2

Harry's dad and the A45 are an island in a rising tide of cardboard boxes and suitcases at the back gate. Harry and his mother are doing the carrying, and his father is mounting the roof-rack and doing the loading. Something's holding him up, a steady stream of muttering is coming from the car and the ring of luggage is piling higher and higher. Harry knows better than to ask what's wrong. As he leans a golf-bag against the wall his father stalks wordlessly past him. A moment later Harry hears him crashing about in the store.

Harry hangs around for a bit until he hears his mother join the scene. "Just what is it you're looking for, Fred?"

"Nuts. Bloody wee nuts, just like this."

"Last year you were going to put the things somewhere you would remember."

Further crashes and bangs.

"I know," says Harry's mum. "In the car boot. Along with the spare wheel."

Harry is rearranging the golf-bag on the wall when his father walks past him to the car and rummages in the boot. "I've got them! It's all right, I've got them. Now, bash on, crash on and get the job done."

"Good for you, Fred." Harry's mother sets a box of groceries down beside him. "That's the last one," she says. Harry and she stand watching Mr Moore loading, trying out boxes in the boot, then on the back seat, head-shakingly retreating, then on the roof-rack, bashing on, crashing on, getting the job done. Almost everything they need is in the boxes: bedclothes, pots and pans, a dish big enough for the potatoes for two families, a big bowl for the soup, a Primus stove for picnics, golf-clubs and, most important of all, groceries. They take these from the shop because they're a lot cheaper than in the South: cornflakes, trays of eggs, butter, marmalade, jam, tea, tins of fruit, packets of sliced bacon and ham, a roast for the Sunday dinner and a chicken from the butcher's. The groceries have gone into the biggest box, which Mr Moore is now balancing on the roof-rack along with their suitcases.

"Maybe we should give him a hand," Harry's mother says, as his father throws a sheet of tarpaulin over the roof-rack.

"I don't think so," says Harry.

With a blowing of horns a blue Corsair crunches into the fair hill, loaded down, and moves towards them.

"Here they are," says Mrs Moore, a big smile spreading across her face. Harry's dad is tying complicated knots into the ropes that hold the tarpaulin down. "Thank God your father's finished. He can't stand Alec giving him advice."

Paddy's tousled head is up against the back window of the Corsair. He's only fourteen, two years younger than Harry. He has the same shock of curly hair and his open mouth often reminds Harry to shut his own. Harry and Paddy are double cousins, for their dads are brothers and their mums sisters.

That makes Paddy more like a brother. They look alike, but Paddy's shoulders are broader than Harry's, although he's younger. Harry envies them. Paddy's good at sport too, that's another difference. Give him a ball and he'll spend the whole day running after it, dribbling, juggling, doing tricks. As the car comes nearer Harry sees Paddy's older sister Marjorie in the back seat, bent over something, a woman's magazine no doubt. She's eighteen and has no time for the boys. It used to be different. Harry can remember when she was a kind of older sister to him, too. The three of them went swimming together until Marjorie started to need a bra, about five years ago. She was so proud of her new breasts that she showed them to Harry and Paddy one memorable day behind the rocks on the beach at Port Braddan. Once, and once only, in spite of all their cajolings and pleadings. Marjorie has been having boyfriends for a couple of years now, big, stupid prefects, bank clerks, assistant librarians, all unhappily in love with her, all with cars.

The Corsair pulls to a stop and three doors open.

"Hello, Eileen, hello, Harry." Uncle Alec flaps a hand at them and struts off with his banty-like gait to the A45. He's a couple of years younger than Harry's dad, but smaller still, and balding.

"Guess what, Harry." Paddy comes round from the far side of the car. He slaps his hip. There's a padded sound.

"You've got your trunks on," said Harry. He slaps his own hip. "Guess what, so have I."

Paddy grins, the same horsy smile Harry knows from his own reflection. "Great minds think alike."

"Fools seldom differ," comes Marjorie's cool voice from the car. She's the only one who has stayed put, still reading, not even looking up. Her hair is cut like Twiggy's and its bouncy black tresses hide her face.

"Pay no attention to her," grunts Auntie Flo. She's man-oeuvring her girth to the edge of the seat. Her stocky legs squirm into view and then her podgy hands, tugging at the hem of her skirt. "Lady Muck's been acting up for days," she says, her head still invisible. "Thinks she's too old to go on holiday with us. Says she can't leave the boyfriend alone for so long. As if he'd do away with himself. Tears, locked bedrooms, we've had the lot these last few days." Her face, red from exertion, emerges. "You can thank your lucky stars you've only got the one, Eileen."

"They say parting's the test of true love, Marjorie dear," Harry's mother says.

Marjorie looks up, nods, and goes back to her reading.

"True love my aunt Fanny," says Auntie Flo, brushing down her skirt. "I give him a month at most. Until somebody comes along with a bigger car."

The two women set off towards the A45. Marjorie's thumb flicks to the next page, she folds the magazine in the middle, pushes her hair behind one ear, and starts to read.

" 'Mary Maryatt's Problem Page'," Paddy reads, squinting in the window. "Is there a letter from you in it, sis?"

Marjorie's hand appears at the window, giving Paddy the fingers.

"Up yours, too," says Paddy. The boys stroll after the two women, hands in pockets, kicking stones.

"Who's the latest?" Harry asks.

"A Ford Anglia, would you believe? A real weed."

"We're getting a Cortina. We'd have had it for the holiday only it's not in yet."

"New?"

"Nearly. But I'm still trying to get the old man to buy a Victor. Better for courtin' in."

"Yeah."

Harry's dad is placing the final cardboard box on the back seat as gingerly as if it were an unexploded bomb. He retreats out of the car. At the far side his brother is tugging at the roping and pushing at the load. Then he kicks at the tyres and nods to himself.

"Alec, what did I tell you on the way up?" Auntie Flo calls.

As the boys catch up with the women Harry overhears her mutter, "Honest, Eileen, if it's not the weans."

There is something between the two men. The way Uncle Alec looks around the shop when he comes in, and the way Harry's father goes all tense. He's the older brother, and he got the family shop. Uncle Alec went into auctioneering, and drives the newer car now.

"I don't know how Fred manages it every year," says Auntie Flo. "All that luggage."

"Right, that's it, then," says Harry's dad, clapping his hands, and adds in an American accent, "Let's get atta here."

"What about my bike, Dad?"

Mr Moore turns around and looks at it, propped against the wall. It has the remains of a 007 sticker on the front mudguard that Harry got free in a comic when *Goldfinger* came out, and tried unsuccessfully to scrape off a week later, after Big Archy said it must be the bike James Bond leaped on to make his escapes. "That'll have to wait," he says. "I'll bring it up next weekend."

"First one up puts the pan on," says Uncle Alec. He says that every year.

No doubt about who'll be putting the pan on. Harry watches the A45's speedometer needle lodge at the 30 m.p.h. mark. It will stay there for the whole trip. His father is hugging the steering-wheel like he's driving an articulated lorry. Further up the long, straight road from Kilmartin to Ballyvagh his uncle's Corsair is disappearing into the distance. In the fifties, when the two families started going up to Donegal, it was different. They both had black Ford Anglias then, the old upright ones, and Harry's father led the convoy. The journey took the whole day, the two cars chugging through the hills of Donegal like the

funeral of somebody not very popular. All that changed the year
Uncle Alec bought the Victor, when Harry was eight, and
overtook them with a toot of his horn going up Benvenagh
mountain.

"Did you see that, Eileen? Did you see that?" his father hissed,
his knuckles white on the steering-wheel. "So that's the way of
it, is it?" The first few days were terrible, you could have cut the
atmosphere at mealtimes with a knife. Harry's dad bought the
A45 after that holiday, the one he still has. Uncle Alec has since
changed to the Corsair.

"Travel in leisure, that's my motto," says Harry's father.

"We've got the heavier load, of course," says Mrs Moore.
Then she starts to sing quietly.

> *"I to the hills will lift mine eyes,*
> *From whence doth come mine aid."*

This is an old trick of hers. Sure enough, Harry's dad joins in
with the bass he sings in the church choir.

> *"My safety cometh from the Lord,*
> *Who heaven and earth hath made."*

It's quite pleasant actually, listening to the pair of them. As
long as nobody else is there Harry doesn't mind. He starts to
hum along, too.

> *"Thy foot he'll not let slide, nor will*
> *He slumber that thee keeps.*
> *Behold, he that keeps Israel,*
> *He slumbers not, nor sleeps."*

They finish the song, and Harry's mother turns to him "You're to be sure and be nice to Marjorie this year," she says. "None of your fighting like last year."

"That was Paddy, not me," says Harry. It wasn't Harry's fault Paddy started smoking last summer, he hadn't forced him to, he could have been content to keep on watching Harry. But then once Paddy started he made a game of finding out where Marjorie hid her cigarettes so that he could steal them. That was why Marjorie had smouldered and huffed her way through mealtimes and outings. Of course she couldn't say. "Those two know why," was all the grown-ups could get out of her.

"Anyway," Harry's mum says, and turns back to the front.

In Derry Mr Moore steers the car on to the lower tier of the Craigavon bridge. The planks thud and the blue girders flash past, dissecting the dreary views of the docks. At the far end they turn off to the left along the shore and drive out past the old deserted shirt factories. A tricolour is painted on the wall to the left-hand side. Harry's dad clicks his tongue against his teeth as they drive past it, and his neck settles into folds. Then they're out of Derry, climbing up the hedged slopes above Lough Foyle. In the car, conversation dies out as they labour up the long hill to the customs post at Killea. They're all thinking about the big box of groceries on the roof-rack. Up to now no customs officer has bothered to undo the knots. The car pulls to a stop at the Northern Irish border post and the customs officer leans in the window. "Where are you going to, sir?"

"Port Braddan. On holiday."

"On you go, sir."

They pull away.

"That's one, anyway," sighed Mrs Moore.

Her husband glares at her. "For God's sake. It's the Free Staters that are the bother on the way out and ours on the way in. I could have a pig in the boot for all these boys care."

"All this fuss for a wheen o' groceries."

The road dips down to the stone bridge across the burn that marks the border. In the middle the hum of the tyres becomes a crunch as the smooth asphalt gives way to loose chippings.

Any minute now his dad will say it. *Here it comes.*

"You know you're in the South anyway, the state of the roads. Painted on the rocks more like."

But now they're pulling up the hill from the bridge. Ahead they can see the Irish customs officer stroll out of the hut, putting on his hat. Mrs Moore is clutching her handbag like a lifebelt and Mr Moore's neck has settled into folds again. When the car stops the customs officer puts both hands on the car roof and peers in at the window. "Nice day that."

"Isn't it just?"

"Any goods with you, sir?"

"No. Just our luggage." Mr Moore smiles.

"No groceries at all?"

"Nope." Now the smile is tighter. The officer steps back and views the roof-rack. He pulls at the flap.

"What's all this?"

"Pots and pans and so on. Just things we need."

"It's well tied up."

"Better safe than sorry."

A rap on the roof. Mrs Moore starts. "Safe journey."

"Kewp," says Mr Moore and lets off the hand-brake. The engine stalls and dies as he lets out the clutch.

"Glory be," mutters Mrs Moore. Then the engine sputters and starts and they move away from the border post. There's a sound like a kettle boiling as Mrs Moore breathes out. She turns to Harry. "It's not really lying, you know," she says. "It's not as if the groceries are stolen. We have to save where we can."

Harry nods. He lies on a daily basis to teachers and mates, you have to really, when stubborn silences and distracting manoeuvres don't help. It's just something you do when you're young but grow out of, he thinks, like blushing. Or wanking. He isn't sure whether to be disappointed or relieved.

"Oh, well," says his mother, "this is where the holiday really starts."

3

THEY MOVE ALONG the hedgerows of border Donegal, through the sleepy hamlets with the big, old-fashioned shop fronts.

Mrs Moore has gone silent, turning her head this way and that. "Do you see that mansion up there with the long drive?" she says to Harry, pointing to a dark-windowed ruin with a collapsed roof. "The longest drive in Ireland. That's where Lord and Lady O'Neill used to live."

"I know," Harry says. His mother tells him this every year.

"On his birthday the drive was full of ponies and traps all the way down to the road. Everybody who was anybody was there. Your grandfather was invited every year too. They toasted him with real champagne and drank French wine for dinner. It's as well the horse knew the way back to Ardbane on its own."

Sunday afternoon at Movanagher farm. Perched on the ancient leather settee in his grandparents' kitchen, legs dangling out of their short trousers, scratched by the horsehair stuffing, eight-year-old Harry listens to his parents and grandparents. Torpid from the dinner roast, they're listlessly picking over the events of the week. The afternoon stretches endlessly ahead. Harry wants to get outside to the barn, where he can play in the bales. If Grandpa says yes his mother won't dare refuse him permission. "Show me the pictures, Grandpa," he says. His grandfather Hutchinson, a small, handsome man with finely chiselled features and a neat moustache, sets down his pipe, reaches up to the shelf above the

*kitchen table, and fetches down the old brown album from its place beside
the enormous radio.*

*"Come over here, young fellow," he says, slapping his thigh. Harry
climbs up, immersed in the smell of pipe tobacco, and follows his
grandfather's finger as it points its way through the sepia photos. The
fingernail is scrupulously scrubbed for Sunday, but there's a thin line of
black that the brush can't get at right in at the quick, and a burnishing
of nicotine along the side of the knobby finger, because Grandpa smokes
Woodbines as well as a pipe. Harry knows the photos off by heart.
Here's the big, ivy-grown house. The trees along the drive. The flax mill
and the shy-looking workers standing in front of it in their Sunday best
on the day of the annual excursion to Bundoran. Harry's great-
grandparents, looking anxiously into the camera. Grandpa as a boy at
the piano in the parlour, although he never learned to play a note,
wearing something like a cake doily round his neck, his mother standing
proudly behind him. Harry reads the copperplate captions out loud:
"'Boxing Day Meet 1913', 'The North Atlantic Fleet in Lough
Swilley', 'The Lord Lieutenant's Visit'." Harry's mother has joined
them, although she must know the pictures even better than Harry does.
Harry's dad and his gaunt and bony grandma are sitting silently near
the fire, he leafing boredly through the* Farmers' Weekly; *she knitting,
needles jabbing and clicking, and her jawbone working away in silent
irritation.*

*Harry looks up at the poky kitchen they're sitting in, and asks,
"Why didn't you stay at Ardbane, Grandpa? It's much nicer than
here."*

*"Och, now," says the old man, puts away the album, and starts up
a new pipe, staring out of the window.*

*In the car on the way back Harry's father explains, while his mother
remains silent. Went bankrupt the old man did, him and his handmade
shirts and shoes from Dublin. Comes from hunting too often with the
quality and not working on the farm. If his brother in America hadn't*

helped him out and bought him the farm in Kilmartin they'd have ended up on the streets, all four of them. Bit of a come down for His Nibs, rubbing shoulders with the great unwashed at the cattle-markets in Ballyraine.

Ardbane is a ruin now. The farmer who bought it had let it go to seed. The last time they visited it all that was left of the big house was a one-storeyed cow stall with a corrugated iron roof.

"There wasn't a man in the country could have pointed a finger at him," his mother says.

"A fat lot of good it did him," says Harry's father.

At Newtowncunningham they have their first view of Lough Swilley as they swing round the slopes on its southern shore. The sun, chased by a cloud's shadow, bowls along its glistening sands. Beyond the lough the Donegal hills rise in tiers that lighten from brown in the foreground to faint blue in the distance. Waves of fat clouds, their bottoms soaked black with rain, move across from the west, jostling with blue spaces. Harry smiles. Funny thing, he can't remember what the weather was like yesterday in Kilmartin.

"There's Muckish," says Mrs Moore.

The way she says it Harry knows she's been waiting for the first sight. He strains forward to get a better view. Now he sees it, suddenly dominating the landscape, rising gently from its western slope to the steep drop at the east. Like an old watchdog rising slowly to its feet. You can see its massive brooding hump from the house, in fact from almost anywhere in Port Braddan, even if as often as not its upper slopes are swathed in mist or clouds.

As they pass the southern shore of Lough Swilley towards the steeples of Letterkenny Harry is gauging the ripples and surgings of the water between the rushes at the shoreline and the dryness of the sand above it. The tide's coming in. I'll be able to go in off the harbour with Paddy tonight.

After Kilmacrennan Harry knows every corner and hedge. After the few scattered houses of Termon comes the long straight bit that takes you right up to the foot of the hills. The stone walls snaking down from them like roots. The road skirts the hills for a time as if looking for a way through them. A few new concrete bungalows, in garish blues, reds, yellows and greens, have sprung up these last years on the lower slopes. It isn't only the roads that look painted on, the topsoil looks as if it has been dusted on as an afterthought. Rocks poke through it near the houses. Like knuckles clenching the thin topsoil of their marshy gardens. On the hills up above the new houses you can see the ruins of the farmhouses where the parents and grand-parents of the owners lived.

Just ahead the road looks as though it's going to peter out at the foot of Stragaddy Mountain. It feints to the left then suddenly sweeps back to the right, and there's the pass that takes you through the hills, the ancient, speckled rocks showing through the moss shoulder right up to the road. "They take a good look at passers-by before letting them through," his mother used to say. A lonely farmhouse to the left and on the far side of the road opposite it a tiny, green-painted wooden hut, which once boasted the sign "Ireland's smallest shop", now boarded up and flaking. At the far end of the pass the black pillars of the old railway viaduct straddle the road like a last line of defence. And then they're through, coming out on to the plain dominated by Muckish Mountain, the southern end of their holiday world.

After Carrigart they come to the last part of their journey. The A45 chugs up the last hill before Port Braddan, and the vast panorama of Horn Head butting out into Sheephaven Bay pushes up into their view like a huge, mossy-backed whale surfacing. Mr Moore stops the car at the place he always does and they get out. The wind is blowing into their faces from the west, whipping up white streaks across the bay. They can see the white froth of the Atlantic rollers beating against the black knob of the Little Horn that fronts the larger mass like a ship's prow and washes round the cliffs at the side. You can't hear the boom of the waves, it's too far away. Like watching TV with the sound turned down.

This is the scene Harry used to paint from memory, the greens and browns of Horn Head, the grey fields of scree, the stone walls netting the fields further down in a grey mesh. When he was feeling homesick for Donegal, in Kilmartin, in winter. He knows how his mother feels. This is the real Donegal for them. This stretch of sea, rock, scrub and heather from Horn Head to Muckish.

This is where his mother grew up, in Horn Head's shelter, for Ardbane is only a few miles round the coast.

Harry looks at her and she smiles back.

"No sense in hanging about here all night," says Mr Moore. They get back into the car and start the last part of the drive to the house. Nobody speaks. It will be the same as always. The smell in the hall is the first thing you notice. It's mostly of the turf fire that will be burning in the living room, with a touch of mustiness from the old books and dampness from the big, whitewashed dining room, the smell of pine from the panelling up the staircase and gas from the cooker.

They pass Sessiagh Lake and turn up the lane to the house.

That's the clump of grass in the middle, hissing against the exhaust pipe, and here comes the whin bush in the stone wall that taps at the car's side; now for the rattle of the cattle grid and the crunch of gravel. They swing in beside the Corsair in front of the house. The lights are on in all the rooms and the front door is open. When Harry opens the car door the smell of a fry wafts in.

After tea Harry and Paddy set off for the harbour under a sky veined like thin-cut streaky bacon. Paddy keeps straining ahead like a dog on a leash, Harry hurries after him, holding back when he remembers he's sixteen. Across the road at the bottom of the lane they go to the slight dip in the stone wall on the far side where they can clamber up. The same stones sticking out as steps that Harry remembers, the rounded one with the ridge on top, and the flat one near the top with the dash of tar on it. Then through the fields squelching with rainwater and up to the wooden gate that hangs, collapsed on its hinge, like an old man in an armchair. The same old wire clasp that they carefully replace when on the far side. Into the cow-path now, avoiding the fresh pats splattered generously along it. Now it's Paddy who's hanging back, kicking at the tufts of grass. He bends down and picks up a big flat stone. Then he lobs it on to one of the fresher pats. The skin bursts with a satisfying splat and the dollops scatter, oozing brown. He looks around for another stone. "Stop arsing about," Harry says. "The tide will be going out." The pungent smell hangs in the damp air as they walk along the lane, while in the distance the sea strains and sighs, like a huge, restless animal.

It's mostly for the way from the house to the harbour that Harry and Paddy need their bikes. The other families from the North take houses down by the harbour, but the house the Moores rent under the slopes of Lacky Hill is bigger and cheaper because it's further away from the sea. Two summers ago, fed up with having to wait for their parents to leave the house, and with being hurried up by them to leave the harbour, Harry and Paddy started to take the path. It gets them down to the harbour in fifteen minutes; if they run, in ten. It takes them five minutes on the bikes, although the way by the road is longer.

Now they are approaching the modern box of the Dunbreaghy Hotel. Through the big bay windows they can look into the well-lit dining room at the waitresses moving about in their green uniforms and the families at their tea. Most of the cars parked outside have a Dublin registration. The hotel is a different world from Harbour Road. Harry's parents and Auntie Flo and Uncle Alec go there with some of the other people from Harbour Road for an evening meal once every year. The women are excited all day, making a big fuss about what they will wear. It's incredible and fascinating that people can afford to stay there for a whole week, or longer. And even have their meals there. Harry tries to imagine it. Sitting in the bar you can see from the other side. Like Patrick McGoohan from *Danger Man*. Harry likes him because he has the same narrow shoulders. He tries the wry smile, curling up the left corner of his mouth and crinkling his eyes. A dark-haired girl in the dining room puts aside her menu and looks straight out at him. He looks away quickly, in case she thinks he's leering at her, and moves away from her view before she can see his blush. Who does she think they are? Locals? Farmers' sons, even. The back of the hotel is less prepossessing: they can look into the steam-filled kitchen and the laundry. Here they leave the path because it veers away from Port Braddan, back up the hill. They climb over the stone wall at the side of the path and walk over a field to the hotel car park. Paddy is heading to the right, towards the cars. He likes to check out the foreign makes among them; you see a lot more of them in the South than in Northern Ireland. Harry follows him. As they cross the field at the back of the hotel Paddy says, "Look at that. A Citroën."

They climb over the wall to the park and go up to it.

"It's a real French one. Look at the numberplate," says Harry.

"Yeah. The steering-wheel's on the other side and all." By now Paddy is peeking in at the dashboard through the driver's side window. Just like a kid, Harry thinks. But there's something fascinating about the car, right enough. Something living. He goes to the other side and looks in, too. He has to rub at the film of condensation his breathing makes. It's like a plant, that's it, with its grey bulbous form, the curved tuber of the steering-wheel sprouting out from the dashboard with its one spoke, the way the upholstery swells out marrow-like between the seams.

A few intriguing foreign details; a blue packet of cigarettes Harry has never seen before in the console, a book that looks like a red Bible on the passenger seat, a yellow-backed paperback on the back seat.

"Can you see how fast it goes?" Harry asks.

"Two hundred."

"Jesus."

"That'll be kilometres, though."

"Still."

"Yeah."

"Look at that front seat."

"Yeah."

"Great for a court." Harry straightens up.

"Hi, you boys! Get away outta that!" Wee Sammy, the crew-cut barman, is gesticulating from the hotel porch. With as much nonchalance as they can muster, Harry and Paddy ignore him and saunter down the drive, trying to look like hotel guests. They cross the road at the bottom and turn into Harbour Road.

There's not really much to it. Harry remembers thinking the same thing every year. Just a patchily tarred bend of road with a row of small holiday houses on its right and a grass slope down to the beach on its left. At the far end of its curve the harbour

points back towards them. Funny that you can spend so much
time looking forward to being here. But the sea is shouldering
into the bay, already covering all but a thin strip of sand, and the
harbour lies low in the water like a heavily loaded ship. Harry
feels the old excitement rise in him. It'll be great for diving off,
too short a distance to overbalance and fall on your back.

He and Paddy are moving at a trot again, registering as they
pass the houses which families are there and who isn't up yet.
The Mulhollands' house, the only two-storeyed one, is ablaze
with light. He's the owner of the tweed factory in Carrigart; the
house belongs to them and they come every weekend. The next
house is still dark and no car is parked outside, but the boys stop
to check, because this is the one the McClellands rent and Brian
McClelland is their special friend. Nobody in. Then on faster
past the Bryces' house. Two cars are parked outside, a Hillman
Imp, that's hers, and a big Humber. The Bryces are moving
about inside, carrying boxes. Mr Bryce is a vet, a big, shambling,
mild-mannered man a good deal older than his wife. They keep
a bit apart from the other holidaymakers. Harry and Paddy go
on, past the caravan park where the families live who can't afford
a house. The Fosters from Strabane are up, too, apparently just
arrived, their unruly brood of children spilling out into the
garden while the parents unload the car, a new Triumph 2000
estate. A couple of years ago you would have known which
families were up by one glance down Harbour Road. People
had their cars for years on end. Now they seem to change
constantly and you can never be sure what kind they will be
driving from one year to the next. All except Harry's dad. He's
the only one who still has the same car he had eight years ago.
And the only one who can't stay up for the holiday.

They pass beyond the houses and slow down to a walk, self-
conscious again as they approach the harbour.

★

The boys are standing in their swimming-trunks on the stone slabs that pave the harbour, looking down at the slow swell of the sea at their feet. They're shivering and holding their arms crossed in front of their chests in the soft drizzle that envelops them. Horn Head lies in a shroud behind them. The holiday-makers have all taken to their houses, lit up in a row along Harbour Road facing them. The drizzle has pearled the ropes that sway from the rusty rings to the jostling boats at the harbour wall and coated the marble slabs in a slippery film. It muffles the sounds of the sea, the cries of the seagulls and the creaks of the boats at the ropes, and it thickens the smell of fish and diesel.

"Jesus this is awful," says Harry. "Are we wise?" He chatters his teeth at Paddy.

"The first time's the worst," says Paddy. It could just as well have been the other way round. They say something like this every year.

"On the count of three, right?" says Paddy.

"Right."

They move back a couple of paces.

"One – two – three – go!"

They slap barefoot across the smooth stones and push off the rounded stone at the edge. The leaden, heaving sea looms up before Harry's eyes: he shuts them and holds his breath. *And . . .*

The cold! They surface again, releasing the shock in a laugh. They splutter and snort the sea water out of their noses and mouths, then strike out for the harbour steps. The holidays have started.

At the top of the house, up a steep flight of stairs more like a ladder that leads up from the first floor where the other bedrooms are, Harry and Paddy are standing at the two windows

at the gable end of the attic bedroom they share. They've gone
to bed early to savour the first night in the house. They have
switched off the light, the better to see in the dark, for the sky
has cleared. Down below, a yellow oblong of light from the
living room on the ground floor falls on the garden. The adults
are still up. Beyond the garden is the drystone wall, and behind
it a rocky field descends into the gloom to the road that leads up
the side of the hill. Between the road and the sea across the fields
beyond it everything is in darkness. The sound of the waves
breaking on Killyhoey strand reaches them and they can see their
white crests as they sweep in towards the paler sand. Horn Head
is black against the red-tinged sky; the lights strung across it
deepen the surrounding darkness.

The boys have pushed down the upper sashes of their
windows. They are leaning on the wooden frames, resting their
chins on their crossed arms, and gazing out into the night. They
are feeling warm after their swim off the harbour and pleased with
themselves. The six weeks stretch infinitely ahead of them. At the
back of the room Radio Luxembourg wafts in and out of fields
of static in Harry's transistor radio. Twin clouds of cigarette
smoke billow out from their windows.

"How's the love life?" Paddy asks.

"Fair enough, fair enough."

The summer before, Harry had told Paddy the facts of life. He
had been suitably appalled. Since then Harry has kept him
informed about his own progress in the field.

"Still Mavis McWhirter?" Paddy asks.

"Yip."

"Well?"

"See at the pictures last week. Don't ask me what was on. She
was going wild. God knows what we'd have done if we'd been
in the back of a car."

"As bad as that?"

"Fuckin' apt. Couldn't go the whole hog in the pictures. I had a hard-on fit to bust."

"You're a wild man, Harry."

Harry smiles out into the darkness. Their cigarettes are down to the last couple of drags.

"Ready?" Harry asks.

"OK."

Since Paddy started to smoke last summer too they've had to get rid of their butts from the bedroom, so they've started to flick them over the stone wall at the end of the small garden. Out of that has grown a competition about flicking the butts the furthest. In the night they have to do it simultaneously, so that they can compare landings.

"One – two – three – go!"

The butts flash out from their hands. Paddy's takes a high trajectory but Harry tries the more difficult shot, with the force going into the distance rather than the height. His butt narrowly clears the wall and hits a rock with a shower of sparks just before the field slopes away into the darkness. Paddy's falls like a red tracer to the ground well short of it.

For an instant they're quiet, watching the embers die out. In the silence the sound of the sea comes to them again.

"One–nil," says Harry, and pulls up the sash.

4

WHEN HARRY COMES down the next morning the two men are silently eating their cornflakes. Paddy has already finished his. He raises his eyebrows in warning at Harry and nods in the direction of the kitchen. "Is that you, Harry?" his mother calls, through the sizzles of frying.

"Yeah."

"We were just saying we could all go down to the harbour together this morning."

"And go for a nice wee drive this afternoon," Auntie Flo adds.

Anything the women describe as nice and wee is to be avoided like the plague. It's a remnant from the holidays of other years when the boys were younger and the families did everything together. It's part of the women's conspiracy to stop the world in its tracks, to keep Harry and Paddy in short trousers. It means going and coming when the grown-ups want; standing about while they chat interminably to other grown-ups; driving round the countryside for hours on end. And no sneaking off for a quiet fag.

"We'll just walk down to the harbour, won't we, Paddy?" says Harry casually.

"Yeah, that's what I said," says Paddy. "No sense in taking two cars."

Marjorie appears from the bathroom, her hair wrapped in a

towel. "Why is everybody so quiet?" she asks. "Somebody died?"

Harry pulls on his nylon trunks and winces as the still damp cotton inset settles round his balls in a cold, clammy grip. He looks at the grey sea. This is the acid test. It will be drawn-out torture. The freezing water creeping up his thighs. The horrible anticipation of its shock on his balls. *Jesus. Only one thing for it.* He scampers off, diving-mask perched on the top of his head, past a startled, still changing Paddy, down the beach and into the sea. He takes the first waves in hurdling style but the deepening water slows him down and the next wave is peaking in front of him at a level with his waist. He flings himself recklessly against it, but convulses straight out of the water on its far side and screams. Then he falls his length in the water and emerges again with another whoop. He does this a few more times in diminishing spasms until he turns, swimming, to face the shore and Paddy, who's watching with his mouth open.

"Come on in," he shouts, "the water's lovely."

Coming out is even worse than going in. Harry runs up the beach, his body starting to feel as though a million pinpricks are goading it as the wind chills the film of water on it. His lower jaw falls open involuntarily and begins a staccato rattle. At the rocks where their clothes are lying he whips off his trunks, disregarding the few families who lie scattered about the beach. His prick has shrunk so much it's probably invisible to the human eye from any distance over a few yards anyway. Then a furious pummelling with the towel and into his clothes. He pounds off barefoot along the hard part of the sand as fast as he can, over to the harbour and back again. By the time Paddy's blue-tinged, trembling figure emerges from the waves

Harry is starting to feel great, glowing through and through, feeling his body right out to the ends of his nerves.

"The McClellands won't be up until next weekend now," says Paddy.

"Fucking nuisance. I wouldn't mind getting out in a boat."

They cross the road to the hotel drive.

"There's the Citroën," says Paddy. It's approaching them on the Dunbreaghy road. They stand and watch it. Normally they'd give the Northern greeting – the wink of the eye and swivel of the head – but the car's foreignness inhibits them. Just as well, because the people inside ignore them as they whoosh past. The boys see a dark man with sunken features and a strictly coiffed woman looking straight in front. In the back a dark-haired girl doesn't look up from whatever she's reading. It's the girl Harry has seen in the hotel. The general impression is one of boredom.

"Fuck," says Harry. "That reminds me."

"What?"

"This afternoon. The drive."

"Oh, God, aye. I'll bring my rugby ball along. Maybe we can get a bit of practice in."

"Yeah," Harry answers. Football's bad enough but at least you can keep out of trouble. In rugby it seems to him as if everybody's trying to get themselves seriously injured as soon as possible.

"Maybe there'll be some other boys there and we can get a game going," Paddy says.

Not if I can help it, Harry thinks.

Harry's mother has bought strawberries for the picnic. That's because of Mrs Mulholland of the tweed factory. And it's the reason why Harry's father is in a bad mood. He isn't saying anything, but Harry can tell by the set of his jaws. Mrs Bryce has come along, too. Her husband isn't with her, they're seldom seen together, he spends most of his time on the golf course. She's somewhere between Harry's parents' and the Fosters' age, a dark-haired, attractive woman with a slightly plump figure and quite pronounced teeth just short of being rabbit-like. She looks straight at you when talking but you often have the impression that she isn't really taking you in. She's a bit of an outsider, an amateur painter, seldom about Harbour Road because she's always driving around the countryside in her Imp, looking for views to paint.

Now they're all huddling on the slope of the dunes that leads down to the broad beach, changing in silence, working away under huge towels with fixed smiles on their faces, as if they're enjoying the wind that tugs at their towels, wobbling from one foot to the other, trying not to lose their balance. Harry and Paddy are changing too, although Harry has no intention of going into the sea. It's much too far out, for one thing, meaning a freezing walk or an ungainly scamper across the vast stretch of sand, and too rough today for another. The breakers are sweeping in from the open Atlantic and pounding against the beach with such fury that the water will be a turmoil of sand impossible to see anything in.

Harry is covertly watching the women. Amazing what you can see out of the corner of your eye when you concentrate on it. Looking directly is too obvious but when you're changing you can stare down at the sand and kind of sensitise the corners of your eyeballs. If they think nobody's looking the women sometimes take a chance and you'll be rewarded by a tantalisingly unfocused glimpse of breasts between towels and bathing-costumes. But the few glimpses he's had of Auntie Flo were more frightening than stimulating; Mrs Foster is the opposite, with breasts so small Harry thought he'd missed them somewhere and peeked so obviously she caught him at it and gave him a shy, embarrassed smile; Mrs Mulholland is too old, she'll have desiccated breasts like the ones on the mummy in Belfast Museum, if her chest is anything to go by; he doesn't feel right peeking at his mother, so Mrs Bryce is the best bet.

Now, as he tugs at his Y-fronts under his towel Mrs Bryce bundles up her frock in a preoccupied manner over the tops of her stockings. An indistinct gleam of white thighs at the periphery of Harry's vision slows his movements to a standstill.

"Liz! The children are watching!" hisses Auntie Flo.

"Sure they'll be seeing me in my swimsuit next, what's the difference?" Mrs Bryce answers equably.

There's a bloody great difference. Snap, snap go the clips and now she's rolling the stockings down. Nice, the way she points her foot.

"Are you feeling all right, Harry?" Paddy's voice from behind, exaggeratedly concerned.

Harry feels the awful flush start to prickle at his cheekbones.

"I thought you were going to be sick there, the way you were bending over," Paddy goes on remorselessly. Clutching his towel Harry shuffles round to face Paddy so that the others won't see his crimson face.

"Catch!"

The rugby ball is corkscrewing straight towards his midriff. He catches it and the towel falls to his ankles past the Y-fronts tangled round his knees.

"God, you should have seen their faces." A wild cackling from Paddy's bed.

"Ha-ha." Harry is still a bit miffed but has got over his initial mortification. He was just reviewing the episode for its comic content, thinking about the best way to tell it to Brian when he comes up.

"What in the name of God made you do it?" he asks Paddy.

"I didn't stop to think. I couldn't help myself." Another hysterical splutter. "You standing there starkers holding the ball. The look on your face." Hacks like a smoker in his last throes.

"I didn't know what to do. As long as I held the ball it hid my dick, but then I couldn't pull up my pants or the towel. So I tried to hold it with my knees and kind of bend down."

"It looked like the most enormous dong." Waves of laughter rack the two of them.

"*'Would you hold this a minute?'* he says to Mrs Foster." A series of moans, like a cow giving birth to a calf, comes from Paddy's bed. The door at the bottom of the staircase opens.

"Will you boys quit that codology and quieten down up there?" Harry's mother hisses up the stairs.

"All right, Mum."

Brimming silence for a while. Then out of the darkness comes Paddy's whispering voice again. "Did you hear about the woman who married a gypsy with crystal balls?"

"What about her?"

"She had jelly babies."

They try to laugh silently. It sounds like an upended bottle emptying itself.

"What about the world's fastest wanker?"

"Don't know."

"He came before he went."

"Jesus." Harry can't laugh at that one.

After a while Paddy's voice comes again, quieter.

"Harry."

"What."

"This wanking business."

"What about it?"

"It doesn't work with me."

Harry sits up and looks across. The pale blur of Paddy's face looks back at him and then turns towards the ceiling.

"I can rub it for ages and nothing happens."

"It's no good just rubbing it," Harry says. "You have to think of tits and things."

There is silence, apart from the rustling of bedclothes.

"How's it going?" Harry asks.

"Nothing yet."

"It takes a while."

Silence again. Then Paddy says, "Mine doesn't work. I'm giving up."

"Nonsense. Think of Marjorie that time." This is a fail-safe method with Harry.

"It's getting smaller. I'm going to think of somebody else."

"Anybody you like."

After a while Harry hears panting sounds. "Nice, isn't it?"

"Yeah."

"Who are you thinking of anyway?"

"Mrs Bryce."

Harry is piqued. "I was just thinking of thinking of her myself."

Paddy's breath is coming faster. "Get your own," he says.

5

Time has flown, and is now standing still. Saturday already, the first week past, a blur of bathes, drives, cigarettes. But now Harry seems to have been staring into the bracken-coloured water that comes up to his shins for an eternity, whereas it can only be half an hour at the most.

He and Paddy are shuffling barefoot along the stream that flows through the golf course to the beach. They started back-to-back in the middle and have moved slowly apart, Paddy in the direction of the sea and Harry towards the road, shuffling in zigzags to cover the whole bed of the stream. Harry has delegated his consciousness to the soles of his feet and the rest of him is bored to death. For a short time he has pretended to be a Chinaman in a ricefield, but that is even more boring. A man picking his way through a minefield, then. *One wrong step . . .* That is no good either, because Harry wants to find something, not avoid it. He's waiting for the tell-tale rub of golf balls on the soles of his feet. Paddy wants to play with the ones he finds but Harry wants to sell his for sixpence or a shilling, according to their condition, at the clubhouse.

Ah! There it is. The sensuous round hardness, poking through the silt. You'd never see it, the water is so brown, that's what makes the barefoot approach essential. They have learned the trick from the local lads. Boys on holiday wouldn't stoop to it because rumour has it that the stream is really sewage from the hotel.

Harry is bending down to grope for the ball when he hears the whoosh of the approaching Citroën. By now the holiday community is fully informed about the French family. He's a buyer for a big clothes chain store combining a family holiday with visits to the Donegal tweed factories. They're all supposed to speak very good English.

As Harry straightens up to watch the car, the man, and the woman in the front shoot him disapproving glances and as the car draws alongside the girl in the back looks up from her reading. Her eyes meet Harry's and as the car swishes past she turns to look through the rear window. Harry sees her face framed in the window as the car retreats; large, observant eyes, high cheekbones and lips slightly parted. She seems to smile before she turns away. Watching the car disappear Harry becomes acutely conscious of the ridiculous figure he cuts with his jeans rolled up, his shins streaked with mud and his windcheater pockets bulging ludicrously with golf balls. What will she suppose he has been doing? He can almost hear her bursting into laughter in the car. Thank goodness she can't see his face do its traffic-light impression. What is he thinking of, messing around like a kid here anyway?

"I'm away to the clubhouse to sell my balls. Are you coming?" he shouts at Paddy's retreating figure.

Sunday morning. Church. The air is filled with the ringing of the bell, the whisperings of the ushers and wooden clacks as the people are asked to move up closer and the aisles lined with folding chairs. The church is overflowing with holidaymakers. The road outside is lined on both sides with cars that have unloaded droves of frocked, hatted and handbagged ladies, and shaved, suited and tie-bearing men. Now they're sitting, on their best behaviour, conversing in quiet tones and nodding to people they haven't seen since last year. Through the open windows a light breeze wafts stray scents of hair-cream, shoe-polish, nail-varnish and eau-de-Cologne. The bell's ringing starts to die off in diminishing peals. The congregation falls silent as the black-clad figure of the minister emerges from the vestry and ascends the creaking stairs of the pulpit. He spreads his arms wide in a sudden, dramatic fling. "Let us pray."

In front of Harry heads bow with a rustle like waves breaking on a beach. He shuts his eyes. In his retina the light from the windows reappears as yellow rectangles, darkens into purple and disappears. Sometimes interesting monster-like shapes form on the insides of his eyelids, but today he isn't going to keep them shut long enough. Where are the McClellands? If they had come up yesterday they would be here today. But he hasn't seen them in church. If they don't come today they won't be up till next week. Maybe they aren't coming at all. At least his dad has brought his bike. He opens his eyes and squints up at the Reverend McLeod. He's still standing in the same posture like a black vulture, his face screwed up theatrically to suggest some kind of pain, or maybe it's only the effort of keeping his eyes shut. The long strands of hair that he cultivates on the left side of his head and combs up and across to cover his bald pate are hanging down in front of his face. You can always tell when the prayer is going to end because he'll sweep them back shortly beforehand.

Harry turns to where Paddy is sitting on the far side of his mother, trying to keep his neck from rustling against the nylon of his shirt. But Paddy has his eyes shut. Beyond the flowery bulk of Auntie Flo Harry's gaze falls on Marjorie's legs, protruding from a shimmering green mini. With a bit of luck she'll cross them later and Harry can watch them during prayers.

The minister is winding down, no more questions rising in tone but shorter, affirmative sentences. Harry watches for the hair-restoring sweep of the minister's hand. There! When he pronounces "Amen" a ripple of throat-clearings, sniffs and rustles of clothing passes through the church. In its wake a late couple and their son move quickly up the aisle to the front and slip deferentially into seats left vacant by the choir. As they sit down the boy turns round and shoots a big-toothed grin back in their direction. It's Brian McClelland. Thank God.

Marjorie refuses to cross her legs, the set of her mouth revealing her awareness of Harry's attentions, so he spends the sermon deliberating on the back of the Reverend McLeod's wife, who's sitting directly in front of him. She has that round-shouldered look that comes from holding her hands in her lap, and by the way her shoulders are working she's ceaselessly rubbing them. The women say she has trouble with her nerves, and apart from church, she's never seen anywhere outside the manse. She's wearing a white nylon blouse, which various undergarments crease into intriguing contours. At its upper limits fat pink arms and shoulders shimmer through, but then comes a ridge of something about an inch in towards the middle, which transforms the broad expanse of her back into a white area, like an unexplored region in an historical atlas. In the middle of her back rises a further carapace about as wide as a hand. Her standings-up to sing and bendings-over to pray are accompanied by an orchestra of stretching, snapping, slithering sounds. Below the material of her blouse at each shoulder the outline of three straps can be seen, one twisted. *What in the name of God has the woman got on? And what does she look like when she hasn't?*

After the benediction the congregation has to remain seated until the Reverend McLeod has passed with flapping robes down the aisle and taken up position in the vestibule. He insists on shaking hands with everybody as they leave, which causes a congestion up the aisles, like in Kilmartin cinema. Harry thinks the Reverend McLeod is a bit of a phoney but the adults, especially the women, are always going on about the way he has about him.

Marjorie is right in front of Harry and when it's her turn the Reverend McLeod takes her outstretched hand in both of his. "Marjorie! I almost didn't recognise you. Quite grown up, hasn't she?" he says to the other Moores. He passes over Harry with a vague smile, having obviously forgotten his name, and he is released into the sunshine.

Outside Harry and Paddy move through the crowds. They spot Brian standing a bit away under a tree at the same time as he sees them and they saunter towards each other, hands in pockets, deliberately casual. Brian is the same age as Harry and, but for his straighter, darker hair and spade-like front teeth, could pass for a brother of his and Paddy's. He's wearing the smart, blue blazer of a school team.

"Hi, Brian. Long time no see," says Harry.

"Hi, men."

"Neat blazer," says Paddy, fingering the blue material with the school crest on it.

"Yeah, they made me a monitor this year. Because of the rugby. Medallion fifteen and all."

Rugby teams are idols at Ballyraine Boys' too, but Harry has never been any good at rugby and has given it up to join the sorry bunch of cross-country runners that traipse around the roads near Ballyraine Boys'. The teachers all look down on them. *A lot of weeds. No fancy blazers for being a bus-boy and a cross-country runner to boot.* He'll have to keep an eye on Paddy and Brian, or they'll be organising games of rugby all over the place.

"When did you get up, anyway?" Brian asks.

"Last week. We've been waiting for you all week," says
Harry.

"Yeah, my gran was sick. We couldn't get away. It was a real
bore."

"Is she better now?"

"No, dead. Are you coming down tomorrow afternoon? We
could get the boat out."

"What do you think, Paddy?" Harry asks, careful not to seem
too keen.

Paddy's trying to keep his grin under control and he answers
in the same flat tones: "We might as well."

At dinner-time Harry's mother corners him. "You're not to go
gallivanting round the harbour the one day your dad is up. You
know how much he appreciates it when you come on a run
with us."

They're trundling along the road to Carrigart at the statutory
thirty miles per hour. The other car has long since disappeared
over the horizon. Harry's mother is sitting with folded arms. He
can imagine the little smile on her face. This is what she likes,
the three of them going somewhere. Funny how she doesn't pay
any attention to the warning signs Harry sees in the tension in
the back of his father's neck and his grip of the steering-wheel.
She's different in Donegal. At home she'd be getting nervous,
trying to keep up a conversation.

"The way some folk tear about the countryside you'd wonder
if they look at the scenery at all," Mr Moore says. "Look at that."
They come out of the copse that enfolds the road down to
Lackagh Bridge. The tide is still coming in and the water is
rippling up below the old stone bridge from the bay to their left.

The sea is already higher than usual.

"It's the spring tide today," Harry says. He loves it when the sea reaches out that little bit more and brims over the brown seaweed and the black rocks that fringe the fingers of land, covering the grey, lichen-speckled ones higher up, too, lapping right up to the green fields. It looks so clean and generous. At the harbour the tide will come right up to the third step from the top, maybe even the second. You can just step off.

"When are we going home?" he asks.

6

"I'M SORRY TO hear about old Mrs McClelland," says Harry, as his mother has instructed him. The boys are standing on the doorstep of the McClellands' house in Harbour Road, chafing to get out in the boat.

"Yes, well, I think it was really a relief at the end for the old dear, actually. Are you boys staying for dinner? If you are Brian will have to go to the shops."

"No, they aren't," says Brian, appearing from behind her. "They're going back up the hill for a big fry. They don't understand 'dinner', anyway, Mummy. They have dinner at lunch. You have to say 'tea' . Isn't that what you call it?" He winks at Harry and Paddy. Brian's always trying to press-gang them into his guerrilla war on his parents. "Why do we call it 'dinner', Mummy? Grandma always said 'tea', too." Even the way Brian always says *Mummy* and *Daddy* to his parents is cheeky.

But Mrs McClelland is impervious to Brian's provocations. She's a small, mouse-haired woman with an off-putting way of concentrating on some things and ignoring others, above all her son. Now she's looking past Harry and Paddy with her intent stare. "Who are those people?" she asks. Harry looks. The French family have just turned into Harbour Road with the measured step of people out for a stroll.

"Those are the French people that are staying up at the hotel," he says.

Mrs McClelland starts down the garden path. Harry and Paddy follow Brian into the garage.

"Right, lads," Brian says. "There are the oars, the hand-lines and the life-jackets. You take them outside and I'll look for the rowlocks."

Harry and Paddy pile the things in a heap at the bottom of the garden, where Mrs McClelland has taken up position, watching the approach of the French family with a fixed smile. They go back into the garage.

"Christ," says Brian, rummaging through boxes of tools, "if we've forgotten the bloody things we can forget the boat for the holiday. I don't remember seeing them yesterday. Fuck, fuck, fuck."

Mrs McClelland's voice carries up the garden. "Glorious day, isn't it?"

Low rumblings in reply.

"Just out for a walk, are you?"

Further indiscernible rumblings.

"Next thing she'll be asking them in for a cup of tea," says Brian.

Her voice flutes up the garden. "Why don't you come in for a cup of tea?"

At the sound of the garden gate being swung open the boys turn to watch through the open garage door. Mrs McClelland is holding the gate open with one hand and waving in the direction of the house with the other. Now the French family are coming up the path in a phalanx with the girl at the front and Mrs McClelland herding them from behind.

"What's your name, dear? Ah, *comment* . . ."

"Marie."

"Oh, Marie, how charming. You must be awfully bored. The boys are just going out in the boat and I'm sure they'd love to take you. Wouldn't you like that, Marie? Brian!"

"Shit a brick," says Brian, looking up. "Would you credit it?"

"What's up?" he shouts, through the open garage doors. "We're busy."

"Come out and say hello to these nice French people."

"Fuck the nice French people," Brian mutters. He drops a spanner with a clang on the concrete floor and trudges outside. Harry and Paddy follow.

In the daylight by the door Harry sees the rowlocks nestling in a box among a bicycle pump, an electric torch and a Primus stove. He snatches them up and troops out after the other two.

"This is my son Brian and two friends of his, Henry and Patrick. This is the Fischer family."

"Harry," says Harry.

"Brian, Marie would love to go out in the boat, why don't you boys take her out for a nice little row round the harbour? You can practise your French! You know what your French teacher wrote in your report."

Brian is looking up at the sky, shading his eyes with his hand, as if checking the weather. "Daddy always says the boat's not safe for four," he says.

"Nonsense, Brian, not if you're only staying in the harbour."

Mr Fischer looks at his watch and then at his wife. Harry squints down his nose to see if his embarrassment is showing. No sign yet. The girl doesn't seem to be affected. She watches the boys calmly, occasionally tossing back her dark, windswept hair.

"Anyway, we can't find the rowlocks," says Brian. "We must have left them in Belfast."

"I found them," says Harry, holding up the missing items.

"Good for you, Henry," says Mrs McClelland. "Off you go, then, boys. Be sure to look after Marie." She ushers the Fischers into the house. Brian picks up a hand-line, and starts to work at it, glowering at the knots at its end.

Marie walks forward to the boys, smiling at Harry and Paddy as though they're sharing a joke. She has nice dimples at the side of her mouth, as if she's suppressing an even wider smile. She's wearing a blue sweater and jeans, clothes that an Irish girl wouldn't be seen in.

"We've seen you before," says Paddy. "In your car."

"I've seen you too. You are the boys who walk past the hotel with the towels every day. Are you brothers?"

"Double cousins," says Harry. "Two brothers married two sisters."

"I see. But you are like brothers. Harry and Patrick."

"Paddy," said Paddy.

"And you are Brian."

Brian grunts, and goes on unfurling the line.

"Are you communists?" Paddy asks.

"No, we are big capitalists. Why?" says Marie.

"Isn't that Mao Tse-tung's *Little Red Book* in your car?"

"Do you mean the *Michelin Guide to Britain and Ireland*?"

"Maybe, yeah."

"There's about two pages for Ireland."

"Tell us a good French curse word," says Paddy.

"*Putain* is good. You can say it almost always."

They try it. "What does it mean?" Harry asks.

"Whore."

"Isn't it just for girls, then?" Paddy asks.

"No, no. For everybody."

"Like *hoor*," says Harry. "Hey, Brian, you oul' *putain*. What did your French teacher write in your report anyway?"

Brian grunts.

"'Can only grunt', probably," says Paddy.

"Look, I never said I wanted to go out in your boat. It was all your mother's idea," says Marie.

"I know," says Brian. "You don't want to go out in the boat. We don't want to take you. Your parents don't want a cup of tea. Six people doing things they don't want, just to please her. Christ almighty."

Marie's brown calves are sandwiched between Harry's and Paddy's pale shanks. Their trouser legs are still rolled up from launching the boat. She's sitting in the stern, facing Harry and Paddy on the middle seat. Behind them Brian is sitting in the prow. The boys are rowing, and the boat, smaller than Harry remembers, scuds along, the fibreglass floor and sides juddering with the passing water. The rocks of Breaghy Head slide across the harbour, blocking the view from Harbour Road.

"That's far enough," says Brian. "Fag time, lads."

They pull in their oars, and the boat rocks gently. It's a dull, overcast day; the tops of Horn Head and Muckish are shrouded in cloud.

"My round," says Harry, and brings out a packet of ten *Silk Cut.*

"Try a French one," says Marie. She holds out a blue packet, open at the top.

"They've no filters," say Paddy.

"Filters spoil the taste."

None of the boys say anything to that. The only kind of cigarettes Harry knows without filters are brands the farmers in Kilmartin buy, kinds the boys wouldn't normally be seen dead smoking. Paddy turns the packet over in his hand.

"Gaw . . ."

"Gauloise."

"Gauloise. *Putain*."

"Very good."

They light up. The smoke sears Harry's throat like the time the wet bales of hay at his grandpa's farm caught fire. Tears spring to his eyes.

The boat swings slowly round in the current. Suddenly Paddy leans over the side and retches into the sea, rocking the boat. His face is greenish-white.

"It's the bloody boat," he mutters, before retching again.

"I think he is too young to smoke," says Marie. Harry flicks his half-smoked cigarette overboard while she's watching Paddy's heaving shoulders. Paddy slumps back on his seat, still clutching his cigarette. He looks at it, his face greenish-white, then takes another drag from it as though nothing has happened.

"Great fag," he says.

Two hours later they come back into the harbour, and see the three adults waiting on Harbour Road. They've been to Breaghy Head, caught twenty-three mackerel that shat rings round them, and Harry has shown Marie how to row. They carry the boat up the beach, the fish slithering about in the bottom. At the foot of the slope they put the mackerel into a bucket and start to climb up, stumbling a bit because each of them is carrying their shoes, an oar, a hand-line, a rowlock and a life-jacket. Marie is ahead of Harry. Her jeans are still rolled up, and the folds round the knees are dark with wet. Further up the jeans are lined with salt where the water has dried, and thin streaks of mackerel shit. The boys look more or less like this every time they come back, but Marie's parents haven't been expecting it, to go by the looks on their faces.

Brian is holding up a mackerel. "They shit all over us, Mummy. Or is it shat?"

"We'll be going, then," says Mr Fischer. "Thank you very much for the coffee."

"And for the banana sandwiches," his wife says.

"What are banana sandwiches?" Marie asks.

"Slices of banana on buttered white bread with sugar on top," Mrs McClelland explains. "The boys love them. You can make them with oranges too, if you can't get bananas."

"Then they're orange sandwiches," says Brian.

Mr Fischer turns to Mrs McClelland and shakes her hand briskly. "Goodbye."

"So nice of you to call in. Do come again any time!"

"Bye," says Marie, and goes off after her parents.

"We'll be going out again tomorrow," says Harry. He wants to see her again, this French girl who doesn't make a big thing out of being in a boat with three boys, and dead mackerel sloshing about her bare feet. Marie turns round and calls something but Harry can't understand it.

"Such nice people. Pity your father wasn't here," says Mrs McClelland, still waving at the retreating backs.

"Sounds like a waste of banana sandwiches to me," says Brian.

"Maybe they'd be happier eating snail sandwiches," says Paddy.

"Frogs' legs sandwiches," says Harry.

"I'm not having those fish in my kitchen," says Mrs McClelland.

Lying in his bed in the anonymous darkness they prefer for talking, Harry is waiting for the review of the day's events with Paddy. Harry is on his stomach, arched backwards on the old, worn-out mattress like one of the day's mackerel frozen in mid-flap. His chin is propped up on his pillow, his hands grasp the upright bars of the bed's headboard, his head poking between two of them. Across the room Paddy is lying on his back, holding his head in his arms, elbows sticking out into the gloom, watching the slope of the roof as it closes in over him. There has been no repeat of the wanking session. They haven't even mentioned it.

Harry says, "It was nice in the boat today."

"Yeah."

"What did you think of Marie?"

"Nice girl."

"Pretty, isn't she?"

"Yeah."

"Do you think she'll come tomorrow?"

"Dunno."

Suit yourself. "Makes you tired, doesn't it, the sea air?"

"Yeah."

"Goodnight, Paddy."

"Goodnight, Harry."

But as he stares wide-eyed into the darkness Harry is feeling anything but tired. Those knots of wood in the panelling straight ahead, they're just like the dimples at the side of Marie's face when she laughs, the grain in the panel just below curves the same elegant way her calves do, and there are the lines at the back of her knees. How they flexed when she climbed up the slope ahead of him. When he closes his eyes impressions of the day flood his mind – the pressure of her thigh against his when she sat beside him while he was showing her how to row; the peal of her laughter; her hand dangling in the water. Her face keeps floating up out of the darkness, her lips moving towards his. His breathing seems to be speeding up rather than slowing down, and he has a slightly queasy feeling as if he's inhaling more than he's breathing out and the surplus air is seeping into his stomach.

He knows what it means: he's in love.

7

WHEN HE WAKES Harry is surprised to see the sun already high in a cloudless blue sky. He must have fallen asleep some time after all. Paddy's bed is empty and made. Outside he can hear the clip of wood on golf balls. Paddy is practising his drive on the old ones he hasn't been able to sell.

When he comes down into the dining room his mother fries him some eggs while watching the stew she's cooking for dinner. Everybody else has already gone down to the harbour.

"Are we having the mackerel tonight?" he asks.

"No. They'll keep till tomorrow. We have to eat the two chickens your father brought up first."

"Can Brian come up for tea tomorrow, then?"

"His mother wouldn't let him keep his mackerel, is that it? Yes, why not?"

"That French girl might want to come, too."

"What French girl?" His mother appears from the kitchen, wiping a plate.

"The one from the hotel."

"Where did you fall in with her?"

"At the harbour. She was out in the boat with us."

"Was she now? Fancy that."

"Can she come?"

"Would she eat mackerel?"

Harry nods casually.

"I suppose she might as well. We've far too many anyway. What's her name?"

"Marie." He tries not to smile when saying it.

His mother is still looking at him. "Is she a nice girl?"

"Nice" is the sum of all the things his mother thinks a girl should be. It includes going to a grammar school, singing in a church choir, not giggling, not showing too much leg, not wearing makeup, in short being the kind of girl it isn't worth having a wank about.

"Yeah, very nice."

"Well, all right, then. Aren't you going to finish that?"

"No."

"Waste of a good egg."

When they arrive at Harbour Road Harry leaves his bike conspicuously on the mossy ground opposite the McClellands' house. Does Marie know they have bikes? He joins Paddy who's wheeling his bike up to the McClellands' garage. Brian comes out of the house. "About time, too," he says. Paddy follows him into the garage and Harry takes a last look outside. Then he hangs around just inside the door while the other two start to gather up the oars, rowlocks and life-jackets. They're taking ages. Asleep on their feet. Marie could appear now, see no one about and go away again. She might be there just now. He sticks his head outside. No sign. A wooden clatter comes from within.

"Am I to carry all the bloody oars on my own?" says Brian. Harry dashes across and picks up the two that Brian has dropped and is outside again. The other two emerge and make off across the road and down the slope.

"I'll close up here," Harry says. "Go on ahead."

He closes the garage door, then wheels his bike into the McClellands' garden and props it up against the wall, then wheels it back out again. Still no sign. He puts the bike where it was before, then turns it the other way round.

"Get a move on, Harry!" Brian calls from the beach.

"Keep your hair on!"

Brian and Paddy have already got the boat into the water and are fitting the rowlocks and the oars.

"What's the rush, for Christ's sake?" Harry says, as he joins them. "What about a smoke before we go?"

Brian stares at him. "Are you wise? We smoke when we're out round the head, like always."

Paddy holds the boat steady while Brian jumps aboard.

"Didn't that girl, what's her name, Marie, say she wanted to come out with us?" Harry says.

"Well, she isn't here, is she?" says Brian. "Anyway, I want to go across to the Horn and four's too many in the boat. Come on, Harry, what are you waiting for?"

"Seriously, lads, I'm not feeling too well. I'll just hang about here for a bit until you get back."

Brian rolls his eyes towards heaven then looks to Paddy for support but he's busying himself with the fishing-lines. "Have it your own way," he says, "two's even better."

They clamber aboard and are soon pulling away from the beach. Harry watches them but they don't look at him. He turns away and walks along the beach. He has to stay in a vantage place where he can see Marie coming. Or where she can see him. The best place is the beach. What will he tell her if she does turn up? Why has he stayed behind? He could be looking for sandworms for bait. Good idea. Marie won't know that there aren't any sandworms on this beach.

Half an hour later he's kneeling beside a row of arm-deep

holes in the sand when he hears a shout from Harbour Road. "Harry!" He looks up quickly, but it's only Marjorie. *Fuck.* What's she doing here? He gives a kind of preoccupied wave, to show how busy he is, but she comes down the slope and walks up to him.

"What's this going to be when you're finished? Or are you just measuring the length of your arm?"

"We're all out of sandworms, so I said I'd stay behind and dig for some."

"There aren't any sandworms on this beach. Even I know that. Have you fallen out with the other two? Come on, Harry, what about going for a fag? Mum and Dad are up at the shop."

"Not just at the minute, I think I'm on to something here." He gropes around, lying with his face in the sand.

"Please yourself." She walks away.

Harry waits until she's gone, then he gets to his feet, annoyed at himself for having turned her down the one time she'd offered. There's no sign of Marie. She isn't coming in a month of Sundays. And Brian and Paddy will be better friends when they come back and start playing their bloody rugby. A feeling of failure like gall is rising from his stomach. He kicks at the sand in disgust at himself.

"Guess who we saw this morning," Paddy asks. They're having an after-dinner smoke up in their room. The grown-ups and Marjorie have gone out for a drive.

"Moby Dick. How would I know?" Harry has spent the rest of the morning looking through the paperbacks in the chemist's shop in Dunbreaghy, until the chemist chased him off.

"Marie."

"My arse you did."

"Ask Brian. She was down at the harbour when we came in.

She went for a fag with us. We had a great chat."

"What about?"

"Lots of things. She's from Dalmatia."

"Since when's that a part of France?"

"Alsatia, maybe. Something like that. Some place where they have dogs."

"Brilliant."

"Want to know why she speaks English so well?"

"Well?"

"Her grandmother's English, that's why. And she said Marie had to learn English from a very young age."

"Why do they all do what she wants?"

"Because she has the money. The spondulicks. She owns the firm. She was a governess in one of the houses Marie's grandfather used to visit. There was a big scandal when they married, because she was below his station. His family cut him off and he started a shop of his own. Now the old man's dead, and the grandma's the boss."

"Was Brian there too?"

"Yeah. You should have seen him slobbering all over her."

"I can imagine."

"Know what else she said?"

"How would I?"

"She said she was glad she'd got to know us."

"You?"

"That's what she said. She wants to come out to Horn Head with us some time. She said it's deadly boring driving around with her father when he visits all these tweed factories to look at their stuff, and it's deadly boring up the hotel with all those old faggots. They're staying for nearly five more weeks, just like us. Know what else?"

"For fuck's sake."

"She's coming in for a swim off the harbour with us tonight."

"Pull the other one."

"Honest to God. And Brian isn't coming. He'd been spouting off for about ten minutes what fools we were, that it would freeze the balls off a brass monkey, and then suddenly she says she'd love to come, so he couldn't very well change his mind."

"Just looking at it makes me shiver," says Marie.

"The first time's the worst," says Paddy. "You just have to not think about it and dive in."

The three of them are standing at the edge of the harbour, looking down at the water lapping half-way up the harbour steps in sullen oil-streaked ripples.

"I said I'd try it once," says Marie.

They retreat to the shelter of the harbour wall to change. Nobody is about. Harry has hardly spoken yet. It's the being in love. He can't talk off the top of his head any more to Marie, like he did the other day. He keeps turning over every sentence in his mind until the chance to say it is long past. And the worry on top of that. He's been worried all afternoon that Marie won't turn up, but no sooner did he see her waiting at the end of the harbour than he started to worry about how to organise their next meeting. How can he blether away like Paddy when he might never see her again? He starts to unbutton his shirt, thinking of how he can ask her about the mackerel.

Marie has turned her back to the boys. She's reaching under her blue skirt and wriggling with her hips. "Where were you this morning, Harry?" she asks. She tugs her slip down her thighs and steps out of it.

"You get fed up messing about in boats." This is another sentence he's been chewing over in case she asks until all the flavour has gone out of it. He has to choke the end off because his voice has taken on a life of its own, rising like a fire siren starting.

"Brian and Paddy have already promised to take me out to Horn Head some time," she says. "Won't you be coming then?" She's holding her costume at arm's length, turning it this way and that.

Fool. Paddy has already said. "I might. But we still have all the mackerel to eat from the last time. Why don't you help us out?" This time his voice comes out all leaden.

"Yes, I've already asked my parents. They say it's all right." Marie is squirming into her costume. She unbuttons her blouse, takes it off, and looks down at her stomach. "Can you never sunbathe here? My tan will soon be all gone." She's standing in a white brassière that shows up against her brown skin and a black swimsuit whose top is hanging down over her hips. She turns to Harry. "Look." She holds her forearm against his pallid stomach. He can feel the fine hairs touch his skin, and almost simultaneously a stirring in his pants. "Hardly any difference. I'll soon be as pale as you." She turns away again, and undoes the strap of her brassière with deft movements. The muscles of her shoulders flex as it comes away and the supple stretch of her back is bared from the bob of her hair to the upper globes of her buttocks. Harry's prick gives another lurch. *Please, God, don't let me get a hard-on.* He eases his trousers down over his knees and steps out of them. Thank God, no sign of life in his Y-fronts.

"Come on, you two, get a move on!" shouts Paddy. He's standing shivering at the edge of the harbour.

An awful realisation dawns on Harry. He has absent-mindedly unwrapped his trunks over by the steps, trying to think of witty things to say, and he's left his towel there. Now he's standing like an idiot dressed only in his underpants. He should have kept his shirt on, of course. How is he going to get his trunks on? He catches Paddy's eye and nods frantically at the towel. Paddy looks at it and back to Harry, shaking his head. He's smiling. *Bastard!*

Marie is fastening her top behind her back. *Now, you fool!* Quickly he pulls his pants down over his knees. His prick is a tiny, shell-less snail. One leg out, *oh, Christ, no,* he's over-balancing, hand on harbour wall, *that was close, where are the trunks? in your hand, you twit,* and he's pulling them up as Marie turns to him.

"Ready, Harry?" He can only nod and push out his chest.

They walk over to where Paddy is waiting, now clutching his shoulders against the wind. Paddy's face brightens as he turns to face them. He points at Harry. "Look who's got his trunks on inside out," he says.

"Nice figure, hasn't she?" says Harry to the ceiling.

"Yeah. Nice tits."

Harry lies there for a while and then he sits up suddenly. "Did you see them?"

"Yeah, from the side."

"The nipples and all?"

"Yeah."

"Jesus." Harry flops back. He waits for the tell-tale swishing sound of the blankets from Paddy's bed and is relieved when he hears nothing. He settles down to concentrate on the image he's been saving up: the way Marie looked at him when they left her at the hotel, something dancing in her eyes that matched her laugh, and then changed into something else.

Something searching and then finding. And the shy smile as she looked away.

8

Harry has never felt so removed from the house and every-body in it. It all looks so different framing Marie: the cavernous old whitewashed dining room, the huge, black-slated fireplace, the uneven stone slabs on the floor, **Remember the Sabbath Day to keep it holy** crocheted and framed hanging above her head beside the calendar from Craig's Mill and the photographic mural of some loch in Scotland, the old Singer sewing-machine table in the corner they set the huge bowl of potatoes on.

What must she think of it all?

He's desperately trying to tune in to what she is saying, but he can hardly hear her for Paddy's and Brian's dronings about some pathetic rugby match both of them have been to. They're sitting on either side of him, but he's leaning so far forward over his plate of mackerel that they can comfortably chat behind him, leaning on his back, digging their elbows into it. Marie is sandwiched between Harry's dad and his uncle on the far side of the wide table. The two men are lapping up her every word. Her father has driven her up, and will fetch her again later. She has entered the house like a humming dynamo that draws energy from everything else, making Harry feel grey and drab, reducing him to a mumbling nonentity who had no say in where she was to be seated, hanging about the perimeter of what's going on. Which is why he has ended up as far away from her as possible.

Harry pokes at his mackerel, as if making sure it's really dead. Occasionally he lifts a tepid morsel and chews it for an age. Tantalising snatches of what Marie is saying waft in and out of his hearing, like Radio Luxembourg on his transistor radio at night.

Something about everybody speaking two languages in Alsace. French and English? No, French and German. But no German in their house. The grandmother again, forbidding it. Her husband's family, the ones who cut him off when he married her, spoke German, so her grandmother refused to learn it. Even her mother, who speaks German with her own family, isn't allowed to speak it when the grandmother is about.

Something about her father's business. Expanding. Buying tweed for a big chain.

Now she's talking about the other day, when they caught the mackerel. She must be telling them about the mackerel starting to shite because her lips are quivering before laughing, the way they did yesterday with Harry's trunks, yes, there she goes, so infectiously that the two men are laughing along with her.

"She's a real looker, that one."

"What?"

Marjorie, leaning forward, talking to him from the far side of Paddy. "Who's she going with anyway, you or Paddy? Or Brian? Hardly."

"She's not going with anybody." He wishes she would keep her voice down. He can't hear what Marie is saying.

"Off your food?"

"Ssssh."

Now they're talking about the hotel. The two men are looking all worldly-wise, as if they were in and out of the place every day, rubbing shoulders with the nobs from Dublin. But Marie is shaking her head. She looks across the table, straight into Harry's eyes, and smiles at him. Everything around her swims out of focus and the table seems to fall silent. "I like it better here," she says.

"It's you she's after, all right." Marjorie again. Harry feels the blood rise to his cheeks and has to lower his face to his plate again.

"Maybe Marie would like to come for a nice wee run with us tomorrow," says Harry's mum, out of the blue. *Yes! A nice wee anything!*

"I'd love to," says Marie, "but I have to go with my parents tomorrow and Friday. They are complaining that they haven't been seeing enough of me. Thank you all the same."

"Do you hear that, Harry?" sniffs Harry's mother. "Some children still have a bit of consideration for their parents."

Harry spends the rest of the evening in a turmoil. He's trying to work out a plan, but he finds it difficult to think straight, let alone join in the conversation, because he has the growing impression that, whenever he isn't darting glances at Marie, she's darting glances at him. It's hard to work out how to see her next while he's watching out for her looking at him. There's the hooley at the church hall in Port Braddan on Friday. How can he get Marie to go there if he isn't going to be seeing her tomorrow or the next day? Every last person sitting round this table knows about it, apart from Marie; the Moores go every year, but nobody's mentioning it. It's as if they're doing it on purpose. He leans back between Paddy and Brian, making them move apart.

"Isn't there something on at the weekend?" he asks.

"The Donegal rally," says Paddy. "It's coming round the Atlantic Drive on Saturday."

"At seven o'clock or some unearthly time," says Brian.

"Isn't your man Hopkirk in it?" asks Uncle Alec.

"Yeah. In the works Mini," says Paddy.

"That'd be something, now, boys, wouldn't it?" says Uncle Alec. "Up at five in the morning and off to the Atlantic Drive to see them coming through. Are you game?"

"Yeah!"

"What about you, Harry? You don't seem too keen." Marjorie again.

"Yeah, sure."

"Or was it something else you were thinking of?"

Fuck off. He takes a mouthful of cold mackerel.

"I'd like to go to the hooley at the church hall on Friday," she says to the table at large. "You promised me last year you'd teach me the slow waltz, Uncle Fred."

Harry's dad brightens. "What about it, Eileen? We haven't been to a hooley in ages."

"I'd have to go to the hairdresser's in Dunbreaghy. What do you think, Flo?"

"Oh, yes, come on, let's go. We'll get appointments for Friday morning. It won't do you boys a bit of harm either."

"But we can still go to the rally on Saturday morning, Dad?" says Paddy.

"No bother," says Uncle Alec. "Sure when I was young there were nights I didn't get to bed at all."

Nobody seems to think of asking Marie to come to the hooley. Have they no manners, the lot of them? There's a grating beep from the front of the house.

"That's Papa," says Marie. "I must go. Thank you for a lovely evening." She stands up and starts to go round the table, shaking everybody's hand. In behind Uncle Alec to Auntie Flo, then back to Uncle Alec and Harry's dad, then his mum and round this way to Marjorie. The nearer she gets the more Harry's confusion increases to a state of near-paralysis. Maybe Brian will ask her out in the boat. But he barely looks up. Then she's shaking Harry's hand. He feels as if his tongue has cloven to the roof of his mouth. It's like the time he forgot the words of the solo he was supposed to sing at Children's Day in church. He stood there all alone, grinning foolishly at the congregation while the organist kept on playing the introduction, until his mother hissed at him to sit down.

Marie smiles at him and moves on to Paddy, the last one. Then she passes behind Harry again as she moves to the door, where she stops to wave at everybody.

"For Christ's sake, Harry!" It's Marjorie, hissing at him. "Do you need a kick in the arse or what?"

He gets to his feet and follows her out to the hall. She's standing in view of the kitchen, putting on her blue wind-cheater. He hovers uncertainly. Everything has gone very quiet. When Harry looks into the kitchen a row of faces is looking back at him. Everybody has stopped talking. Then Marie moves up the hall, and he follows. At the front door she turns. She's watching him with that smile of hers, as if they're sharing a secret.

"They're all listening," she whispers.

Beside them the door to the sitting room is open a crack.

"Come in here," Harry says, and goes inside.

"I've only got a moment," she says, but she follows him and, once inside, leans back on the door, pushing it shut behind them.

"About the hooley."

She laughs. "You're doing it again."

"What?"

She squints down her nose with her eyes crossed.

"Oh, that. I hate it when I blush."

"Are you blushing now?"

"It feels like it."

She reaches out and touches his cheek. "You hardly notice it. I've got something for you. Here." She hands him a packet of cigarettes. "I think you'll like them better than the other ones."

"It's a full packet."

"My mother has whole cartons of them."

"Doesn't she mind you smoking?"

"I told her they were for you."

"Oh."

"What about the hooley?"

"Would you like to come?"

"Are you asking me?"

Her eyes are so bright he can hardly bear to look at them. "Yes."

"All right." She stays there, watching him, her face lifted to his, and so he kisses her, and her lips are as soft and pulsing as in his dream.

"Well, did you get a snog or anything? You were in the hall long enough," Paddy finally says.

Harry smiles to himself. He has been determined not to tell Paddy anything unless he specifically asks. "Yeah. It's a pity we didn't have more time. I asked her to the hooley."

A cloud of smoke balloons into the night air from Paddy's window. A spatter of rain rattles the windows and falls across Harry's face, but he keeps on smiling.

"Great cigarettes, aren't they?"

"Yeah."

Harry has produced Marie's Kents as matter-of-factly as he

could. The butts are almost as long as the cigarettes they normally smoke.

"I think she loves me," he says.

"What makes you think that?"

"You can tell. The way she kept looking at me, for a start. Didn't you see the way she kept looking at me?"

"Yeah . . ."

"Well?"

"Yeah."

"It's great having you to talk to about it, you know."

They smoke on in silence. Over the hump of the black hill, between it and the grey sea is the hotel with Marie in it. She'll be in her room, looking up the hill, thinking of him.

"Are you coming out in the boat tomorrow?" Paddy says. "Brian's dad said he could take the engine."

"Yeah, might as well." It's as good a way as any of getting the day in.

"Ready?"

"Right."

"One – two – three – go!" The butts dart out into the night on similar paths but Paddy's, being slightly lower, careens off the far edge of the stone wall and lands a bit further away.

"I'm catching up," says Paddy. "That's only six to five for you now."

"Luck," says Harry, feeling that the luck is all his.

9

WHEN HARRY AND Paddy arrive down at the beach next morning the boat is already in the water, and Brian and his father are fitting the engine. "Hello, Mr McClelland," says Harry. He hasn't seen Brian's dad this holiday yet. He's a tall, balding, deep-voiced man with a black beard who likes to go around in shorts on his holidays.

"Hello, boys. You keep an eye on this fellow. He thinks he knows it all."

Brian is pouring petrol into the little tank. By the grim look on his face some kind of altercation has been going on. His father is a maths teacher at the same school in Belfast that Brian goes to. Harry thinks that's the reason for Brian's subversive tactics.

"Mind and row out a good bit before you start the engine up," Mr McClelland goes on. Brian's nod is so small you could have imagined it. "And never ever come inshore with the engine still down."

"I'll manage, I'll manage."

"You and your 'I'll manage'. I spent a fortune repairing the fibreglass after last summer. Watch the currents in the bay and don't get too near to the rocks. And you're not to go out past Little Horn."

★

Within half an hour they have scudded across the bay, and the cliffs at the base of Horn Head are looming up in front of them. Brian turns the boat right and heads out towards Little Horn. It's a calm day: they could explore the caves or land on one of the shingle beaches or take the boat right up to Little Horn and climb up its bulbous side, but Brian keeps the boat going.

"I thought your dad said not to go past Little Horn," says Harry.

"Fuck that. He'll never be any the wiser," says Brian. "The fishermen all say Skate Bay's where the mackerel are."

As they round Little Horn a high concave sweep of cliffs lurches into view like scenery appearing from the wings of some vast, wobbly theatre. This is the other face of Horn Head, the gaping maw it presents to the Atlantic, rising sheer to six hundred feet at the far side about two miles away, in the bleak promontory of Great Horn. At its base a white line marks where the rollers from the open Atlantic spend themselves on a submerged plate.

The little boat rises and falls in the powerful waves as Brian steers it to the middle of the bay, and shuts off the engine. Soon they're lying back, smoking Marie's Kents, hands on their lines to detect fish biting, and listening to the seagulls' cries echoing from high up the sheer cliffs.

Harry gives himself up to thinking about the kiss again. It's the only thing that calms him down. When he isn't thinking about it he feels all coiled and tense like a clock that's been wound up too tightly, but still can't run any faster to work it off. He thinks he didn't sleep at all the night before. When the tension gets too much he brings out the memory he's been hoarding, and cherishes it. Her lips parting as he moved to her, her eyelashes fluttering against his cheek. The soft pressure of her hands on his back. The sigh she gave when her father blew the Citroën's horn again.

The rollers are passing under the boat, and carrying it in short sweeps towards the cliffs. Soon they appear, teetering at the periphery of Harry's vision, rising and dipping around them in a dizzying arc. They can hear the waves beat against the rocks with long, lazy booms and dissolve into countless tiny slaps and splashes.

"Got off with Marie yet?" Brian asks.

"I asked her to the hooley."

"Yeah, but did you get the finger up?"

"Fuck off."

"Touchy, touchy. True love, is it?"

Harry is suffused in a mixture of embarrassment and pleasure. "I think so."

Brian grunts and tugs at his line.

"What do you think of Marie?" Harry asks.

"Nice enough."

"Her English is perfect. Better than mine."

"That's not difficult. I'd hardly call it English, what you speak in Kilmartin."

"Hasn't she got lovely eyes?"

"Jesus you've got it real bad."

Thick bastard. Anybody can see how beautiful Marie is. That firm furrow of skin from her nose nudging her upper lip up into two beautiful little peaks. Oh, God.

"Here come the Stevensons," says Paddy. "They're going flat out."

"Taking people out to Tory, no doubt," says Brian.

The blue trawler, low down in the water, is ploughing further out across the bay.

"Jesus, that's some wake," says Paddy.

"Christ, we'd better get the boat turned into it," says Brian. He starts to tug at the engine; it splutters but doesn't start. A double wave is sweeping harmlessly out to sea, but its mirror image, two smooth walls of water about four feet high, is sluicing in their direction. The boat is rocking sideways to them.

"Get the oars, for fuck's sake," says Brian, still tugging at the cord.

"Hadn't we better get the lines in?" asks Paddy.

"Fuck the lines."

The oars are under the middle seat, on which Harry is sitting. He and Paddy bend to get them at the same time. Their heads crack together. In a fog of pain Harry grabs an oar and manages to get it into the left rowlock just as the base of the first wave starts to lift the boat. He plunges it into the water and, pulling with both arms, turns the prow half-way into the wave. As the boat corkscrews over the crest it throws the boys against the gunwale. It dips into the wave and a green wall of water pours into the boat. They lurch along the seats to the other gunwale. Harry is still holding the oar, and as the boat rights itself it comes free, lifting the rowlock out of its hole. It jitters round the oar for an instant and then falls with a plop into the wave's back, where it glints for a moment under the surface before slipping away. The boat sinks sluggishly into the trough, heavy with its extra weight of water, still only facing half-way into the next wave. As the boat starts to rise again Paddy is hauling out the other oar, getting it into the rowlock on his side, pulling. The prow lifts and the water sloshes back down the boat towards Brian, who has his back turned to them, still tugging at the starting cable. As the water rises to his knees he turns, his face a mask of terror as the boat plummets downwards again, lifting him above the line of the clifftops behind him. The water shoots back past Harry and Paddy, and the boat crashes jarringly into the trough. Water sprays up on all sides, soaking them, but the boat stays afloat.

They sit for a few moments, not speaking.

"Jesus Christ, Harry, you've got a head on you like Great fucking Horn," says Paddy, feeling his brow. "I've got a fucking great lump coming up."

Harry feels his head in panic. *That's all I need for the hooley. A lump like Frankenstein.* But he can't feel anything, although his head is starting to throb. "It's OK, I'm fine."

"Oh, well, that's the main thing, isn't it?" says Paddy. "Any more of Marie's cigarettes?"

Harry fishes in his pockets and finds the cigarettes, unaccountably dry. An omen.

"You got that wet bringing the boat out of the water?" Mr McClelland asks.

"You should have seen the waves," says Brian.

"And you didn't go past Little Horn?"

"I promised, didn't I?"

"Did you, or did you not?"

"I didn't."

"Thank you. That's all I wanted to know. Maybe you're getting a bit of sense after all."

Harry and Paddy exchange glances. They're sitting in the McClellands' kitchen in clothes of Brian's that are too big for both of them while theirs are drying in the clothes press. They're struggling with plates of macaroni that Mrs McClelland has served them.

Brian winks at Harry and Paddy. Harry takes a mouthful of the rubbery tubes and chews at them. "Having a spot of bother, lads?" asks Brian, all concerned. "Why can't we have big fries,

Mummy, like the Moores do? Normal food, eh, lads? Things that don't look like worms and slither off your fork."

"It's very nice, Mrs McClelland," says Harry.

"Yes, really," says Paddy.

Mr McClelland puts his knife and fork on the plate, pushes his chair back and makes a church of his hands. He masticates carefully for a while, swallows, then clears his throat. Brian grins diabolically at Harry from across the table. *Oh, no, a story.*

"I'll never forget the time I played a round of golf with your father," Mr McClelland begins. The pupils of his eyes have disappeared up below the fluttering lids and all Harry can see are the whites. He does this when he's trying to remember stories. At his side Brian promptly imitates him.

There's a choking sound from Paddy. He's stifling a laugh. "That went down the wrong way," he says, and clears his throat.

Mr McClelland's pupils appear again, and he gives his son a suspicious look, but Brian is innocuously munching his macaroni.

"So we arrived in our cars, and they were both in need of a wash," Mr McClelland goes on.

Harry remembers the story. It's one of the ones Mr McClelland tells every summer. "So I said to your father, I said, whoever loses has to wash the other's car, right?"

"Whose father?" asks Brian.

"What?"

"Whose father, Harry's or Paddy's? They have two different fathers."

"Harry's. Or Paddy's? No matter. Anyway, it was neck and neck up to the sixteenth green." It isn't enough for Mr McClelland just to tell the story, his eyeballs reappear suddenly at key points, and he stares exhortingly at the boys like the schoolmaster he is until he has extracted a nod or at least a grunt

to show they are paying attention. He takes them through each
shot up to the eighteenth hole where everything depends on the
last putt. Eventually Harry and Paddy feel obliged to put down
their knives and forks and give Mr McClelland their undivided
attention. Brian, munching noisily on a lettuce leaf, waits until
the putter in his father's story is descending on the ball and then
he says, "And you won and when you got back to the car park
both of your cars had been washed by a boy who was hanging
about, waiting for a tip."

Mr McClelland's eyeballs swivel towards his son again. "Do
you know what they say is worse than lugging bricks? Digging
canals. That's what they say."

Brian's smile fades. Once a year he's sent off to a youth camp
somewhere in Europe, where he has to work on some project
for a pittance. His father says it's great for forming the character.

The doorbell rang. "I'll get it," says Mrs McClelland.

There are female voices conversing, first quietly, then
excitedly. Mrs McClelland comes back into the kitchen, arms
folded. "That was Mrs Foster," she says. "She went on the trip
in the Stevensons' boat to Tory today. She said she saw you boys
in the boat right out by the Great Horn."

"Well, well, young fellow," says Mr McClelland, into the
silence, "looks like that's the end of the boat for this holiday.
Where was I? Oh, yes. He missed! A foot or under and he
missed! So I said, 'Fred', or was it Alec? I said, 'That's you up the
creek now. Ha-ha. Without a paddle.' But when we came back
to the cars there they were, both washed. The water still
dripping off them. And here was this wee boy, standing with his
hand held out like this." He snorts with laughter and shakes his
head. "Aye, that's what I said, up the creek. Without a paddle.
And missing a rowlock, no doubt, as well."

10

O N FRIDAY HARRY stays in bed until he hears both cars drive
off, his mum and Aunt Flo in the A45 to the hairdresser's
in Dunbreaghy, and the two men and Paddy in the Corsair to
the golf course. It's the Twelfth of July, so the Moores' shop is
shut, and Harry's dad has come up the night before for the long
weekend. When Harry is eating his toast Marjorie appears. She
fetches a bowl of cornflakes and sits down to eat it, her hair
hanging under her chin like a boar's tusks. After a while she
looks up at him. "What are you doing here so late?"

"There was something I wanted to ask you."

"Fire away."

"You know when a boy asks you out to a dance."

"Yeah."

"Well, what does he do?"

"Not very much the first time, if he's wise."

"I don't mean that. I mean – where do you meet?"

"Have you asked Marie to the hooley?"

"Yeah."

"Well, you pick her up and take her home, of course. Unless
she dumps you at the hooley. But I hardly think she will, the
way she was looking at you the other evening."

Harry feels a glow of pleasure.

"One more thing, have your bath tonight, before the hooley."

"But it's only Friday."
"Still."

Harry joins Paddy and Brian in the afternoon, and ends up
having to play football on the beach. It isn't too bad until the
Fosters' boys and some others from Harbour Road start to play,
running rings around Harry although they're much younger. In
spite of Harry's resistance the others decide to have a proper
game, and Paddy and Brian, as captains of the respective teams,
take turns to pick from the assembled talent. The group around
Harry dwindles until there's only him and the smallest boy left,
and it's Paddy's turn to pick. He picks the small boy.

"Fuck the lot of you," Harry says, and walks off. He goes over
to the rocks and lights a cigarette. He tries to think about the
kiss. It has got him through the Thursday and this morning. But
now with the hooley drawing closer he's unable to stop the
churning in his stomach, and he starts to worry again. It had only
been a kiss, after all. Maybe it doesn't mean as much to her as it
does to him. Maybe he should play it cool this evening, act as if
nothing happened.

When Harry gets back from the harbour Marjorie has already
engaged the bathroom. He retreats to his bedroom. Snatches of
songs, whistlings, rustling and thudding noises come from the
other bedrooms. He misses the bathroom changeover a couple
of times, and by the time he gets in there's a great mixture of
perfumes and aftershaves but only cold water left to bath and
wash his hair in. He's surprised, as always, by the amount of sand
in the bathtub after the water has run off. He shaves carefully,
then can't resist squeezing at a spot that isn't quite ripe. It hurts
like hell and perches throbbing on his chin like a cherry. He
gives it a thick coating of Marjorie's Clearasil and slaps Cedar

Wood everywhere else on his face. Then up to the bedroom to pick what clothes to wear. Paddy's back, and reclining on his bed.

"What do you think?" Harry asks. "The school blazer or the cord jacket?" He tries on both.

"I think the sooner you get down to your shirtsleeves the better," says Paddy.

"You're a big help. I can't pick Marie up in my shirtsleeves."

"The cord, then."

The rest is easy. It has to be the black polo-neck over the white nylon shirt, the grey flannels and the desert boots. He hunkers down to see himself in the sideboard mirror. If he hunches his shoulders forward slightly he really does look a bit like Patrick McGoohan.

"Are you boys ready?" Auntie Flo calls up the stairs.

Harry feels his stomach give a slight flutter. "Coming," he shouts.

Harry leaves the others at the cars outside the church hall and starts back up to the hotel alone. A wind has come up. It whips at his anorak and cord jacket, flapping them around him like a scarecrow's rags. He walks quickly, rehearsing the things he'll say. An embellished version of yesterday's events in the boat will do for a start. Play it by ear after that. Be funny, but don't show all your teeth when you laugh. He tries Patrick McGoohan's smile. Keep your shoulders hunched. Bash on, crash on and get the job done. Keep your head down and bore on regardless.

A light drizzle comes on just before he enters the hotel. The receptionist, a young girl with a farming complexion in a green uniform, looks up expectantly at him and he wonders whether to ask for the Fischers' room, but then he sees Marie standing in a group of hotel guests near the stairs, flanked by her parents.

Harry approaches the group. The men are the well-off red-faced kind who sometimes buy Harry's golf balls, and drive the fancy cars in the car park. The women are of Mrs Cooper's ilk. Marie is talking animatedly, apparently about the new tweed coat she's wearing, because one of the group, a fat white-haired man, is taking the opportunity to paw at it, and the others are listening. Marie is starting to smile. Harry watches the warmth coming into her eyes, and everything he wants to say evaporates. He stands still to prolong the moment. She hasn't noticed him yet, but she soon will. Then a burst of laughter comes from the group, and Marie looks his way, sees him, and moves out from the middle of the others. The warmth stays in her eyes, as she takes his arm and leads him to her parents.

"Good evening, Mrs Fischer. Good evening, Mr Fischer." He shakes hands with them as his mother has told him to.

Mrs Fischer's smile is a poor, crimped thing, like something that has been left out in the rain and shrunk, and Mr Fischer stands drawn up very straight, frowning slightly, like a general inspecting inferior troops. He takes Harry's hand in a vice-like grip. "I think I will drive you in the car," he says.

"Nonsense, Papa, it's only a short walk," says Marie.

"Hmmm. You'll have to see my daughter home, then." He's still holding Harry's hand.

"Yes. Of course."

"You will look after her. We don't normally let our daughter go out on her own. She tells me you are a trustworthy young man." His eyes engage Harry's steadily. He looks as if he's considering applying some kind of wrestling lock. "She has to be in before twelve o'clock." He lets go of Harry's hand.

Mrs Fischer says something in French and pats Marie's coat.

"*Salut*," Marie says.

"*Salut*," says Mr Fischer. "We will wait up for you."

Marie leads the way out of the hotel. They set off down the drive. When Harry looks back at the hotel he sees Marie's father and mother standing at the bay windows of the foyer, looking out at them. "What was everybody laughing at?" he asks.

"It was only that Mr O'Connor. He thinks he's such a charmer. Always on about what he'd do if he was thirty years younger."

"What's that?"

"I don't know. It wouldn't help him, being thirty years younger. Even if he wasn't fat then he'd be going to be. You can always tell."

"That people are going to be fat?"

"Yes. Like Brian. Haven't you noticed? There's a fat man inside him, waiting to get out. He's only a thin fat boy in the meantime. Do you know what I mean?"

"Kind of."

"It works the other way round, too. There are fat thin people. Your aunt is a fat thin woman, wouldn't you say so?"

"Maybe, yes."

Watching her lips move in talk and smiles Harry wishes he could just kiss them. How can they be talking about anything else other than what has happened between them? Isn't she thinking about it at all? They reach the bottom of the drive and turn up the road to the church.

"Lots of film stars and pop singers are short tall people," she goes on. "Humphrey Bogart. Dustin Hoffman. Charles Aznavour. Mick Jagger. Most of them, in fact. Then there are clever stupid people and stupid clever people."

"People here, you mean?"

"No. You don't know them. My cousin is a clever stupid person. Our gardener is a stupid clever person."

"What am I?"

"Normal." Marie turns to look back at the hotel. Is she going to say they're out of sight now? Will they kiss? But they're almost at the church hall, and they can hear shreds of accordion music spilling out from the open door between the gusts of wind. People are getting out of cars and running into the hall, holding their hats.

In the porch Marie combs her hair while Harry pays. He takes her coat and hangs it and his on the hooks by the kitchen door. Marie is wearing a blue dress that flares out from under her bosom and ends just above her knees. They go inside. The hall is half empty. On the stage the band is playing a waltz but nobody is dancing. There's an accordion player, a man at a rudimentary set of drums and an electric guitar player strumming chords. The girls are sitting up the left side, the married couples and a few boys on the right. Some local males are milling near the door, smoking and eyeing the talent. The Moores, the McClellands and the Bryces are sitting up near the stage on the right. The chalked boards echo as Harry and Marie walk across to join them, and Harry feels everybody's eyes upon them.

"Marie!" Marjorie is waving. "Come over here."She pats the seat at her side, and Marie sits down beside her.

Harry goes to join Paddy and Brian, who are standing a bit further up with their hands in their pockets as though to sit down would be taking the thing too seriously. "Hi, men."

They nod, not smiling, looking around. Harry looks around, too, and then back at Marie, now deep in conversation with Marjorie. What will she make of it all? Quite shabby, the whole place, has it always been like this? Drab brown oil paint on the walls, glaring fluorescent lights on the ceiling, the local girls in their old-fashioned summer frocks, the tinny music that twangs across the empty floor.

"Take your partners for the next dance," says the guitar

player, bending down to the microphone, and strums the introductory chords.

"Come on, Alec," says Auntie Flo. "Somebody has to make a start." Soon she's sailing round the floor with her husband firmly attached to her front, smiling contentedly. *A fat thin woman.* Marie is right. Harry looks across to her. She's sitting on her own, because Harry's parents have joined Flo and Alec on the dance-floor and the Reverend McLeod is dancing with Marjorie. Marie looks up and smiles at him. Harry smiles back and looks away again. He listens to the music, and tries to hear what kind of a dance it is. The only one he's certain about is the waltz, and it isn't that. Quickstep? Foxtrot? Can Marie dance them? What will she think of him if he can't? The band starts into the third tune of the set. Harry recognises it. He goes across to Marie. "May I have the pleasure? I know this one." He takes her hand and leads her on to the floor as the guitar player starts to sing.

> *"Trains and boats and planes*
> *go passing by.*
> *They mean a trip to Paris or Rome*
> *to someone else*
> *but not for me.*
> *The trains and the boats and planes*
> *took you away*
> *away from me"*

"I know it too," says Marie. "We call it 'Quand un bateau passe'."

Harry takes her in his arms, and they move away. After a few steps Marie smiles, nods, and falls in with Harry's all-purpose shuffle.

> *"We were so in love*
> *and high above*
> *we had a star to wish upon. Wish*
> *and dreams come true*
> *but not for me.*
> *The trains and the boats and planes*
> *took you away*
> *away from me."*

"It's really a tango, Harry," says Marie. "Can you do it?"

"I don't think so."

"It's easy. Look. Slow – slow – quick–quick – slow."

Harry follows her lead and they move round the floor while the band plays the instrumental bit in the middle. Being a learner means he can look down and watch her legs. Every time she takes the longer strides for the slow steps the hem of her dress rides up well above her knee with a slight hiss. On the last verse the accordion player comes in on vocal harmonies.

> *"Trains and boats and planes*
> *took you away*
> *but every time I see them I pray*
> *and if my prayer should cross the sea*
> *the trains and the boats and planes*
> *will bring you back*
> *back home to me."*

"Is that how you travel?" Harry asks. "Trains and boats and planes?"

"No planes. Just trains and boats."

Will they bring you back? Back home to me?

She smiles back at him, looks away, but moves in closer. She's following his lead now.

"You can hold me a bit lower," she says.

But then the song ends with a flourish of drums.

When they leave the dance-floor Harry sees the hall has filled up a bit. Paddy asks Marie for the next round of waltzes and Marjorie is dancing with the Reverend McLeod. Harry joins Brian. He's still standing, hands in his trouser pockets, the flaps of his buttoned blue prefect's blazer bunched up round his waist in two pouting snouts. "Aren't you dancing?" Harry asks.

"No, thanks all the same. I prefer girls. There's a bit of real talent over there." Brian nods across the hall. The one he seems to mean is a heavily made-up, dumpy girl in a floral mini-skirt who's staring intently at the back of the hall.

"She seems to be more interested in the locals," Harry says.

"That's because she doesn't know any better." Brian straightens his tie, stretches his neck, and sets off across the floor. Harry sees the girl look up in surprise, and shake her head. Brian moves to the girl on her right, who also shakes her head. Harry thinks he's going to go up the whole row, but he only tries the next one, then saunters back across the floor. "Bitches," he says.

Harry is relieved to see that Marie and Paddy aren't talking while they dance, because Paddy is too busy watching his feet. They don't hold hands either when they leave the dance-floor. By now there are enough people for the set dances, and the Siege of Ennis is announced. Harry asks Marie again.

"What would you say Paddy is?" he asks Marie, as he leads her out. "Thin fat? Tall small?"

"Old young."

"What's that mean?"

"He acts older than he is, but he's too innocent."

They have to line up opposite each other, and Marie watches the steps and formations carefully, so there's no further chance for conversation. After that there's a slow waltz round, which Harry sits out. He watches Marjorie dancing with his dad, and Marie with Uncle Alec. She dances perfectly, it seems to Harry. Everything about her is perfect. Her face, her voice, the way she moves. Surely every male in the place has to fall in love with her, just from looking at her.

Shortly before ten Harry goes out of the side door to the toilet. There's a queue that stretches round the back of the hall. He joins its end. When he sees there are only women and girls in it he goes on round to the deserted far side, and pees down the drain, careful to keep the stream in the direction of the wind. Then he completes the circuit to the front of the hall and comes that way, pushing through the crowd of young men at the back. The music has stopped, and tea is being served. A procession consisting of a trolley of white cups and saucers, a boiler full of tea on wheels, and another trolley of cakes and sandwiches is slowly making its way up the side of the hall, escorted by a convoy of women. Marie and Marjorie are laughing when he joins them.

"Five," says Marie.

"Far too good," says Marjorie. They're watching the back of the hall. "Look at that double-breasted navy-blue jacket. The brass buttons. The winklepickers, for God's sake. Three, at the most."

"Out of what?" Harry asks.

"Ten," says Marjorie.

"What'd I get?"

"That'd be telling. More from Marie than from me, anyway. Double the amount, to be precise. Sorry about that. I keep seeing you in those shorts you had on last year."

"Where are Paddy and Brian?" Harry asks, while he thinks about this.

"Out for a cigarette," says Marie.

"Is the sum an even number or an odd one?" Harry asks.

"What do you think, Marie? Is that giving away too much?" Marjorie asks.

Marie shrugs.

"Even," Marjorie says.

The procession reaches them and they hold out their cups.

"Anybody for without?" one of the women says, and fills the cups when none of them retract theirs.

"What about the one with the sideburns?" Marjorie asks.

"I don't know," says Marie. "Do you know Johnny Halliday? No? Something left over from the fifties?"

"The Ted That Time Forgot," says Harry.

"Five points," says Marie, and sips her tea.

"Ah, but look at the way he talks with the cigarette in his mouth. That takes practice. A real James Dean. I'd give him seven."

"What's this?" Marie holds out her cup.

"Tea," says Harry.

"There's milk and sugar in it."

"You have to ask for without. They did say."

"Oh." She sets the cup on the window-ledge behind her.

"What's the most points you've given?" Harry asks.

"I'm not saying," says Marie. The sides of her mouth are puckering again.

The crowd at the back of the hall is swelling visibly. The pub in Dunbreaghy has closed, and an influx of boys is pushing their way to the front, blinking slowly from the drink as they eye the girls, who have become more lively, shrieking and giggling. Brian's favourite is sitting on another girl's knees, whispering excitedly, and casting glances towards the door. Sheets of rain rattle the windows high up in the walls.

The music starts up again. The girls and women form a circle in the middle, holding hands, and the boys and men, fewer in number, form a circle round them. The two circles start off in opposite directions. Harry keeps losing hold of a farmer with big, chapped hands, and having to run to catch up with him. The music stops unexpectedly, leaving Harry facing Brian's favourite, who's obviously as disappointed as Harry is himself. The band starts into a waltz, and Harry shambles away with his unwilling partner. The women who are left over sit down or dance silently with each other, smiling into the distance, as if it's all right to dance with each other as long as they don't talk. Harry sees Marie dancing with Brian. She gives Harry a rueful smile as they pass. Harry tries to fiddle the choice after that, slowing down before Marie appears, and hanging back in her vicinity as long as he can before tearing off round the circle to catch up with her again. But the next time he ends up with another local girl, and finally Mrs Bryce. It's hard to find a place on her back to hold her by that isn't a strap or a fold, and he has to move his hand around a bit before he finds a kind of no man's land between her bra and some other protuberance further down. She's watching him with a slight smile during these wanderings, and looking as though she wants to say something, but she doesn't. While they dance Harry tries to trace Marie in the throng, and finally he sees her, in the arms of a burly farming lad who's holding her as if he thinks she'll break if he drops her. She's talking away and smiling. Harry's stomach lurches. How many points is she giving him? What can that clod have to say to make her smile? If he isn't funny why is she smiling? Isn't Harry funny either, then, if she laughs at the things he says?

"Marie seems to be enjoying herself," says Mrs Bryce.

"Yeah."

"She has all the boys' heads turned."

Harry's glad when the dance is over. He can't find Marie for a horrible moment and then he sees her talking to Paddy. The hall is quite crowded by now, and before he can get to them she's whisked away by the Reverend McLeod for the foxtrot.

"Tell me this," Harry says to Paddy. "If one woman bought double the number of apples another one bought, say from a number between one to ten, and the sum of the two was an even number, what could the higher number be? Seriously."

Paddy looks askance at him. "Are you talking about Marjorie's silly game? Marie gave you eight points. It was just before we went for a fag. She'd probably have given you the full ten, only Marjorie started off with four."

After the dance McLeod leads Marie back with a great flourish and a bow. "Thin fat?" Harry asks. "Clever stupid?"

Marie thinks for a moment. "Definitely good bad," she says.

"Ladies and gentlemen, by special request," says the MC, making three syllables of *request,* "the clap dance." A scattering of whoops comes from the crowd.

"Wait till you see this," Harry says to Marie.

Marie laughs as the dancers take to the floor. "Why are the old men dancing with each other?"

"Wait and see."

Soon the air is resounding with the whip-like cracks of the old farmers' big callused palms.

"Doesn't it hurt?" asks Marie.

"Look at them, they're laughing."

The air is thick with cigarette smoke and sweat, and moisture is running down the walls when the dance finishes.

"And now what we've been looking forward to all evening, Ladies' Choice!" says the guitar player. A few girls start to cross the floor. This is what it's like to be a girl, Harry thinks, the feigned indifference, the awful waiting.

"Oh, I see," says Marie. "May I have the pleasure, isn't that what you say?"

The joy.

The music starts. "It's a polka," says Marie. "Can you do it?"

"It's 'Shoe the Donkey'. I can do that all right."

They join the line and set off. The hall is shaking with the thuds of the dancers' feet. The accordion player is putting all kinds of notes into the simple tune, eyes tightly shut, sweat pouring down his face.

"You'd think it was trying to get away from him," says Marie. It looks like a comic act with a suitcase that's too full. When the accordion player manages to get one part of his box shut it bulges open at another, and cascades of notes tumble out.

Marie says something.

"What?"

She nudges her face right up beside his to talk into his ear. He can feel her cheekbone moving. "One of those boys asked if he could walk me home. I said I was going with you."

After that the band play a couple of pop songs for the young folk. Even their version of "Satisfaction" sounds great to Harry, and for "Massachusetts" Marie comes right into his arms and stays there while they shuffle round the floor without speaking. The hall is absolutely packed now and other couples keep bumping into them but Harry feels a great calm. It's like waking up from a dream when they move apart after the dance.

"Take your partners please for the 'Waves of Tory'."

"I'll have to go," says Marie.

"Just this one more."

"All right."

The lines form up quickly. Everybody wants to dance this one. Harry and Marie join an animated Marjorie with the Reverend McLeod, who keeps sweeping his hair back as he bobs his head to emphasise some point. Then the couples have to part to join the men's or women's lines. When the two lines stretch the length of the hall the music starts up.

Marie learns the dance quickly by just following the others. Soon she's even doing the shuffle with her feet the way the local women do. The two lines of men and women turn towards the stage and start to move off, coming together like a zip at the top of the hall. Harry is worried that he'll end up with somebody else, but there she is, holding out her hand, smiling her smile. *Like fate.* Then they're off into the waves, first ducking under the arch of the oncoming couples' arms, Marie's soft hip against his, then moving apart, still holding hands to make a bridge over the next couple. Harry's whole consciousness is in the fingertips that are holding Marie's, feeling their skin strain together again after each slight slip. Faces loom up out of the murky smoke, fixed in laughs or in grimaces, his parents, Brian, the Reverend McLeod's bald pate below them, all seeming far away compared with the warm pressure of Marie's hand.

When the round is over it is a quarter to twelve. Harry takes Marie to say goodnight to his parents and gets her coat. The guitarist is singing, "The old home town looks the same . . ." when they leave the hall.

Outside the cool wind hits them like a wave. A storm is crashing and thundering over the bay. Behind the broiling clouds the sky pulses yellow and forks of lightning flicker down to the leaden sea, lighting up the whole bay. Claps of thunder roll, sounding like bowls in a quarry. The images of the streaks stay in Harry's retina when he blinks, like threads of gold. "It's going to rain

again in a minute," he says, "we'd better get a move on." It
seems natural to put his arm around Marie. They run off towards
the hotel. The rain comes on as they reach the drive, lashing in
sheets across the lawn. The bent and gnarled trees at the bottom
of the drive creak and groan as they run past them.

"Do you have to go straight in?" Harry asks, as they approach
the side entrance to the TV lounge, now dark.

"We have a few minutes left," says Marie, and they take
shelter.

"I've been looking forward to this all evening," says Harry.
Her face, wet with rain, is turned up to his. He bends down to
kiss her and she closes into his embrace. Her lips are cold against
his and he feels the corners move into a smile.

"I can't forget the other evening, when we kissed," she says.

"I haven't slept a wink for thinking about you," Harry says.

"I was worried that I'd got on your nerves with all that silly
talk about thin fat people. I spent all afternoon thinking about
what I'd say when I saw you again, and once I'd started I
couldn't stop. I was hoping you'd just give me a kiss."

"Everything else seems a waste of time, doesn't it?"

"Yes."

They kiss again. Then she lays her head on his chest and they
watch Horn Head's dark hulk flash in and out of sight.

"I must go," Marie says. "My parents will be waiting."

"Will I see you tomorrow?"

"In the morning?"

"I have to go to church. In the afternoon."

"Two o'clock?"

"I'll pick you up here."

"OK."

They kiss again, and she dashes off through the rain towards
the front entrance. Harry watches her go in, then leans back

against the wall and watches the storm roll and crack across the bay.

This is what peace feels like. He has almost forgotten. He turns up the collar of his anorak and sets off into the night.

He's soon soaked through to the skin. Hefty gusts are whipping the briars against his legs and the stones in the walls are treacherously slippery. He hums "Trains And Boats And Planes" and it sounds as though the wind is blowing harmonies.

"Harry?" A dark shape at the foot of the second stone wall.

"Paddy? Is that you?"

"Thank Christ you've come. I thought you might have taken the road."

"What's the matter?"

"The fucking stone moved."

"Did you fall?"

"Aye. I must have broken something." A flash of light shows Paddy huddling at the foot of the wall, holding his right ankle.

"What did you walk up for anyway?"

"Och, I was that pissed off, I didn't want to wait, sure I've been gone for ages."

"I didn't notice."

"You didn't notice very much."

"Can you get up if I give you a hand?"

"Give it a try, no, Jesus, stop, it's no good."

"I'll go and get the men. We'll come for you in the car."

"They've just gone up. I heard them drive past. I shouted, but it was no good."

"I'll just be a minute. Don't run away." Harry sets off down the path. Then he comes back. "Do you know one good thing?"

"I can't think of one just at the minute, seeing as my holiday's probably ruined."

"You won't be needing your bike."

"What's good about that?"

"Marie can have it."

It takes all three of them to manoeuvre Paddy over the wall and into the car. Auntie Flo kicks up a great fuss, wanting them to drive him to Letterkenny hospital straight away, but Paddy says he's feeling better and can even put a bit of weight on his ankle so they decide to wait until the next day. They manoeuvre Paddy up the stairs, and get him into bed. When the men retreat Harry lights a cigarette at the window. It's the last one of Marie's Kents.

"This one doesn't count," he says.

"Very big of you."

"Do you know when a tooth has just fallen out?"

Paddy sneezes.

"And you poke at the hole with your tongue," Harry goes on. "You know the feeling? That nice kind of pain. That's what it's like."

"What what's like?"

"When she doesn't know I'm watching her."

"For her or for you?"

"For Christ's sake, Paddy. For me, of course. I can't remember what it used to be like. Before I fell in love with Marie. The things I used to think about. The things that used to fill my head. How I used to fill in the day. I can't remember. You see, when we walk arm in arm . . ."

"Yeah?"

"Well, it's like we're moving as one, you know? Not like with other girls that bounce up and down beside you. Like yo-yos. You can't get into step with them, you know what I mean?"

There's no answer from Paddy, and after a while Harry hears his breathing slow and become regular. Harry smokes on, looking out at the night. The storm has passed inland, drawing a heavy curtain of rain behind it that cuts off Horn Head.

11

" AND THEN THERE was nothing wrong with his leg at all,"
Harry says. "Well, apart from it being sprained. But he's
caught pneumonia."

Marie whistles. "That's serious."

"He doesn't know whether he can smoke or not, *that*'s
serious, he could hardly ask with his father and mother there. He
has to stay in the house for two weeks."

"And he doesn't mind about the bike?"

"It was his idea." Harry has wheeled both bikes down to the
hotel.

Marie swings her leg over the bar and pushes off, careering
out over the middle of the road.

"On the left, Marie!"

"Oops!"

A last shower from the previous night's storm overtakes them at
Doe Chapel, but before Creeslough the sun comes out again.
After Creeslough a narrow, pot-holed road branches off to the left
in the direction of Doe Castle. The Tarmac lies in smooth pools
coated with a film of rain through which the underlying rocks
poke here and there. The blue sky and fleecy clouds are reflected
in the water beneath their hissing tyres and it's as if they're flying.
The spongy purple moss stretches away on either side.

Then the road descends into the woods of Dunbally river. They have to brake because of the rocks that break surface through the tar so they have no momentum when the road swings upwards again and have to get off their bikes and push. They enter a thickly overgrown alleyway with high banks of redly glistening fuchsia on both sides. The dense interlacing of leafy branches overhead has held off the previous rain; by now it has filtered its way through and falls in swollen drops that splat lazily on the road. Harry, leading, turns when Marie screams, but it's only one of these bulbous drops that has landed on her neck, she has arched her back in reflex; still in the scream her eyes are tightly shut and her mouth is stretching between a grimace and a laugh. He can clearly see the contours of her bra pushing through her thin pullover and the raised nipples below it.

"I'm getting soaked!" she says.

They put on their coats and push on up the hill. A drop hits Harry between his collar and his neck and spreads down his shoulder-blades, making his whole body twitch. When they emerge into the sunshine at the top of the hill they're soaked.

"We'll dry off in the sun," says Marie, once again removing her coat and shaking out her hair. Harry does the same, trying not to look at how her pullover is now moulded damply to her bra and the nipples, still cheekily erect.

They're still wet when they reach Doe Castle. It's low tide and only a far-off shimmer of silver in the bay shows where the sea is. Marie shivers as a gust of wind comes up. "Is there nowhere we can lie in the sun?"

"Maybe that island out there."

About a hundred yards into the sands of the bay lies an island, a green mound in a skirt of brown seaweed with a few bushes on top. Nobody will disturb them there. They leave the bikes down by the shore, take off their shoes and socks, roll up their jeans and set off across the sand, Harry carrying the picnic basket. Near the island they have to cross the carpet of seaweed. The globules squelch and pop unpleasantly under their feet and then they're climbing up the grassy slopes. From a spur at the top Marie looks down the far side facing towards the bay. "There's a place where I can lie. I'm going to take my clothes off and leave them to dry. You can lie on this side. And no peeking!"

"OK," says Harry, abashed. He retreats down the near side and stands about holding the basket. He can hear zippings and rustlings. Then silence. He stares up the ridge. *I'm going to take my clothes off.* He puts down the basket and moves stealthily up the hill again, moving like an Indian in the games of his childhood, careful not to step on any twigs. As he approaches the top he sinks to his knees then wriggles forward on his belly to the spur of rock Marie has stood on and inches his way forward.

In spite of what he's told Paddy the only breasts Harry has seen were in his father's *Amateur Photographer* magazines. And they were black and white and shades of grey. Marie's are pale pink, rising from her sun-tanned shoulders, and roseately tipped. She's lying directly below, facing the other way, eyes closed, wearing only white cotton pants. Then she looks straight up at him, her inverted eyes attractively Oriental.

"I thought as much," she says, and covers her breasts with her hands.

"There's no sun on the other side," says Harry.

"Really, Harry. Well, you may as well come down now."

By the time he gets down to her she has put on her brassière and is sitting up.

"Sorry about that," he says. "I didn't think you'd undressed that much."

"My brassière got wet, too, you know." She doesn't seem too badly put out.

"Is it dry now?"

"Not quite. I'm not taking it off again, though."

"Wouldn't like you catching a cold."

"Very thoughtful of you. But you can take off your shirt. It must be wet, too."

He unbuttons it and spreads it out on the grass, embarrassed by his pallid white limbs. His jeans are clammy round his legs. He'd like to take them off, too, but that might look as if he's trying to get up to something. He lies back uneasily.

A light breeze rustles the leaves and branches of the bushes above them and above that larks are circling in the sky. Through their chirps and the caws of the seagulls they hear the rasping cry of a corncrake staking its claim in the fields to their backs. In front of them lies the great bay with the strong blue channel of the Lackagh river winding through the yellow sands and beyond that the hills rise in ever lightening layers of blue.

Harry is finding it difficult to attune to the landscape the way he usually does. The image of Marie's breasts is too fresh in his mind, their presence in the white brassière beside him more exciting than in a swim suit.

"Can anybody see us here?" asks Marie.

"Not a soul."

She doesn't say anything to this. He looks at her, then rolls over towards her, takes her awkwardly in his arms and kisses her. The cups of her bra flatten against his chest.

"Your trousers are wet," she says.

"Should I take them off?"

"Don't you dare."

They kiss again and slowly the heart's ease that he felt on Friday comes over Harry again. He opens his eyes and Marie does, too. Hers gaze steadily into his, green–grey with tiny brown flecks, slowly blinking. She makes a little sound and moves against him. He has an erection. He passes his hand over the hard carapace of her bra. She quivers and sits up, breathing hard.

"I have to be careful," she says, and reaches for her blouse.

What does that mean? Has she gone further with another boy? Brooding, Harry puts on his shirt and then his pullover. From the depths of it he asks, "Have you got a boyfriend?"

"Not really."

He tugs the pullover furiously over his head and looks at her. She's watching him with a half-smile, hugging her knees.

"What about you? Have you got a girlfriend?"

"Of course not."

"But you've had girlfriends."

"Only two." He has snogged with two girls after youth–club dances. "What do you mean you haven't really got a boyfriend?"

Marie is lying back again, eyes closed. "I wouldn't call him my boyfriend exactly. He's just a boy I kiss sometimes."

A red–hot poker twists in Harry's entrails. "Who?"

"My cousin."

"The stupid clever one?"

"The clever stupid one, you mean. I only have the one. My parents don't let me go out with other boys. They'd go crazy if they knew I was alone here with you. I tell them there's a whole crowd of us, Marjorie and all. They think that's good for my English."

"But they've no objections to you going round kissing your own cousin?"

"They don't know, of course."

It's time somebody told them. "Well, is he your boyfriend or not?"

"No, no. He's far too old. He's only, well, the boy I kiss, you know?"

"I know rightly. How old is he?"

"Twenty. He's a student. So my parents think it's all right for me to go for walks with him, seeing as he's my cousin and everything. And then we go for walks and then we kiss. I think he's in love with me."

"He should be ashamed of himself. And so should you. What do you kiss him for if he's not your boyfriend?"

"Practice."

Harry lies back and closes his eyes. His mind has gone blank, a numb receptacle of grass rustlings and bird cries. He feels Marie's lips on his again. This time her hand strokes the side of his face as they kiss. "Silly boy," she says. "Haven't you noticed that I love you?"

"If you knew how funny you look with that smile on your face," says Paddy.

"She loves me," says Harry.

"How do you know?"

"She said so." The words have been going round in Harry's head the whole evening. He thinks he sees Paddy rolling his eyes over by his window but he doesn't care. "I've never been in love like this before."

"You say that every time."

"What do you mean?"

"You said that about Pearl Brown, you said that about Josephine McClintock. Then you forget."

His two youth-club courts. Trust Paddy to remember every word he said. "They were nothing compared to this."

"Are you getting any good courting done?"

"Enough, enough."

Harry has caressed her breasts through her bra and then undone it with her help and kissed the little nipples till they stood up. But he doesn't want to tell Paddy that. He's spoiled him with exaggerated accounts of his encounters with girls from Kilmartin, and now that he's actually doing the things he has long since boasted of he doesn't want to talk about them.

12

"Is the Scourge of the Seven Seas still not allowed out in the boat?" Harry asks.

"I'm working on it," Brian says. "Suffering in silence, you know. I don't think the old man can take it much longer." He's sitting on the arm of Marjorie's armchair, reading the *Daily Mirror*. They're all up at the Moores' house with Paddy, listening to Marjorie's record collection on the record-player she has brought down from her room – "A Whiter Shade Of Pale", "I'm A Believer", "Nights In White Satin", "Jumpin' Jack Flash", "Excerpt From A Teenage Opera", and "Sunny Afternoon". She also brought "Honey", but Paddy hid it under a loose floorboard in his and Harry's room before his accident. The adults are out.

"Hey, Marie, bet you don't know who the Prime Minister of France is," Brian says.

"De Gaulle, of course," says Marie.

"Wrong. He's the President."

"Then the other one, Pompidou."

"Wrong again. Monsieur Couve de Melville, since last week."

"Never heard of him."

"Because of all the student riots."

"It's the same everywhere, America, England, Germany."

"Not here. Not in Ireland."

"Oh, yes, it is," says Paddy, from his place by the fire. "We have Civil Rights and everything too. They sing 'We Shall Overcome' and all."

"That's different," says Brian. "That's just the Prods and the Micks."

"Is that a group?" Marie asks.

"Protestants and Catholics," says Harry. "A big thing in Northern Ireland. For the old folk, anyway. When we grow up everything will be different. Anybody got a fag?"

"It's a nice change to be asked rather than just stolen from," says Marjorie. She produces a packet of Silk Cut and wriggles out from behind Brian to pass them round. "Not for you, little brother."

"Ah, come on, Marjorie, for Christ's sake."

"You're too young. And aren't you supposed to be ill?"

"I won't inhale."

"You're still too young. I didn't start until I was sixteen."

"If you don't give me one I'll just go and get one of my own. Up those steep stairs. And the doctor said I wasn't to exert myself unnecessarily."

"God, if Mum could hear her darling little boy."

"Ta. Now all I need is a cup of coffee."

"Marie's Catholic."

"So what?"

Harry exhales smoke out of the window while he tries to think of a suitable response. Paddy's answer was what he had wanted to say.

"Yeah, that's just it, so what?" he says. "It doesn't matter a fuck." But he feels a bit put out. It isn't something to be taken for granted. Lots of his friends wouldn't go with Catholics.

"It would be different, wouldn't it," Paddy says, "if she was Irish?"

"Not a damn bit."

"I mean, if she was, say, from Kilmartin."

Harry has forgotten Paddy can be like this. There's this thran streak about him. You say something really obvious, something that anybody with any common sense will agree with, and he'll start to pick and poke at it, like their grandmother unravelling a pullover with a knitting mistake only she can see.

Paddy goes on, "Like if she was going to the convent school in Ballyraine, just imagine, sitting up at the front of the bus in that grey uniform —"

"Blue."

"— blue, no matter, sitting up there with all the others, away from all you Protestant boys at the back."

"Jesus, I'm sorry I spoke."

"If she was, what do you call that woman from across the street, if she was Mrs McCloskey's daughter."

"She wouldn't be Marie, then, would she?"

Paddy says nothing.

"You should get yourself a girlfriend," Harry says.

"Bit difficult, seeing I can't get out of the house."

"I don't mean now, I mean generally speaking. You're old enough. And now that the old apparatus is in working order . . ."

Paddy makes a sound between a laugh and a grunt.

"Have you ever had one?" Harry knows he hasn't.

"Not really."

"Is there nobody you fancy?"

"There is, actually."

"Tell us."

"She's already taken. Anyway, it's nobody you know."

"Tell me anyway."

"There's no point."

"Unrequited love, eh?"

"I don't know."

Harry lets it go at that. "She's got aitches at the back of her knees," he says.

"She's got what?"

"Aitches. I don't know what you call them. Like the letters. At the back of her knees, where they bend. They're lovely."

"Aitches. Lord God Almighty. I thought you were talking about some disease."

They go to bed, and Harry lies in the dark. He's thinking of the courting session with Marie in the dunes behind Tramore Strand near Horn Head that morning, and his penis is throbbing at the memory of Marie's moist little bud under his finger. He has sworn to himself never to wank again.

13

Harry's mother comes out of the dining room just as he's slipping out of the door. "What do you want that rug for?"

"For the picnic."

"You're not to be getting up to any hanky-panky with Marie. Do her parents know you two go off on your own?"

"Of course."

"It would be a better idea for you to keep Paddy company."

"Sure we were up all afternoon yesterday."

"Well, he'd be alone all morning if it wasn't for your uncle and aunt and me."

"Where's Marjorie going off to?"

"She's taken to practising on the church organ."

"I thought she'd given up the organ."

"Don't go changing the subject. You know rightly Paddy's your friend, not hers, even if she is his sister."

"All right, all right, we were coming up this afternoon again anyway."

"And mind what I said about Marie."

"Does nobody ever come here, do you think?" Marie asks.

"It's so hidden maybe only the farmer knows about it."

"And he doesn't live here any more. We could be the only people in the world."

By chance they have found a hidden beach over on the other side of Horn Head, enclosed by a ring of rocks and sand dunes, with only one narrow channel through the rocks to the sea. It's the hottest day of the summer yet. The outgoing tide is draining the basin of water between the rocks and the sand, and the sand is drying as they watch in the heat of the sun, emerging in a growing crescent form like the waxing moon.

"I'm going to sunbathe," says Marie, and starts to undress.

"We've no bathing trunks."

"So what? There's nobody here to see us except the cows." Marie is already stepping out of her jeans.

Harry unbuttons his shirt. "Do you do this often?" he asks, thinking of the camps he's heard about on the continent, where people run about starkers all day.

"I've only done it once before."

"With your cousin?"

"Maybe." She slips out of her pants, and lays them neatly on her clothes. Then she straightens up, and turns to Harry. "He might have been there. I don't remember. There was a whole crowd of us. It was last summer. We were camping near a lake. It was a lovely warm evening."

Her nipples and pubis stand out in pale swathes in her tan. "He'd remember all right," Harry says.

Marie is giggling.

"What's the matter?" Harry asks.

"It's the socks. You shouldn't leave them to the last."

They lie on the blanket, Marie on her back and Harry on his stomach. After a while he can bear it no longer, and rolls towards her. They kiss. Soon he's on top of her.

"How am I supposed to get a tan?" she says.

"You can get a tan later." His erection is between them, he nudges playfully at her, hesitates when he finds an entrance, and then pushes on a bit, not quite clear in his mind what he intends.

"You'll have to be very careful, it's my first time," she says, and shifts slightly.

"Do you think we should?"

"Yes."

"Was it your first time too?"

"Of course."

"Then you'll never forget me. I read that men never forget the first time."

"I could stay here for ever."

"Me too. I don't know how I'm going to bear going back to France."

"Don't talk about it. We have another two weeks."

"We have to talk about it. I have to know when I'm going to see you again."

"Christmas."

"How? My parents won't let you stay with us, and yours won't let me stay with you."

"But Marjorie's parents will let you stay with them. Then I'll come and stay too."

"It might work. It's a pity there's no exchange between our schools. Then I could stay with you, and you could stay with us in Obernai. Two weeks, every year, with the schools' blessing."

"Yeah." He starts to move again. "What about the second time, did you read anything about that?"

"Thank God you're all here," says Paddy. "The morning was dire. My folks stayed with me. The worst thing was they thought they were doing me a favour."

"My mother was worrying about you too," says Brian. "She

told me to bring you up some old Enid Blyton books she found in the attic. How about *The Mountain of Adventure*?"

"You could read it yourself," says Marjorie. "It would save you reading mine all the time."

Brian is perched on the edge of her armchair. "I like reading yours," he says.

"Well, I don't."

"Haven't you got one for me?"

"Upstairs in my room."

"Come up and show me."

"You'd like that, would you?"

"That depends. On the book." Brian smiles, showing the shovels of his front teeth.

"I can imagine. Don't you think I'm too old for you?"

"I might be prepared to make an exception in your case."

Marjorie shakes her head and goes back to her book. But she has a little smile on her face.

Out in the kitchen Harry asks Marie about it. "Of course she doesn't like him," she says. "Anybody can see that."

"Why does she play along with him, then?"

"She doesn't mean anything by it."

"She keeps looking at him."

"No, no, she's only looking to see if he's looking at her. She's flattered, she likes him to like her even if she doesn't like him. She's just playing a bit with him, stringing him along is what she calls it."

"What you did with your cousin."

"Maybe, yes."

Harry thinks about this for a while. "I know you don't like Brian anyway."

She goes on washing up. "You see, the way he held me when

we danced at the hooley. That's one of the things."

"What way?"

"Close up. You know. A boy should know whether a girl wants to be held that way or not. She shouldn't have to be pushing the boy away all the time."

"Couldn't it be that the girl starts out not wanting that and gets to . . . quite like it?"

"Only with a boy that she would really like to dance with that way anyway. You know, she doesn't know him at the start and then she gets to know him and likes him and that's all right. But a boy should know that too. And he thinks he's so smart. With his prime ministers and everything."

They go on tidying up the dishes. Harry knows Marie's thinking about the morning, too. "Have you asked Marjorie yet?" she asks.

"Haven't had a chance."

"Why don't your parents come down to the hotel some time for a drink with mine?"

"Oh, they wouldn't do that."

"Don't they want to meet my parents?"

"It's not that, they don't drink." Only Catholics do, he almost says. "They wouldn't go into the bar anyway."

"Why not?"

"It's just not the kind of place they go into. They're two different kinds of people, Harbour Road and hotel people. They don't really mix."

"Prods and Micks again?"

"More or less, yes."

"Mrs Bryce is up at the hotel sometimes, though, she seems to know some of the people."

"Well, she's different. I don't mean the people fight or anything, they just tend to ignore each other."

"I see. Like my uncle Ludwig and his wife. They haven't spoken to each other in years but they still live in the same house."

"Would you do me a favour, Marjorie?"

"Depends."

"Would you invite Marie for Christmas?"

"And then Paddy invites you. That's a big favour, isn't it?"

"I'd do the same for you."

"There is something you can do for me, actually."

"Anything."

"I might need you to say that I was with you and Marie some time. Out on Horn Head or somewhere."

"And you'll be somewhere else? Where?"

"Least said soonest mended. It's only an idea I have."

"Have you had a fight or what?"

"Naw, I'm just tired." For the first time Harry would have liked a room of his own.

"How's the courting going?"

"All right."

"Don't want to talk about it, eh?"

"Since you ask, not really, no."

"Aren't you getting as much as you like?"

"Don't talk about Marie like that. You sound like Brian."

"Sorry. I mean, I know Mavis McWhirter's tits as well as if I'd felt them myself. I was just wondering."

"Wonder away."

14

Harry is sitting on the stone wall opposite the drive up to the hotel. In a minute she'll come out of the door. She'll take Paddy's bike from where it leans against the wall among the maids' and cooks' big black ladies' cycles as if it has never done anything else. She'll ride down the drive, she'll probably be laughing like she can't help it. She'll stretch out her right leg at the road to brake. Then she'll straighten up, her body flexing like when they're making love.

They're going back to the Secret Strand on the other side of Horn Head today. They haven't been back there since the first time, and they haven't made love for a couple of days now because it has been Marie's dangerous time.

They're going to make love again. Even the weather is on their side.

"Hasn't she turned up yet?" It's Mr Bryce with his long, springy stride, his golf-bag on his back, flourishing a walking-stick. Harry hasn't heard his approach because of the wind. He leans on the wall beside Harry.

"Where are you two lovebirds off today?"

"Maybe Horn Head again."

"It's great to have the bikes, isn't it?"

"Yeah."

"What about Paddy?"

"He's fine. Gets a bit bored, though. We keep him company in the afternoons."

"Fine, fine." Mr Bryce smiles his big, friendly smile and turns to face the sea. He looks down at the cove on the far side, his bald, freckled pate glinting in the sun.

"There's a nice length of stick down there," he says. "Must have been washed up in the spring tides. Just like mine." He lifts his walking-stick and runs his thumb along it. "Could use it for a ruler. Bit of mahogany that was washed up at Portstewart in 1948, that was a mighty August spring tide that year. Probably off a tanker sunk in the war. Just imagine it, constantly wafted and tumbled by the sea for years, maybe decades, then suddenly it's all over, you're immobilised, trapped. It must be like dying. Unless the next spring tide takes you out to sea again, of course. But one day there's going to be a tide that washes you up so far you'll never get away again. Then you get turned into a walking-stick." He laughs and turns away from the sea. "Well, have a nice day, the two of you. Young love. You're quite the envy of Harbour Road, let me tell you. You bring it all back to the rest of us, what it was like." He starts off briskly and then stops and comes back, rubbing his nose.

"You know, Harry, I was just thinking you're a lucky man sitting there, waiting for her to come. I remember that bit myself. Sometimes I think it was the best part of the whole thing." He gives a dry cackle and moves off again with a wave of his stick.

What do you know about it?

Fifteen minutes later Marie still hasn't turned up. Could she have misunderstood something and gone on ahead? Harry wheels his bike up the drive and takes it round to the back. No, Paddy's bike is there. Has she gone somewhere with her parents? No, the

Citroën is still there, too. He goes inside. She isn't in the foyer. He walks on through to the TV lounge. A few bored men look round at him from a Test match between England and Australia. He returns to the foyer, puzzled.

Clinks of glasses and low voices are coming from the lounge bar across the room. Wee Sammy's domain. He pushes open the door, expecting to be chased off the premises. The sweet-sour smell of old beer and spirits shot through with smoke wafts out. He sees the Fischers at once, sitting facing him at a small, round table, but Marie isn't with them. He starts to back out again.

"Come over and join us, young man," says Mr Fischer, beckoning to the empty seat beside him. Harry walks across. "I must buy you a drink for taking such good care of my daughter. Sit down, please. What will you have?"

Harry doesn't know what to say. Can he order a lemonade?

"A brandy perhaps?" says Mr Fischer. "Hennessy, for the French-Irish alliance?" He smiles gloomily. Harry doesn't know what he's talking about other than that some kind of alcohol seems to be expected.

"Half a pint of lager, please, if that's all right." He has never drunk beer before but he doesn't want to say that. Mr Fischer calls the order to Wee Sammy, who is drying glasses behind the bar, rubbing vigorously at them and glaring narrow-eyed at Harry, like a boxer's second mustering his man's opponent between rounds. Harry waits for him to object but he fills the glass and brings it to the table.

"Cheers," says Mr Fischer, and raises a glass of what Harry takes to be brandy.

"Cheers," says Harry, and drinks from his glass.

"For my stomach," says Mr Fischer. "For the long journey."

The beer tastes unpleasantly soapy. Harry struggles to refrain from grimacing. Mrs Fischer is watching him. She doesn't have anything to drink. Harry tries to think of something to say. "Are you going on a long journey, then?" he asks.

"To Sligo today. Then on to Connemara."

Harry thinks he's made enough conversation. "Where is Marie anyway?" he asks.

"In her room, I suppose."

How simple. Harry hasn't thought of that. He doesn't even know where her room is.

"Packing," Mrs Fischer adds. It's the first time she has spoken to Harry.

"For the picnic?" he asks. He already has the things for the picnic. He always buys them first and they share the expense.

"Picnic?" says Mr Fischer. "No picnic. Her clothes. In her suitcase." He makes a church of his hands. "We are going to Connemara on business and she is coming with us. She doesn't want to but we cannot pay a hotel room just for her. And, besides, she should see more of Ireland than just this place. Other girls would jump at the chance."

Harry feels the blood rush to his face. He bends over his beer and takes another sip, then cradles the glass in his hands. "Are you coming back here?" he asks.

Mr Fischer purses his mouth. "Oh, yes. We had to promise that. Ah, here she is. You must talk sense to her."

Marie is standing in the open door. She's wearing a light blue cape and a matching costume, with white stockings and white shoes. She makes no move to approach them. She's beautiful.

Harry drains his glass, gets to his feet and walks across. His legs are moving of their own accord, as though not a part of him. He follows her when she turns and goes out through the lounge. A brown suitcase is standing at the side of the staircase. They're leaving now, he thinks. They go outside, round the corner to the side entry where they kissed the night of the storm. She turns and comes into his arms. "We don't have much time," she says. "We have to keep our heads."

"What's happened?"

"That priest was talking to my father in the bar the other day."

"The Reverend McLeod?"

"He must have passed us in his car or something. Anyway, my father lost his head when he heard that there were only the two of us on our trips."

"Christ."

"He wanted to go to Connemara anyway to visit some wool factories. Now he insists that my mother and I go with him." Marie is keeping herself firmly in check, Harry can feel it in the stiffness of her body. He tries to stay in control too. But there are so many things he thought he had all the time in the world to talk to Marie about that he doesn't know where to begin.

"How long will you be away?"

"I don't know. A week, maybe longer."

"What if your father says he doesn't want to come back here?"

"I'm going to say I've forgotten my passport and we must come back for it."

"Can't he just ring up the hotel and have it sent on?"

"Not the hotel. I've had the whole morning to think, and this is what we'll do. I'll tell him I left it at your house. And you haven't got a telephone. Here." She's holding out a blue passport. He takes it. "Jesus, Marie, you're great."

"They're coming. Don't forget me, Harry."

"Never."

She kisses him and walks to the hotel, looking down, not back.

Strasbourg

Harry looks at his watch again. Two o'clock. The heat can't be regulated so he has opened a window, but he is unused to the noise of the cars, the batterings of the pigeons on the roof and the gurglings that come from the tacky afterthought of a *chambre de toilette* that stands in a corner of the room like a heap of something the caretaker has forgotten to tidy up. For the first time in years he wants a cigarette. More than that he would like to get some sleep, but every time he tries to calm down a fresh surge of rage comes over him, alternately at Jenny, Baldy Willie and himself.

He squirms in the bed every time he thinks of how he has been taking Baldy Willie's part in disputes with the staff these past months, how he tried to make the others see that he wasn't such a pain in the arse after all. He squirms again when he thinks of the warning signs he overlooked, Jenny's shopping expeditions that ended with nothing bought, or how Ballyraine library seemed to have run out of books. He groans when he remembers recent phrases of Jenny's: *Don't call him that. Looks don't matter in a man. Why don't we have the McNutts in for dinner? Can't you see William wants to stick with the German white?* He tosses and turns when he thinks of her and Baldy Willie together. He thinks of them in bed or in the car, moans, sits bolt upright, and phones Baldy Willie's number again. It rings and rings.

"Yes." McNutt's voice, tremulous but hopeful.

"Sorry to disappoint you. It's only me."

"Moore."

"The same. Did I get you out of bed? I hope so."

"It's a bedside telephone."

"Oh dear, how embarrassing for you. Your dear wife cuddled up in your arms, I trust."

"Actually my wife and I don't – we have separate bedrooms."

"Don't get your end at home, you mean."

"Much like yourself, from what I hear."

"Don't make stupid comparisons. You're fucking my wife, I'm not fucking yours."

"I don't suppose we could talk about this like reasonable people?"

"Why should I? Just tell me this. Why wouldn't you leave old Hatchet Face for Jenny, like anybody with a bit of sense would?"

"I'm not going to discuss that with you."

"Fair enough. I'll just discuss it with you. It wouldn't have anything to do with the fact that you're up for nomination by the Unionist Party for a seat at Westminster, would it?" Harry can hear a kind of a stifled groan at the other end of the line. "Didn't think I'd know about that, did you? I only heard about it the other night. From my colleague and good mate Bertie Tate. Who, as you well know, is chairman of the Ballyraine branch of the Unionist Party."

"It's all only idle speculation at the minute."

"That's not what he said. A foregone conclusion, those were his words. Couldn't understand it himself, knowing you like he does. But it's what people think that counts. A safe seat, Ballyraine. For the fine, upstanding pillar of the community that you're mistaken for. Not for a two-timing wee fart of a body."

"You're one to be talking, Moore. Everybody knows about you and that woman."

"Exactly. And nobody knows about you and my wife. That's the difference."

"I'm sure you'll agree that it's better for everybody concerned if it stays that way."

"Not quite everybody. Not me, for example."

"Think of your wife."

"It's not her name that would be mud. It's yours. Baldy Willie McMud. Anyway, I wasn't quite thinking of putting an advertisement in the Old Boys' magazine, or anything like that. Just a word in my good friend Bertie Tate's ear. And another thing. You can stick the exchange up your arse, you wee slimy Freemason church elder turd."

It's the first time Harry has managed to hang up on somebody tonight.

Love, or passion, Jenny had said. Passion. Rain in Ballymena. Jenny wouldn't get that, not even after all these years.

In the quietest time of the night, between three and five, he wafts off fitfully into sleep. He dreams he is walking through a building that is a mixture of the corridors of his school in Ballyraine, the narrow stairs of the hotel here and the vast, vulgar spaces of a set from the grand finale of an old James Bond film. Teaching colleagues pass but don't see him. He tries to speak to them but he can't, though he pushes, pushes from the solar plexus. The corridors become more and more deserted. He should be going home too but he keeps on pacing. Now he is a pupil again, but not younger; bony-kneed, balding and pot-bellied in his impossibly small uniform. He comes upon another open space, criss-crossed with free hanging stairways. For some reason he has to get up to the next floor. As he ascends the stairway it loses its handrail and elongates, sagging in the middle like a clown's concertina. The whole construction sways and stretches impossibly steeply up to the now invisible next floor and Harry is crawling on his hands and knees. There is a woman up there, sometimes she is Jenny, sometimes she is Marie. The steps are chest-high and he has to pull himself up on his elbows, then they are as minuscule as a row of clips in a stapler and he is balancing like a tightrope walker as they swing and yaw high above the hall. The metal cord snakes up into the darkness at an ever-increasing angle and his feet start to slip. He's shinning up it but his hands are slipping and he's falling back, sliding down towards the torn end of the rope.

He wakes up, bathed in sweat. No prizes for interpreting that one. An electric van is washing and brushing the street outside and the pigeons are bashing about the roofs again. From the pace of his heartbeats he knows there'll be no getting back to sleep so he gets up and pads to the shower. When he's finished it's half past five. At home it's an hour earlier. Jenny's phone is still engaged. He's not to meet Monsieur Bruckmann until nine o'clock. He dresses, leaves the hotel, and walks down the Rue des Grande Arcades as far as the Place Kléber, glad of the cold after the stuffiness of his room. He considers trying to find the hotel he stayed in so long ago, but in the end walks about aimlessly along the streets and canals of Petite France.

Back in his room at eight o'clock he phones Jenny again. The phone rings.

"Hello."

"It's me."

"Well."

"Disappointed?"

There is the sound of air being expelled.

"I've been trying to ring all night."

"The phone was off the hook. I wanted to get some sleep."

"Did you?"

"A bit."

"More than I can say. Were you really thinking of leaving me for Baldy Willie?"

"Don't call him that."

"You called him a little shit and a bastard yourself."

"It's all right for me."

"What'll I call him?"

"William is his name."

"Baldy William, how about that?"

Silence.

"Bald William's my last offer."

Silence.

"Would you really have left me for him?"

"I don't know."

"How am I supposed to work under him now?"

"The same way I work with that bitch of yours, day in, day out. Anyway, he's leaving Ballyraine next year."

"So you knew he was standing for the next Westminster elections? Did you think he was taking you with him?"

Silence.

"Are you suffering? Pining for him? Going through hell?"

"Leave off, would you?"

"What do we do now?"

"I don't know."

"You're waiting for him to come round."

"No."

"I wouldn't, if I were you. I rang up the Baldy One myself last night."

"What did he say?"

"Not very much after I threatened to fuck up his nomination."

"You bastard."

"I thought you never wanted to see him again."

"That's my decision, not yours."

"I was only doing you a favour."

"Like hell you were."

"How could you sleep with a horrible person like that?"

"You haven't a clue what William's really like. He's tender, passionate, all the things you're not."

"I am so."

"Not with me you're not."

"Listen, Jenny, I was thinking. This kind of makes us quits, doesn't it?"

"It's not a bloody game."

"I know, but you know – some people say it's good for a marriage."

"Stupid people."

"Don't you think so?"

"No."

"Neither do I, really. Is that something we have in common?"

"I don't care one way or the other at the minute."

"Think about it."

No answer.

"Are you crying?"

No answer.

"Do you love him?"

No answer.

Harry hangs up.

Harry is taking a conversation class at Monsieur Bruckmann's school, which is just round the corner from the cathedral. The class has read *Lies of Silence* by Brian Moore as a set text for their *baccalauréat*, but Harry hasn't, so he's letting the pupils tell him the plot.

"So the man take the bomb in his car to the hotel, but he tell the police."

"Very sensible."

"Very sensible if he want his wife killed."

"Is she a hostage?"

"Exact. The IRA kill her if he tell the police."

"Why did he tell them, then?"

"Because he were innocent tourists in the hotel. French, like us."

"Not like us. From the Bretagne." Laughter.

"So he puts his wife's life at risk to save innocent tourists? A difficult decision."

"Maybe not so difficult, he is in love with another woman."

"He will leave his wife anyway. Probably."

"Would he have acted the same way if his girlfriend had been the hostage?"

"This is the question indeed."

"Well, what do you think he should do?" Harry asks the class. The pupils look at each other. Harry has to keep reminding himself that they wear the sweatshirts and jeans they have on every day, not just today to annoy him. But in the jacket and tie he automatically puts on for school he still feels cheated in some way, like the only guest at a fancy-dress party who turns up in a mask.

"Is there anything he can do that is right?" he asks again.

Blank faces. One boy raises his hand. "The best thing is, he go away in the car and blow himself up. But then there is no book."

Harry is waiting in front of La Maison Rouge on the Place Kléber, as he had arranged with Marie. There's a despondent drizzle, and a fog that could be inside or outside his head. A green Renault Twingo sweeps up to the kerb. Marie is leaning across to open the passenger door. He tries not to stare at her neat legs in the tweed skirt as he gets in.

"That's not sensible," she says, as they drive off. "Standing in the rain like that without an umbrella."

"A real Irishman doesn't carry an umbrella."

"They aren't much use against Irish rain anyway. As far as I can remember."

"That's right. If the rain sees you with one it just whips around and gets you from the side."

In front of them a German-registered Mercedes is wavering in the middle of the two-lane one-way street in indecision. The driver's head is swivelling from one side to the other.

"You'd think he's at a tennis match," says Harry.

"We're all tourists somewhere."

The right half of the windscreen is filled with a flapping street map held by the German's wife. Occasionally the whole thing buckles and collapses, and then is painstakingly reassembled sideways or upside down. On a clear stretch of street Marie touches the horn briefly, and pulls neatly past with a smooth gear change and a friendly wave, as the Mercedes wobbles to the right.

"Guess what my wife told me on the phone last night," says Harry.

"She's pregnant?"

"God forbid. She's having an affair. With my headmaster of all people."

"Oh dear. Is it serious?"

"Oh, yes. She's not the kind to have one if it wasn't."

"I don't suppose anybody is."

Harry shrugs. *Maybe I am.*

"Is she going to leave you?"

"She said it was finished, but you never know. These things tend to drag on."

"You sound quite an expert. As if you've had an affair yourself." Harry looks down his nose to see if he's blushing.

"God, Harry, you still do that." Marie giggles. "Sorry. I mean, surely you have some say in the matter too. Do you want to stay with her? Do you love your wife?"

"I don't know. I don't know what love is. Whether there's such a thing. The older I get the more I think it's just something else in disguise. Sex, or loneliness. Or ambition, or boredom."

"Very cynical. I think there is such a thing as love. I know that I love Annie."

That's not what I want to hear. What about us in 1968? Did you love me then?

They channel into the *autoroute* and bowl out through the suburbs.

"Do you think your wife loves this man?"

"I don't know how she could. He's so horrible. He looks ugly, he's not funny, he's boring . . . But I suppose she probably must."

"He must have some positive sides."

"He can't be any good in bed either," Harry goes on. "I've seen him trying to dance. It was awful. In fact, I should be relieved it's only him she's fallen for. There's absolutely nothing to be jealous of."

"Lucky you. Just imagine how much worse it would be if it was someone really good-looking. Or rich. Better in bed. Someone superior to you in every way."

Harry ponders glumly on this, and on the belt of super-markets, sports complexes and apartment buildings that girdle the city, all swathed in a fine veil of rain. "Did you love your husband?" he asks.

"I think so, yes, at one time."

"Why did you get divorced?"

"He had a girlfriend he didn't want to give up. So I set him a deadline. He still couldn't make up his mind, so I threw him out. Sometimes I wonder if I did the right thing. Maybe it was only a silly test of wills."

"Do you ever wonder how our parents' generation did it?"

"Did what?"

"My mother never looked at another man, and neither did my father. At another woman, I mean."

Marie shrugs. "I am not so sure. My mother, no, but my father . . . Sometimes there were fights, locked bedrooms . . ."

"Well, people in Northern Ireland didn't use to . . . carry on like that, anyway."

"That's not how I remember it."

"Yeah, well, it was just about then that they started, maybe – 1968, make love, not war. Love-ins, and all that. Everybody was at it."

Marie doesn't say anything to this, and they are silent for a while, as the car zooms out into the country. It has stopped raining. Vast tan fields of maize, recently harvested, the shredded stalks sprawling limply, disappear into the fog. Distant skeletal copses are a fine etching in the haze.

"Tell me about your wife. I can't picture her."

"She's English," says Harry, and then hesitates.

"Well? Is that all?"

"No, of course not. What do you want to know?"

"When did you meet her?"

"1970." *Two years after you said you never wanted to see me again.* "I met her at Canterbury University. In England. She was studying French too."

An autumn day like this; the colours washed out, drained. Harry's first day in Canterbury, leaving the students' quarters to walk into town and have a look round, walking down the drive when a big Jaguar pulls up beside him. The window sliding down reveals a face the colour of a plum, with flabby jowls so weighty that they drag the lower eyelids down, revealing a strip of pink under the eyeballs, like bulldogs have. "You look as though you know your way around, young man. My daughter here . . ."

"Father!" A girl in the back, rolling her eyes.

"If you could show her the ropes, where to sign in, that kind of thing . . ."

"Oh, for God's sake." A flurry in the back of arms, a coat, and a bag, and then the girl is getting out at the far side to Harry, shouldering a duffel-bag, striding away.

"Jenny! Be sure to ring." The mother, waving out of her window, as the car reverses away. Harry sees her face, slack-jawed, eyes wells of despair, as she turns to the blustering toad at her side with whom she will spend the rest of her life.

None of Harry's business. Not very much was, in those days, two years after that summer. Harry's business was getting out, and staying out. Out of his family, away from his mother's unsettling smile as the money the new supermarket brought in got her the respect she'd failed to earn otherwise. Away from his father's bewilderment. Away from visits to his Auntie Flo in the mental home. Away from Kilmartin, where the first bomb went off on the day Harry's A level results came out, the first bomb in a series that spilled the houses and shops of Main Street like breaking waves into piles of rubble that were carted away, leaving more and more gaps. Away from the soot that came thumping down the chimneys and billowing out through the rooms. Away from the windows bursting on to the streets. Away from the plywood boards with "Business as usual" painted on them that the rain corrugated and then soaked into the raised humps, in darker stains in the brown, like a mouthful of rotting teeth.

All none of Harry's business. This girl, who wanted to get away from home as much as Harry did, who was now stomping away in the wrong direction, the same way Harry had gone on his arrival a couple of hours before, towards a set of official-looking buildings that looked like they belonged to the university, but were in fact the seat of the Wessex Water Board, the administration offices being behind Harry, incognito in red brick; that was none of Harry's business either.

Only she turned out to be in Harry's French seminar. The next morning she was already there in the corridor, waiting for the lecturer to turn up, when Harry arrived. And, instead of being embarrassed at Harry's witnessing of her discomfiture, she wanted to know why he hadn't pointed out her mistake, and shook her head at his answer. "None of your business," she repeated. "If I'd been heading for a cliff would that have been none of your business too?"

Interested in Harry. Intrigued. Because he kept himself apart. Because he didn't give a damn. The year they were both assistant teachers in France Harry hitch-hiked from Normandy to St Girons near the Spanish border to see her.

"*So you do give a damn,*" *she said, when she opened the door.*

"Why did you go back to Northern Ireland? It can't have been a very nice place to live in the seventies."

"It was better than you might have thought. Ballyraine was always very quiet."

"Still, she must have loved you to go there."

"Well, it was a good way of getting away from her parents as well. Her father can't stand the Irish."

"What does she look like?"

"She's good-looking. Tall, as tall as me. Strong face, high cheekbones. Red hair, and the temper they say goes with it."

"Do you fight a lot?"

"Sometimes." *Only when one of us has an affair.*

"Well, you loved her, then."

"You could say that."

"That's a funny way to put it."

"It was love. Only . . . I was very careful. I didn't want to let it in so close to me after that time with you."

Marie nods slowly, but doesn't look at Harry. "And you have looked at other women, then, as you put it?"

"One affair."

"What was that about?"

"God knows. I thought it was love at the time."

"Were you going to leave Jennifer then?"

"I thought so for a time." He sinks back into the seat. Helen. Love so certain it drove me mad for half a year. The real thing, just like it had been with Marie. Or so I thought. Crazed, sweaty passion on the back seat of the Ford Escort. Letters, poems, pledges. A miracle that evanesced so thoroughly you couldn't be sure it had ever existed. I exorcised it on my own, only I got it wrong, I exorcised the miracle, and was left with the demon. Myself. As punishment for lack of faith.

"The worst thing wasn't the falling in love. I was quite relieved about that, that I was still capable of it. It was the falling out again."

"I don't understand."

"There was nothing left. It had vanished so completely I wondered if it had ever been there. It made me feel empty. Like an impostor. Do you know what I mean?"

"A bit, maybe."

"Did you never only think you were in love?"

"No. Well, as a young girl, maybe."

"With your cousin." *Not with me, say it.*

She laughs. "Yes. Fancy you remembering that."

Maybe I'm only a fake. Have been all my life. Or turned into one. When? Accretions of guilt, they're hard to avoid over the years. Like sclerosis. "Oh, God, sometimes I think it would be great to be accused of something you can be absolutely sure you haven't done," Harry says.

"Oh, Harry."

"It must be such a relief, so refreshing." *Wrongfully imprisoned. Framed, for the murder of Baldy Willie. Imagine the burning righteousness.* He shakes his head. What rubbish he's thinking. "I don't know if I can trust myself. Whether my feelings are true."

"You seem to be worried enough about your wife."

"That's different."

"Why?"

"Oh, God, I don't know. I feel tired. I hardly slept last night. Is there anywhere we can go for a walk? Get some fresh air."

"I know just the place."

They are climbing up through the Vosges mountains. Primeval pines fade into the veil of fog and then suddenly the car is bathed in sunshine.

"It's often like that," says Marie. "When you get up above it." She turns into an almost empty car park that is surrounded by boulders.

"Where's this?" Harry asks.

"Mont Sainte Odile."

"I've read something about this place. A monastery, right?"

"A convent."

"Something about a saint, a woman who was blind, and got her sight back."

"That's right."

They get out, and take the path up from the car park that winds through the boulders.

"Annie wasn't even in when I got home last night. I needn't have dashed away like that," Marie says.

Last night seems so far away to Harry.

"I think she's got a boyfriend," Marie goes on.

"Wouldn't she tell you?"

She gives a tired laugh. "I tell her everything, but she keeps her secrets."

"Marie!" Up ahead a nun dressed in white has seen them approach. She waits on the path. When they draw level she and Marie embrace. Harry walks on along the leaf-lined path. He wonders if the woman is some relative of Marie's, some aunt probably. Not a bad idea for old spinsters, being a nun. Keeps them in company. Ahead of him a red-brick complex unfolds. A stone figure stands above its grey-slated roofs, one arm is cradling a crook and the other is raised in benediction. Harry looks back. Marie is still talking to the nun, both leaning back with folded arms, laughing at something. *That laugh of Marie's. Bloody attractive.*

He walks on under an archway into a courtyard lined with linden trees. A few tourists are standing about with guidebooks, pointing out various features of the church to the right of the main complex. A sign points to "La sarcophague d'Odile" but Harry wants to stay in the open air so he skirts the buildings to the right and follows a path round the outside that brings him to the front. A series of terraces leads down to a wall. Some people are standing here, looking over the parapet. Harry joins them.

It's a marvellous scene. The buildings are standing on a sheer cliff that falls into a sea of mist hanging in motionless swathes. Humped hills of golden brown and dark green trees poke through it. It's like standing at the prow of a mighty liner inching its way through a chain of islands.

Marie comes up and stands beside him. "There's a great view from here on a clear day." She points out across the sea of fog. "You can see right across the Rhine valley to the Black Forest."

"Tell me about this place."

"Ste Odile founded it in the eighth century."

"I'm afraid I'm not very well up on saints."

"She is our local – patron? – saint. She was blind at birth and her father wanted to kill her. Only a daughter and then blind on top of that, this was too much. But her mother hid her and when she was being *baptisé* – baptised? – she got her sight."

"She didn't get turned into a boy, though?"

"No, this miracle was asking too much." Marie laughs. "Her *source* – spring? – is just down the hill. It's a nice walk."

"Good. That's just what I need."

They follow the wall to the other side of the monastery, where a path leads down the side of the cliffs. Before long the mist engulfs them again, draining the forest of its bright autumn colours. Huge, mossy boulders loom up out of the pastel shades. Soon they reach the spring, behind a metal gate let into the rock face. The round basin into which it bubbles is filled with coins.

Harry reads the inscription at the side of the gate. "What's this about a blind man? I thought she was the blind one."

"It was another baby. An old man carried it up here and got lost. Odile appeared to them, struck the rock with her staff and water came out and cured the baby's sight."

"I see."

"People with eye problems come for the water."

"Are you religious, Marie?"

"No. But I like this place. There's something about it. When I was a child we came here every Sunday."

"It feels like a Sunday kind of a place."

"I don't come as often now. Annie says it gives her the creeps, so I come on my own when I've got time."

"To see your relative?"

"What relative?"

"I thought that nun . . ."

"Oh, no. I know a lot of the nuns here. I stayed here once."

"Is there a hotel?"

"Yes. A kind of hotel."

They start back up, walking more slowly because of the incline. From down in the valley they hear the bark of a dog and a crow's cawing, muffled by the fog. Harry thinks of the car waiting to take them back to Strasbourg. "So you're happy enough," he says after a while, without looking at her.

"Oh, yes."

"Good. I thought about you for years." He keeps his eye on the path. Then he feels her hand on his arm. They come to a stop and turn towards each other. Her hand slips off his arm but Harry takes it and draws her to him. They embrace. He strokes her hair. "Did you ever get to read my letters?" he asks into her hair.

"Yes. They were in my father's drawer. I found them when he died. He kept them from me but he didn't destroy them. I still have them. In a box."

"Lucky you. I never got any from you."

"I did write to you once."

"When?"

"When I had to go away with my parents that time to the south of Ireland."

"I never got it."

"It's probably just as well. I'm sure it was a load of sentimental rubbish."

"Sounds great."

She's gone all still, and as he bends to her face she looks up and they're kissing, tentatively at first, and then urgently, so that when she turns her head away to rest it on his chest they're both taking deep breaths of the damp, mouldy air. He's remembering an awful time he had forgotten completely. Nobody had taken any photos that summer but he could call up her face at will, starting with the eyes. Then, after about six months, it became more and more difficult. Her features started to slip away into oblivion. He had tried to draw her, but that had banished her completely. In desperation he had taken his father's car and driven up to the holiday house they had rented in Donegal every summer until that last one. He had told the owners he had left something in the attic room he slept in and they had let him go upstairs. In front of the wooden panelling on the wall he had got down on his knees and looked for the pattern in which he'd seen her face the summer before, lying in his bed those nights before going to sleep. He couldn't find it. She was gone.

"Marie, I never . . ."

"Sssh." She touches his lips with a finger.

They stay like that for a while and then start to walk up again, holding hands.

"Let's not go back yet," says Harry.

"Of course not," says Marie. "I thought we could drive along the *route du vin*. It's very beautiful at this time of year." They emerge from the fog into the sun under the figure of Odile.

The *route du vin* twists through the hilly vineyards at the foot of the Vosges mountains and connects the wine-growing villages with German names like Mittelbergheim and Blienschwiller. The houses are painted in the colours of autumn leaves and though it's late in the year their windows are still burgeoning with geraniums and chrysanthemums. The falling dusk enhances the warmly lit windows of the restaurants and *Winstubn*.

"I'd better give Annie a ring so she doesn't worry," says Marie.

"Are we going to eat out?"

"If you like."

"Then I'd better phone the French teacher. He was going to take me out this evening."

They stop at a phone box. Marie goes in first. Her body, all stillness during the ringing tone, suddenly swings Harry's way, her face lighting up, when Annie answers. Harry remembers the feel of her against him on the path up to the monastery. Now she is watching him as she talks into the mouthpiece, a smile playing around her lips. He would like to sleep with her.

"I think I've worried Annie," Marie says, holding the door open for him. "She asked me if you were nice and I said, yes, very nice."

When Harry telephones he is relieved to get Madame Bruckmann. He tells her that he is stuck in Colmar, having travelled there by train in the afternoon, and it now transpires that the earliest train back gets into Strasbourg at ten o'clock. He declines an offer to pick him up and expresses his desolation.

"How easily you lie," says Marie, when he comes out. "I suppose you got a lot of practice when you were having your affair. What if they check the timetable?"

"But the next train is at ten. I checked at the station before I walked to the Place Gutenberg. Just to be sure."

They drive on. It is quite dark now. Banks of fog slow down their progress. The villages are enchanting with their half-timbered houses and winding streets, like a dream of the middle ages.

"What does 'Neuer Siaßer' mean?" Harry asks. "It's the third time I've seen that sign."

"It's the new wine of the season."

"*Vin primeur?*"

"No, not as matured as that. It's still fermenting. It can be sweet or sour, depending on what stage it's reached. Often you get chestnuts served with it. Would you like to try some?"

"Sounds great."

"I know a place."

"How much time have we got?"

She looks across at him. "The whole evening."

Harry feels very detached and peaceful. A silence has fallen upon them that doesn't demand to be broken. Everything seems possible. The lower part of her face is illuminated by a closing fan of light from the street-lamps in the villages as they approach them, her eyes a liquid gleam above. Harry would like to caress the line of her chin. Her lips pucker in amusement as she catches him watching her and she pushes the hair away from her neck.

"You should be looking at our beautiful Alsatian villages," Marie says.

"I prefer looking at you," says Harry. His voice comes out slow and thick. She shakes her head and smiles across. She slows down and peers out at the fog.

"Everywhere is so full at this time of year," she says. "There's a place near here, if I can find it." Up ahead a signpost materialises. "Dambach, there it is."

They are sitting in a restaurant in the first floor above the village square, silent as the waitress clears away the *Baeckeofe* they've had. The Germans who filled the dining room shortly before have now funnelled noisily down the narrow steps into a coach rumbling below. Its doors close with a snort and Harry and Marie watch it move off through the narrow streets. The building reverberates with its passing. It stops at a corner, shunts back and forward like a bewildered bull, and then slips past. They look at each other and smile in the silence. There are only a few people left in the restaurant.

"Did you hate me that time?" Harry asks.

"No. Only . . ." She pauses. "You see everything in black and white at that age. I thought if you love a person you do not sleep with somebody else."

"Did you really love me?"

"Oh, yes." She breaks open a nut, looks at it reflectivel,, then up at Harry, resting her chin in the cup of her hand. "In fact, I still think you don't sleep with somebody else if you love a person. Why did you sleep with that woman? Why did she sleep with you, for that matter? I mean, you were only a young boy. Not exactly very – experienced."

"She was only using me to get even with her boyfriend. She thought he was two-timing her."

"Oh, I see, you were a victim. A pawn in her game. You poor thing."

"It was one time. But I only loved you," says Harry. "I would have done everything to get you back. Why didn't you open the door that time?"

She turns the nut over in her fingers. "Did you ever go back to that place, Port . . .?"

"Braddan. Only once. Jenny didn't like it." They'd stayed at the Dunbreaghy Hotel, only by that time it was a forlorn box in need of a fresh coat of paint, with showers and toilets in the corridors and laminated wooden furniture with chipped edges, a none-too-tidy lounge with slashed seats and a deserted dining room where indifferent food was trundled out on trolleys like in a hospital. It's like Portrush without the nightlife, Jenny had said. Never again.

"All our friends were bringing back suntans from Greece, Spain, Yugoslavia. And it rained the whole time."

Marie nods. "Just like that summer."

Harry is shocked. "It did not. Didn't we make love in the open air?"

"And got soaked every time."

"I don't remember." Harry can't think of anything to follow this up with. "I'll be coming to Strasbourg every year if the exchange comes off," he says.

"Is it really pure coincidence that the partner school is in Strasbourg?"

"Well, not really. I kind of pushed it through."

"Aha. But you didn't know I would be here."

"I knew the shop was. I've seen it in telephone directories. Every time I come to France I check up." He reaches out and takes her hand. She doesn't take it away. "Do you know how many Marie Fischers there are in Strasbourg? Eleven. And seventeen M. Fischers."

The tips of her fingers close around the back of his hand.

"Would you have hung up if I'd rung up?" he asks.

"Oh, yes. And changed my number. Moved away. But there wouldn't have been much danger of that."

"Why not?"

"My name isn't Fischer. It's Bonnardot. You forget I was married." She is biting her lip to keep from laughing.

"I was sweating blood outside your shop."

"You poor thing." Marie takes his hand and lifts it to her mouth. He feels her lips move up and down the hairs on its back. "What would you have done if I'd still been married?"

"I don't know."

"Just what are you suggesting, Harry?"

"I can be here for two weeks every year."

"And then go back to your wife? If she's still there."

"What else? I can't stay here."

"Maybe she can arrange to go off for the same two weeks with your headmaster. What would you say to that? Oh, Harry." She shakes her head at him, kisses his hand and sets it back on the table. "We should stop acting like teenagers.

Madame is watching from the kitchen, and she is a customer of mine."

She reaches into her handbag and brings out a packet of Gauloises.

"I think I'll have one too," says Harry.

Marie stops the car in front of Harry's hotel.

"Come up to my room," says Harry. "There's nobody at reception at this time of night."

"I can't. Annie said she'd wait up for me."

"Come up for just a while, then." He caresses the back of her neck.

Her eyes are gleaming in the dark. "Harry, tell me this. Would you really sleep with me while you're worrying whether your wife is with that man or not?"

"I would kind of just enjoy the moment. Let tomorrow take care of itself."

"Aren't we too old for that?"

"No."

"Maybe tomorrow, Harry." She rubs her cheek against the palm of his hand.

"When?"

"Not in the afternoon. I have to go to Obernai."

"I'll come with you."

"No."

"Is it on business? I won't be in your way, I won't try to get you into bed. I'll go and look up that policeman. See if he remembers me."

She gives a little laugh. "It's just not possible." She's looking out of her side window, away from Harry, but he can see her reflection. She looks very tired.

"Another man?"

"No." She turns to him. "We can't have you worrying about your wife and about me, too."

"Tomorrow evening?"

"I'll ring you when I come back."

Harry has a beer in the nearest bar. It's almost empty apart from a drunk slumped at the counter, watching the TV with screwed-up eyes and mumbling to himself. There's a talk show on with some fat French celebrity Harry vaguely recognises. Some kind of an actor. He is boasting about how long he can make love to a woman. "And how do I do it?" he asks the interviewer, whose mouth is hanging open in a sycophantic grin. "Mathematical equations!" he gleefully answers his own question. "Old mathematical equations from my schooldays. I'm doing like this and I'm thinking about mathematical equations." He stands up to demonstrate, pumping away with his midriff. The audience applauds.

"Such a whore," says the drunk. "And what did he think about when he was doing his mathematical equations at school? About cunts, I bet, like the rest of us."

15 1968

I F Sunday afternoons have a colour, Harry thinks, it's light brown. Like the roast beef they've had for lunch, whose stale smell is still hanging in the air. Like the colour of the old wallpaper in the living room, where the Moores are lying round about, propped up in various attitudes, reading.

The day is like lead. Amazing how long it takes for an hour to go past. If he could just sleep for a week and wake up when Marie was back. His record for not looking at his watch is five minutes twenty-seven seconds. Set yesterday. He thought he had waited a quarter of an hour at least. And the things people say. Why they bother. You know what's coming before they open their mouths. His father is glaring at the second page of the *Sunday Press* as if daring it to bite him in the nose. It's bound to be something about civil rights. "Listen to this," his father says. "Singing 'We Shall Overcome' demonstrators were moved on by the police. 'We Shall Overcome' indeed. Who do they think they're going to overcome? Us, that's who." He rustles indignantly to the next page.

Over by the window his mother is hovering, peering out. *A nice wee drive would do us all good.* She turns to the assembled Moores. "Just the day for a nice wee drive, what does everybody think? Do us all good."

Come on, Auntie Flo, that's your cue. She puts down her Barbara

Cartland paperback. "We haven't been to Bloody Foreland this summer yet," she says brightly.

Now nothing can save them from a bloody drive round bloody Bloody Foreland. None the less one of the men will be against the proposal and the other, as a matter of honour, for it. Uncle Alec's bullet-headed dome appears above an ancient copy of the *National Geographic*. "I was thinking of having a game of golf," he says.

But Harry's dad is already laying the *Sunday Press* aside, saying, "I'll go and get the Primus ready."

Harry plays his last card. "I'll stay here and keep Paddy company."

"Paddy's coming too," says Auntie Flo. "It's about time he got out. The doctor said it's no problem if he keeps himself warm. It'll be a real family trip."

"Count me out," says Marjorie, flicking languidly through *Woman's Own*. "I'm trying out the organ in Rathmelton today. It's supposed to be the best one in Donegal."

"How are you getting there?" her mother asks.

"It's all arranged. The Reverend McLeod has some things to see to over there."

"He's reading that rubbish again," says Harry's dad, to the slanting grey landscapes of Bloody Foreland that are inching past the car window. Harry has bought a paperback in the shop that morning after church on the strength of the picture on the front and he's now trying to get interested in it. It's the first book he's tried to read since meeting Marie. Now he ignores his father's comment. "That rubbish" is everything he's read after Enid Blyton, from the *Sad Sack* and *Casper, the Friendly Ghost* comics of his childhood through *Superman* and *Batman* to the James Bond novels of last year.

For the last couple of years he's only been interested in paperbacks that look as if they have lots of good bits in them. He has to be careful here. His father's disapproval of his reading matter is total, but impassive. His mother's the one to watch. She let pass the vermin-oozing skulls and the ghoul-infested mists of *The Pan Books of Horror* Harry bought a few years back but his copies of *The Virgin Soldiers* and *Peyton Place* disappeared very quickly. She'll leaf suspiciously through anything with big bosoms on the front or "steamy", "sultry", or "hot-blooded" in the blurbs. The good bits are always easy to find because the gummed spines are cracked through Harry's repeated attentions. Now he's careful to hold the paperbacks so as not to bend their backs.

"What's that you're reading Harry?" she now asks. Seething with fury he hands her the Angélique novel. He feels like shouting that he's already slept with Marie and it isn't like anything he's ever read in any bloody book. Her mouth sets in hard lines as she regards the huge bosom spilling out of the heroine's dress on the front, and even more as she reads the description on the back. But Harry isn't worried as she starts to flip through the pages. He has already leafed through the whole book in a frantic, vain search for a single good bit. He has forked out three shillings and sixpence in vain.

There's a parp from behind them and a car pulls out to pass. It's Mrs Bryce in her Imp, giving them a wave but not a glance before she drives on. "Where's she tearing off to?" asks Harry's dad.

"Probably away painting somewhere," says Mrs Moore, back to perusing Harry's book. "Not that you ever see any of her pictures," she goes on. She hands the paperback back to Harry. "Looks more like a girl's kind of book," she says.

He doesn't bother to find his place again. He glazes his eyes

and tries to think of Marie. Incredible that she has only been
gone two days. Already last week seems like another world to
him. He was another person then, something like the person he
has always tried to be. Now that other person is a ghost and he's
the old Harry again, the one he hates, who goes for drives with
Mum and Dad. Marie's face is hovering out there on the edge
of his consciousness, not quite realised.

"For goodness' sake, Harry, would you buck up a bit and try
to enjoy the beautiful day?" says his mother.

"What's Marjorie doing with herself anyway?" Brian asks.
"Never see her around."

"She's practising away at the organ. Like mad. I don't know
what's got into her," says Harry.

They flick their finished cigarettes over the side of the boat.
They land with a hiss and wobble drably on the water. Brian's
father has relented on the boat, and Harry has started going in it
with him again, although he doesn't really want to get back on
the old footing after seeing him through Marie's eyes. It would
be a kind of betrayal.

They've been into Dunbreaghy on the full tide this morning,
and mooched around a bit. Now the boat is drifting in the
middle of Sheephaven Bay, the hills at the rim of the bowl
rocking gently. The sky is covered by a uniform layer of white
cloud and in the diffused light that seeps through it everything is
drained of colour.

"What about a spot of fishing?" Brian says. Harry can taste the
dismay in his mouth. It seems everything has slipped back to
how it was before Marie came, and nobody has even noticed
there had ever been a change.

"Why don't we take the boat back in and go up to the
Dunbreaghy Hotel?" he asks.

"What for?"

"A drink."

"What if we get caught?"

"Who'd catch us? Sure none of our folk would be seen dead in there."

So they start going into the Dunbreaghy Hotel for drinks. There's nothing to it, really. Harry feels as though he has a stake in the place since picking up Marie from it. And that's the whole secret. You have to walk in as though you had a right to, breeze in through the foyer past the receptionist and make straight for the bar like a resident. The first time he felt very nervous approaching Wee Sammy. But he took their order with a single, unflurried bat of the eyelids. Now Harry wonders why he was ever in such awe of him.

It's a quiet place in the afternoons. A few people sit at the bar and at scattered tables conversing in subdued tones amongst the rustlings of newspapers and the clinks of glasses. The smell of spirits is always the first thing you notice and a bit off-putting, but after a while you don't notice it. In spite of the big bay windows overlooking the bay it's always darker than outside because the lights aren't put on until the evening.

At first they drink half-pints. Harry still finds the soapy taste unpleasant but he likes the swimming feeling it induces in his head, it's even better than when he started smoking. Cigarettes taste better with the drink, too. He and Brian sit there drinking and smoking, not talking much. Brian sometimes fetches the paper from the lounge or stays there to watch the horse-racing and Harry often sinks into reveries about Marie. Around four the bar fills up and they watch the people.

This is a different world from Harbour Road. The people speak with soft southern accents that seem to go with the money they have. They're the drivers of the Mercedes, Alfa Romeos and Volvos whose side windows would have borne the marks of Harry's nose in former years. The men stand around in relaxed camaraderie at the bar, dressed in slacks and V-necked pullovers with various club emblems. The women sit about smoking and talking with expansive gestures. They say "grand" a lot. They're like the people you see on TV or in films, the kind Harry wants to be like. It's certainly a far cry from the kind of place his mother imagines pubs to be, Hellfire Clubs full of drunken Catholics.

The talk is of different places from the ones the Ulster people visit, places like Dungloe, Bundoran and Buncrana. Harry wonders what they are like. Sometimes, when he's watching them, one of the well-dressed men looks back at Harry. Can they see that Harry and Brian are Ulster Protestants?

He sees himself sitting here with Marie, and the people admiring her and envying him. He wonders if it will ever come to that.

The two boys are smoking a lot more and Harry begins to worry about his finances, especially when Brian starts to drink pints and Harry has to keep up.

The worst part is always coming out into the still bright day after the dark bar. There's something wrong about it, a funny dislocating feeling that makes Harry feel even more drunk. He always thinks of Marie when the fresh air hits him. He sees her hair in the branches whipping in the wind and the hedge's movement at the corner of his eye and looks around, hardly noticing Brian going off down Harbour Road. On the way back up to the house the wind and the realisation that Marie isn't there work through his numbness and sobriety come back again. That's when the pain comes, a searing pain like breathing through your nose when it's all inflamed.

★

"You see, when you have two pints . . ."

"Yeah."

". . . you pish like a fire-hose."

"Huh."

"Wee Sammy just says, 'The usual,' now. And 'Coming up, sir.'"

"Sir?"

"Yeah." Harry looks across at Paddy's face, faintly lit by the moon. He's trying not to look impressed and the effort is furrowing his brow. He looks very young. "If I didn't have you to talk about Marie to I think I'd go mad."

"Mmm."

"I don't know how I'm going to get through the autumn without her. Do you think they have a few days off in France in November, like we do?"

"Dunno."

"Like potato-gathering holidays."

"Frog-catching holidays, maybe."

"I think I'll study French after my A levels."

"Hardly your best subject, is it?"

"But you know the way you have to spend a year in the other country when you study languages? Do you think they'd let me start with the year?"

"Dunno."

"Just fancy. A year in Strasbourg, with Marie."

In bed Harry pulls out Marie's passport from under the mattress and opens it. He has established a ritual. First he reads the address: Rue de la Paix, Obernai, Strasbourg. Peace Street. That's because of the peace he gets when he's with Marie. Obernai is a village just outside Strasbourg, and the Fischers' house is perched on a hill overlooking it, Marie has told him.

There are vineyards beside it, and the head of a saint painted on a wall. He tries to imagine it. But the only pictures he can conjure up are from his aged French schoolbook; broad boulevards with sparse pre-war cars, a cycling Frenchman with a beret on his head, hung with onions and wielding a stick of bread under his arm like a lance.

Then he turns to the photograph. It's the instant before breaking into a smile, her lips are going that way and the corners of her eyes are crinkling. He thinks of the times she's done that, often just before they made love, kisses it, then stows it carefully away, and switches out the light.

16

Harry yanks his head up just before he can glance at his watch. Not yet, not yet. It has to be at least fifteen minutes since he's looked at it. A new record. And only another day to go until Marie comes back. He surveys the lounge, but there's nothing there to divert him, apart from Wee Sammy reading the newspaper behind the bar. There's horse-racing on the TV and the men who usually frequent the bar are in the TV room. Brian is with them.

Harry feels his eyeballs being dragged down as if by gravity. He looks at his watch. Twenty-two minutes past three. "Fuck," he whispers. A minute short. Now it'll take him another fifteen minutes to wait a quarter of an hour. He's smiling inanely at this thought when Mrs Bryce comes into the bar, straight into his field of vision. Hastily Harry bows his head over his table. Too late. He can hear her swift footsteps approaching him.

"Hello, Harry. All alone?"

"Oh, hello, Mrs Bryce. Brian's about somewhere, too." Maybe she'll think the beer and the cigarette in the ashtray are his.

"Where's Marie?"

She has to be the only person in Port Braddan who doesn't know.

"She's somewhere in the south with her parents. She didn't want to go. She's coming back tomorrow."

"Do you mind if I sit down for a moment?"

Fuck. "Of course not."

She sits down, crosses her legs and glances back to the door. Then she looks back at Harry, catches him looking up her pleated skirt, and tugs at its hem. He sees her looking at the glass of beer and cigarette, presented on the table between them like the pieces of evidence in the Perry Mason films. Harry makes no move towards either of them. Wafted by the draughts from the tilted window behind him the spirals of smoke from the ashtray are now describing the most intricate patterns in front of Mrs Bryce's face, almost as if the cigarette is showing off. Harry feels his cheeks start to tingle.

"You'd better smoke that before it sets the place on fire," she says.

Harry lifts the cigarette with a nonchalant movement to his lips, but the smoke goes into his eyes and they start to water. He takes the packet from his windcheater pocket and offers it to Mrs Bryce.

"No, thanks," she says. "But you could get me a drink."

"Sure. What would you like?"

"A gin and tonic, please."

"Sure." Jesus Christ. What will that set him back? Maybe he'll be able to nip out and cadge some money from Brian. But she's bound to notice, the way she keeps glancing towards the door.

She hands him a pound note.

"No, no, it's all right."

"Come on, Harry, don't be silly."

Relieved, he takes the note and goes to the bar. Wee Sammy folds his paper shut with a sigh and takes his order without looking at him. He studies his face in the mirror behind the counter while waiting for it. Not too red, he thinks. And it doesn't look as though Mrs Bryce is going to go running to his parents.

When he returns to the table with her drink Mrs Bryce has moved to his seat, and is sitting with her back to the big bay window, facing the lounge.

"You don't mind, I hope," she says, and flaps her hand over her shoulder. "The view was getting me down."

Harry passes her the drink and her change and sits down.

"Cheers."

"Cheers." He can't see anything out of the window that would get anybody down. Just the usual scrawny fields and scattered houses. The hill in the background is just about to be blotted out by a dark cloud of rain, fair enough, but there's usually a patch of rain about somewhere.

"So this is where you spend your time now," she says. "I wondered why we never see you around the harbour any more."

"Yeah, it got a bit boring, messing about with boats."

"I can imagine," says Mrs Bryce. "There can't be much for young people to do up here. Wouldn't you rather spend your holiday somewhere else?"

"Not really. Port Braddan's the nicest place. Downings is not much more than a big caravan park and Falcarragh Town is like something out of the Wild West. Too far away from the sea, anyway." Harry is gaining confidence, already thinking about how best to present the meeting to Paddy that evening. He expels the last smoke from his cigarette and stubs it out in the ashtray.

"I was thinking of somewhere completely different. Like . . . Guernsey, no, wait, like Mallorca, or Ibiza. Somewhere with sun and cheap wine."

"We've been coming up here since I can remember."

There's a burst of noise from the door behind Harry. He recognises the bantering voices of a group of golfers. Mrs Bryce's gaze flickers over them before returning to Harry.

"Have you ever been abroad?"

"Not really, no." He's been on a day trip to Scotland as a child once with his parents. Across on the boat to Stranraer, and then up the coast to Girvan by train. They were back in Kilmartin the same evening. He can hardly remember anything about it. "I might be going to France next year, though."

"Hardly with your parents."

"No. Visiting Marie."

"I can't imagine them in France. Fred and Eileen, I mean." Is she trying not to smile? Harry doesn't know much about how people from Belfast like the Bryces live. Maybe they think the Moores are very backward. Maybe they make jokes about them.

"This place really gets on my nerves after a while, anyway," she says.

"The hotel?"

She sits back and makes an encompassing gesture with her hands. "Donegal. The whole place. It's like a weight pressing down on you. There's no getting away from it. All this open space."

"That's what I like about it," says Harry. "It makes you see you're not important."

"When you get to my age you don't need a landscape to tell you that. And it's not only me. You'd be surprised at the number of people who commit suicide here. They try to cover it up, of course, mortal sin and all that. Only the other week, my husband was telling me – have you seen him, by the way? Or the Reverend McLeod?"

"No."

"Well, the other week a wee girl from the hospital in Letterkenny, a nurse, took herself out to a strand on Malin Head, a beautiful place, lay down facing the sea and gave herself an injection. Was dead when they found her." Her hands make a brushing-away motion. "Or the amount of people who can only stick it with tranquillisers, like Mrs McLeod." She smiles at him as though she's proved something.

Only another day, Harry is thinking. Tomorrow he'll be with Marie again. He needs to get away from Mrs Bryce before she drags him down into her gloom. "I'd better be going," he says, and gets to his feet.

"You haven't finished your drink."

"It's no odds. 'Bye, Mrs Bryce." He walks out through the foyer, not bothering to tell Brian.

Outside, the dark blot of rain rises up the escarpment behind Sessiagh Lake and moves further inland. Across the bay the greens and browns of Horn Head look freshly washed and painted in the light.

Why does the woman spend so much time painting the landscape if she can't stand it?

"Only one more day," says Harry.

"What makes you so sure?" Paddy asks.

In an awkward mood again, are we? "She said a week."

"A week, maybe longer, you said."

"She'll get her father talked round, don't you worry. She'll probably not be there till the afternoon, but I'll go down in the morning just in case."

"She didn't write or anything, did she?"

"How could she? She doesn't know my address."

"'Harry Moore, Port Braddan' would have been enough."

"How's she to know that? What are you getting at, anyway?"

"Nothing. All I'm saying is she could have dropped you a line, that's all. I mean, it's been a whole week."

"Are you trying to say that she's not coming back or what?"

"All I'm saying is it's wiser not to count on it."

"And since when have you been such an expert in the field? Have you done a crash course or something?" You that couldn't even wank two weeks ago.

"It's only common sense."

"Do you think you're the only one with common sense?" It makes Harry mad, Paddy giving him advice. It's one thing Harry pretending he wants it, and another Paddy thinking he needs it.

"Never mind," Paddy says.

The worst thing is that Harry has been thinking exactly the same thing himself.

17

Harry must have fallen asleep because the next time he notices he can pick out the details of the room in the grey light. It's five o'clock. He has the same feeling he knows from childhood on Christmas morning, a mixture of excitement and exhaustion, and he knows that there's no chance of getting back to sleep. He gets up and sits at the end of the bed, watching the grey breakers slog their dreary way to the beach in the drizzle.

At eight o'clock he's up, laying the table for breakfast, when his mother appears in her dressing-gown.

"What's the matter with you?" she asks, yawning. "Is it your diarrhoea again?"

"Marie's coming back today," he says tersely. "And she's expecting me."

"Still doing a line with her, are you?"

Trust his mother to put it that way. "She'll be visiting us at Christmas or before. Or else I'll be going to France."

She stares at him, then rubs her eyes and pads out to the kitchen. "Your father's coming up today, so don't forget you're not to be running all over the place with Marie the whole weekend, although she's a very nice girl."

"She'll just have to come with us, then."

★

The Citroën isn't in the car park. Harry slows down to a trot. He hasn't really expected it to be so early. The receptionist looks up in surprise when he comes into the foyer. He makes for the bar as usual but the door jars in its frame and he bumps his forehead against it.

"It's not open till half past ten," the receptionist calls across.

"Right." Harry takes a few steps back into the foyer and puts his hands into his pockets. He would study the postcards at the reception desk but that would give the girl the chance to see his crimson face in close-up. He has never been in the hotel so early. He feels very much an intruder. Bags of laundry are propped up against the banisters of the staircase and there's the distant hum of vacuum-cleaners. He walks into the lounge, trying to look casual. It's empty at this time of the morning. From the far side of the door he can hear the clinks of the guests at their breakfast. He sits down in one of the big armchairs and stares at the blank screen of the TV. Too early for horse-racing yet.

An acrid pong starts to rise from his sneakers. They're streaked with brown. He has walked, or rather run down across the fields, because Paddy is going to Letterkenny for an X-ray today, and if his lungs are all right Harry will have to bring him back his bike, and he's been in too much of a hurry to avoid the cow-pats in the lane. He hears whispering out in the foyer and turns around. The manager, a florid-faced, white-haired man who looks like a retired film star, is conferring with the receptionist. Both are looking at him. The manager buttons his jacket and starts to come in Harry's direction. Harry turns back to the TV. The manager's polished shoes come into view.

"Look here, sonny," the manager says, "we don't mind you coming in here in the afternoons as long as you behave yourself.

But we can't have you messing up our carpet with your shoes."
Harry looks up at him in time to see his nose wrinkle. "Now
listen, you'll have to be out of here before the people come out
from breakfast."

"Can I come back in the afternoon?" Harry asks.

"Surely to God, yes, now go on with you."

He stands back to let Harry get to his feet. In the foyer the
receptionist pretends to be engrossed in her paperwork.

Outside the drizzle is cool on Harry's face. It doesn't matter,
Harry thinks, nothing matters as long as Marie comes back. He
walks down to the harbour, hoping that he won't meet Brian.
He goes out to the end of the pier. The rain is coming on
stronger, pocking the skin of the waves as they roll slackly into
the bay. He looks down into the water, wondering how he'd
ever been able to dive in there. He leans on the wall and looks
across the bay to the hotel. From here he can see the car park.
Still no Citroën.

He turns up the collar of his windcheater. He thinks about the
manager. How he pointed to the door. Like in a film. He thinks
about his own abject tone of voice asking if he could come back
that afternoon. God! He feels his cheeks start to burn.

In the afternoon a woman is on her knees, cleaning the carpet.
Harry steps around her and walks up to Reception. There's no
sign of the manager. The girl is on the telephone. She looks
through Harry as he approaches, and taps at the desk with a biro.

"Yes, right, Father, eight o'clock."

He wonders if she should be telephoning home from work.

"Yes, I've got that, we'll make you up a very nice table, but I
can't promise anything about the cake, Father, we'll do our best,
you're welcome, 'bye." She expels air in exasperation. "Would
you credit it?" she asks Harry. "Where am I to get a birthday

cake for Father Columb's sister for this evening?" She shakes her head.

"The priest?"

"Yes. Father Columb." She looks at him as if he's hard of hearing.

"Sorry about this morning," Harry says.

"Don't worry about it. I see you have clean shoes on now."

"Could you tell me if the Fischers are expected?"

"The French family from last week?"

"Yes. They wanted to come back."

She checks her register. "They didn't make a booking."

"Oh. Thanks." Harry walks uncertainly into the TV lounge. Then he goes back. "I know they didn't make a booking but they might have rung up."

"No, they didn't, sorry. Not a word."

He clears his throat and walks out of the hotel as if he has an important date.

Out in the bay a small boat is creeping slowly towards Horn Head. It's the McClellands', Harry recognises the white fibreglass hull. There are two figures in it. Brian and Paddy.

"Did you ask at the reception if they've booked?"

"Of course I did. Do you think I'm stupid or what?"

"No joy?"

"No." *If he says I told you so I'll push him out of the window.*

"So are you going to hang around all day tomorrow on the off-chance too?"

"Yeah. If I have to."

"Now I know what Brian was going on about."

"I'm all ears."

"He was saying you've been a bit of a wet dishcloth all week."

"Fuck Brian. All he thinks about is boats and balls."

"Jesus Harry, knowing you you'll have forgotten all about Marie in a couple of weeks anyway."

"Fuck you too."

The weather picks up the next day. A blue sky pushes the last clouds out to sea over Horn Head.

The receptionist waves to Harry as soon as he comes into the foyer. "I've got good news for you." Harry feels his lips part in an uncontrollable grin. She's smiling too. "Mr Fischer has just rung up. They're booked in for Monday."

"Morning?"

"He didn't say. I expect some time in the afternoon. It was Sligo exchange put him through."

"Thanks."

"You're welcome."

Harry could kiss her ruddy cheeks. He smiles and nods and turns to go. Then he turns back. "How long are they staying for?" he asks.

"Till Saturday."

"Thanks again."

Outside the wind has finally died away. The lowing of cows from across the fields is strangely loud in the stillness. The stones in the wall surrounding the car park gleam whitely as they dry off in the sun. It looks like they're in for a spell of heat.

Harry is watching the men and boys playing cricket down on the harder sand, grinning and laughing like a pack of idiots. Paddy, Brian, Harry's dad and his uncle, Mr McClelland. Mr Foster and his brood are fielding.

They're on Falcarragh beach again. Paddy's mum has asked Harry's dad to fry the picnic. To make up for the beach being Uncle Alec's idea. *Jesus*.

"Why don't you go and play with the others?" Harry's mother asks. It makes him sound about ten.

"I'm fine."

"Don't be such a spoil-sport. You should join in some of the time at least." She's looking at her knitting, not at him.

"I said I'm fine." Only this one more Sunday afternoon to go, thank God.

She drops her voice. "If you don't watch out Brian won't bother asking you any more now that Paddy's up and about again." She casts a furtive glance at her sister but Auntie Flo is chattering away to Mrs Foster and Mrs McClelland. The women are all sitting further up the beach in the warmer sand, all in their bathing-costumes except for Auntie Flo in her cotton dress, her calves jutting out from it like legs of ham in the sand. Mrs Bryce isn't there, nor Marjorie, so there isn't anybody to ogle. Not that Harry would, but it would be nice to have the temptation at least.

"Who cares?" Harry says. "I'm going for a walk."

"Don't go too far. Your father will be starting the fry in an hour. And don't be going into the sea on your own."

Harry stands up and brushes the sand off the seat of his jeans. He skirts the group of cricket players. Paddy is squaring up to bat Mr McClelland's artful lob; Brian is hunkering down behind him, swaying importantly at first slip. "Hi, men," Harry says, but neither of them looks his way. Paddy and Brian are now close friends, taking the boat out further and further. The other day they went all the way across Sheephaven Bay to Downings. Now they're planning to go right round Horn Head to Falcarragh. *Real hard men.*

Harry wades through the stream that flows down the beach, walks to the end of the beach and climbs up the rocks. There's another bay on the far side, curving round to the neck of Horn Head, enclosing a beach like a yellow scimitar. No roads lead down to it and it's completely deserted. As Harry leaves Falcarragh behind him and the clunks of the cricket bats fade he feels his irritation slip away.

He can put up with anything as long as Marie is coming back.

Half an hour later he's lying in a sunken nook in the dunes up behind the other strand. It's another quiet place he will be able to come to with Marie. He's had a pleasant walk across a rocky headland and then a grassy rise with not a soul in sight.

He closes his eyes and feels the sun on his face for a while. It would be nice to have a tan when Marie comes back. A bronzed god. Then he gets bored and reaches for the anorak he has discarded in the heat. He takes out Marie's passport from the inside pocket where he keeps it and opens it at the photograph. This time tomorrow she'll be looking at him like that again. They'll maybe come back here, or go to Doe Castle. Or the

Secret Strand. Paddy will have to go out in the boat with Brian or something so that they can have his bike.

Just when he's about to go back he hears the voices. This couple probably think they're all alone in the world, too. There must be another way down to the beach, they've probably parked their car somewhere. At first they seem to be having a normal conversation, though Harry can't understand what they're saying. Then the woman's voice starts to cut through the man's vibrating, placatory bass, and soar above it in screams, like in the kind of experimental opera you get on BBC2. As they draw nearer he can make out the shouted bits.

". . . take me for a fool . . . bloody well what you're up to with that wee bitch . . . like an old rag . . . another think coming . . . two can play at that game . . ."

The woman's voice, although distorted by rage, seems familiar, but it's the man's indiscernible rumblings that Harry recognises first, by their timbre alone. After all, he's made a fine art of ignoring its individual words in endless sermons. It's the Reverend McLeod's. And the other woman isn't his wife; this isn't an argument between a married couple. Harry is used to his parents' arguments, long-suffering, bloated things that are mostly silent, submerged, that you have to guess at, like whales wallowing just below the surface of the sea, bumping lazily against each other. There's an electric, dangerous quality about this argument. Anything could come of it.

Harry crawls forward and parts the marram grass. McLeod moves into his field of vision from under the dune, walking towards the far end of the strand with rapid strides, patting his hair into place after every few steps, not looking back. Where's the woman? Christ, wait till Paddy hears about this. McLeod must be having an affair with some woman.

"What are you doing here?"

Harry twists round. Mrs Bryce is standing behind him in the middle of the nook, wearing a flowery cotton dress and holding her shoes in her hands. She's come up the sandy track from the beach. Her face is all creased up and her mouth is jerking as though she's trying to stop herself crying.

"Nothing," says Harry.

"Have you been spying on us?"

"We're all here," he says.

"Oh, God." She clambers up to the top of the ridge to look at the other end of the strand.

"Not here. Over the hill, at Falcarragh. It's about a mile away."

"What are you doing here, then?"

"Taking a walk."

She gives a great quavery sigh and turns back to Harry. "I suppose you heard everything."

"No."

"Of course you did. I can see it in your face. I was shouting like a maniac." She looks up the strand, shading her eyes against the sun, one shoe dangling from her hand. McLeod's figure is disappearing into the dunes at the far end. She has obviously come up to see if he is going to turn back. Suddenly she stamps at the close-cropped grass with such force that Harry feels the earth judder. She crooks her arms at the elbows clumsily and flings her shoes as far as she can, which is only about half-way down the dune. Then she makes a strangled, pressing sound like somebody wanting to curse really obscenely, sinks to her knees, her face crumpling like a child's, and starts to sob.

Harry looks away. He fancies he heard a car starting up, but it's hard to tell because Mrs Bryce is sobbing so loudly. After a while it ebbs away to a kind of distant moan like the vacuum-cleaner in the hotel the other day.

"Are you all right?" he asks.

"Thinks he can throw me away like an old rag. The *bastard*!"
She pulls up her knees, buries her face in them and starts sobbing
again, her whole body trembling. She doesn't seem to care that
this exposes her white thighs. She isn't wearing stockings. Harry
looks away again, as if he's seen something very interesting on
the horizon. All he has to do is think of something sensible to
say and leave. That shouldn't be too difficult. He clears his
throat.

"I'd better be going or I'll miss the fry," he says.

"Don't go yet." Mrs Bryce looks up again. The mascara has
run from her eyelids into dark blotches under her eyes, giving
her the appearance of a panda. "I don't suppose you have a
hanky."

"No, sorry."

"I must look an awful mess."

"Not too bad."

She sniffs. "Don't stand there like a statue, Harry. Come and
sit down."

"I'd better go. Honest."

"Just for a minute. I have to talk to somebody."

Harry hunkers down awkwardly beside her, out of the wind's
reach. Mrs Bryce fumbles in her bag and takes out a packet of
Benson & Hedges. She opens it with trembling fingers, puts a
cigarette in her mouth, and gives Harry one. Fair enough, Harry
thinks, three minutes to smoke this and then skedaddle. He takes
out his lighter and lights hers, his hand steadied by the sight of
her trembling one. As she bends over the flame a tear falls off her
eyelashes and lands on the back of his hand in a dark splodge.

She pulls greedily at the cigarette and then blows out a cloud
of smoke without inhaling, as if she can't wait to talk. "If only I
hadn't started to shout." She's staring straight ahead. "I lost my

head. It was him acting as though you can be all bloody reasonable about everything that made me mad. It must be obvious to you what's going on."

"Yeah, sure," Harry starts glibly. "You're . . ." The only expression that comes to mind is his mother's ridiculous "doing a line". ". . . having an affair with the Reverend McLeod," he finishes.

"Exactly. I was, anyway. And now he wants to finish it." She draws on her cigarette. "Says it's getting too dangerous and it's bound to come out and so on, but the real reason is that he's got his eye on somebody who's much younger than me. And now he wants me out of the way." She's looking at a pellet of sheep's dropping on the ground, nodding slowly as if it's some kind of proof. "He's so despicable, such a worm. But I'll show him."

"Aren't you well rid of him, then?"

She turns to Harry and looks at him as if she's seeing him for the first time. "He's the only reason I come up to this bloody place. I spend my whole time looking forward to the summer and then when I'm here I can't enjoy it because I'm dreading leaving. It's ridiculous, really." She gives a small, bitter laugh. "It'll be four years tomorrow. I have the present and everything. Jesus."

"Doesn't his wife mind?"

"She doesn't know anything about it. Or doesn't want to know, maybe."

"And your husband?"

"The same. So that's the situation. The whole thing in a nutshell. The whole miserable thing. Pretty shocking, isn't it?"

"No." Harry snorts in what he intends to be a disparaging manner.

"Happens all the time in Kilmartin, does it?"

"Well, our minister kept getting anonymous letters. He got

the police on to it and they turned out to be coming from the postmaster's wife. They tried to keep it quiet, but it got out. She's eighty-four."

"I see. Not quite the same thing, maybe."

"Maybe not."

"Do you sleep with Marie?"

"Yeah." Harry has answered without thinking. He feels his face going red.

"Here?"

"No."

"You realise that if you tell anybody what you know I'll be ruined."

"I won't tell anybody."

"I've always liked you, Harry. There's something different about you." She's watching him closely now, her gaze shifting disconcertingly from one of Harry's eyes to the other. "You don't think I'm an old bag, do you?"

That's just what her face looks like close up, in fact, with the pouches under the eyes, the crow's-feet at their corners, and the hint of a double chin.

Harry starts as she runs her hand across the front of his jeans. She withdraws it and something like anxiety crosses her face. It's dead still in the nook. He could get up and walk away now, but he doesn't, he just sits looking at her, and then her expression clears, and her face looms up before his, the crow's-feet at the corners of her eyes fluttering from the strain of staying closed, and he feels her hand tugging at his zip.

"Harry!" Paddy's voice from somewhere in the dunes. Mrs Bryce's eyes flick open, and stare into his, so close he can see the grey flecks in the blue irises. For a moment they lie perfectly still.

"Harry!" Closer this time. With sudden irritation she pushes at him and he withdraws clumsily. Then they're on their feet, silently weaving and hopping like shadow boxers as they struggle frantically with their clothes.

"Harry!" Moving further away. Harry straightens up, breathing heavily. Mrs Bryce is going into contortions with the zip at the back of her frock. He moves towards her to help, but she shakes her head and frowns without looking up, and it suddenly seems like an impossibly intimate intention. She pulls it up, and as she straightens up their eyes meet. "You wait here a bit," she says.

He nods, and she goes over the edge of the dune.

"Harry!" Paddy again, getting nearer. "Mrs Bryce!" he shouts. "Have you seen Harry?"

Harry grabs his anorak and goes down the track. Down on the sand he sees Mrs Bryce turning away and heading back towards the far end of the strand with her slightly waddling gait, holding her shoes again. Paddy is watching her go.

"What's all the fuss?" Harry says to Paddy's back.

"And you're certain sure Marie's coming tomorrow?" Paddy asks.

"Want to bet?" Harry says.

"No. I hope she is. Honest to God. It'll stop you moping about like a sick dog."

"That sounds like something Brian would say."

"Yeah. His words."

"He hasn't got a clue."

"Well, I thought you pushed it a bit too far today myself. You should have seen them, dashing off like chickens with their heads cut off. I told them, I said Harry's only mooning about somewhere. And so you were, wandering along that beach like, like . . . like Sir Patrick Spens or whoever the fucker was."

"I couldn't stand that crowd any longer, to tell you the truth."

"Your mum was really worried. She thought you were half-way out to Tory, or the sharks had got you."

"Ach, she worries far too much."

"It was the picnic that upset everybody more than anything else. When the eggs got burnt because your dad went off to look for a phone. That's what annoyed Brian so much. You know how he likes a big fry and never gets one at home. That's why he started giving off."

"Did he indeed?"

"He said you should wise up and grow up."

"Him and his Boy Scout stuff."

"What do you mean?"

"Messing about in boats. Playing cricket with a load of kids."

Paddy is silent while that sinks in.

"So you were doing something really grown-up, then?"

"You could say that, yeah."

"Having a wank in the dunes probably."

"That's all you know. I wasn't alone."

"You don't expect me to believe that, do you?"

"Please yourself."

19

WHEN HARRY WAKES up in the early morning the thoughts he's blocked off come flooding in, and he lies turning from side to side and sweating. How could he have done it? As if he'd never been in love with Marie. As if his brain had been switched off, or overridden. Jesus. And she only did it to shut him up, they hadn't even got properly undressed.

It had become clear fairly quickly that the whole thing was a mistake, but still too late, while their arms and legs bumped like in a dance with both partners trying to lead. She had finally pulled him on top of her, probably more out of desperation than anything else. If only she'd kept her eyes shut, or he. It was her eyes that had put him off. When he'd looked at them they were watching back dispassionately. Like the nurse's that time as a child when he'd been in with the broken leg in the hospital. That was how she'd looked at him when she'd set him on the potty. *Are you finished yet?* And he hadn't been able to finish, it had seemed so pointless after a while.

Maybe it doesn't really count, then. He turns on to his belly to look for the knot of wood that reminds him of Marie's smile. There it is. That soft look she has sometimes when they're with the others and he catches her eye. She'll lower her head a bit and smile at him and he'll know that she's thinking of their lovemaking too. How different that is, with all the kissing, how familiar her body is, as if hers and his are branches of the same tree. Jesus, Jesus. He turns on to his other side.

"Would you give over for Christ's sake and let a body get some sleep?" Paddy mumbles.

Harry turns on his back and lies staring wide-eyed at the ceiling. The main thing now is to make sure that Marie never finds out.

After breakfast Harry clips *The Lord of the Rings* on to the back of his bike and rides down to the hotel. He checks that the Citroën isn't there, then rides back down the drive, leans the bike against the wall opposite and takes up position on it, out of reach of the manager. He can see the whole stretch of road to Dunbreaghy, where the Fischers will be coming from.

He leafs through the book, trying to find a place to start reading, but he can't concentrate and eventually he lays it aside. Today is still sunny but gusts of wind are rippling at his pullover.

A small inner voice is heckling him. You don't love Marie, it's saying, you can't, or you'd never have slept with Mrs Bryce. When you see Marie again you'll feel absolutely nothing. You'll have to think up excuses for not going away on the bikes with her on the days until she leaves, you'll be glad to see her go and you'll never write. Harry fights the voice down. Shut up, he says, the whole core of my being is saturated with love for Marie. But what if the voice is right? He tries plumbing his own depths to find out, but it's like diving in murky water. He'll know when she comes. In spite of the wind his brow is starting to sweat.

"Another fine day." Christ, it's Mr Bryce, on his way to the golf course again. He leans companionably against the wall. "Look at those colours. Like a postcard. Perfect day for painting. Liz could hardly wait to get out and away."

"Have you ever seen any of her paintings?" Harry says, without thinking.

"Hardly ever, to tell you the truth. She's very touchy about them." Mr Bryce is still smiling but his brow is creased as if he has a headache. Harry looks round for something to change the subject.

"Those cows are certainly enjoying the sun." A herd of Friesians are basking on a little grassy headland up the road a bit, flicking lazily with their tails.

"Just don't make the mistake of trying to get down to the beach through them," says Mr Bryce. "That big black fellow's a bull."

"Really?"

"I bet you think he's got the life of Reilly among all those cows. You couldn't be more wrong. Absolute stress, that's what it is. Those poor beasts are completely at the mercy of their sexual instincts. You should see their eyes when they're rutting. Complete panic. It's no fun, I can tell you. We vets really do the young ones a favour, putting them out of their misery."

"Poor things."

"Not down, out of their misery. Castrate them, that's what I mean." Mr Bryce laughs. "Nothing to go all red-faced about, Harry. We human beings are different, thank God." With a wave of his stick he's off again.

Something in the air, a distant familiar whoosh. Harry jumps up on top of the wall. The grey Citroën is loping like a greyhound along the road from Dunbreaghy, rounding the corner below the Moores' house, heading straight towards him. Two heads in the front, could they have left Marie behind somewhere? No, a third head is peeking between the other two, a hand waving, and then Marie is smiling out of the side window as the car slows

down and turns up the drive. Harry starts to walk up the drive
after it. He hears car doors opening and shutting, the creak and
slam of the boot, voices talking. When he reaches the top Mr
and Mrs Fischer are walking towards the hotel, and Marie is
standing by the car.

She looks different, older, with a new hairstyle, combed back,
wearing a very smart tweed skirt and jacket. She's watching him
very closely, her arms folded, a slight furrow between her brows,
and the lines at the side of her mouth that pucker when she
laughs are only hinted at. There's only a small, hesitant smile on
her face. She looks very vulnerable. Harry is flooded with love
for her. How could he ever have doubted it?

"Let's go somewhere," he says, reaching for her hand.

She comes with him to the side of the hotel where Paddy's
bike is, and once they are out of sight Harry takes her in his arms,
and tries to kiss her, but she holds him at arm's length, and looks
into his eyes. "Do you still feel the same?" she asks. "Please tell
me if you don't. Tell me now."

"More than ever. And you?"

She nods, and they kiss.

"I was so afraid you'd stopped. You looked so funny."

"I'll never stop."

"I was worried that I'd used it all up, thinking so much about
you, but when I saw you it all came out again."

They kiss again.

"Did you get my letter?"

"No."

"I wasn't sure how to address it. It's probably got lost."

"You're wearing perfume."

"It's called 'Tweed'. I got it with the costume. My father is
mad about the passport. He knows it's a trick."

"How long are you staying?"

"Till Saturday. Not much time. I'm dying to sleep with you."

"Can we go to that beach again?"

"The Secret Strand?"

"Yes. I've been thinking about it all the time."

"This afternoon? Paddy will just have to lend us his bike."

"Marie!" Her mother's voice. "*Viens, à table.*"

"I've got to go, I can't afford to annoy them. Come down after dinner, and whatever you do, don't forget my passport."

Harry dashes up the stairs to the bedroom. His anorak is lying draped over the chair by the window. He feels the pockets. Nothing there. He turns them inside out to be sure, then checks that nothing has fallen out on to the floor. No passport. Fuck, fuck, fuck. It has to be in the nook.

He clatters down the stairs again and runs into Paddy coming in the front door.

"Tell the others I won't be in for dinner," he says, and runs out to the bike.

In Dunbreaghy he has to slow down. He's been standing on the pedals all the way from Port Braddan and he has a stitch in his side, a knot more like, in a hawser. He hasn't done any real riding or swimming or rowing for ages. Maybe there's something to be said for sport after all. At the far side of the town he takes the main road to the left towards Falcarragh rather than the road to Horn Head. He'll look for the lane that Mrs Bryce and the Reverend McLeod must have driven down, it'll save him the long walk through the dunes. The only thing worrying him is what to do if the passport isn't in the nook. If Mrs Bryce has somehow bundled it up in her clothes.

Please God let it be there. I'll never doubt your existence again.

He has misjudged the time it will take him to ride round the New Lake. He's never been out this way on his bike before and the lake is much larger than you notice from the car. But he finds the lane sure enough and bumps down all its bends until it ends at a stone wall. Then he sets off at a jog across a marshy field at whose far end he can see the beach.

The passport is lying in the nook, its blue cover so obvious on the green grass that he'd have been hard put to explain forgetting it to Marie. On his way back to the bike rain-sodden clouds are jostling in from the Atlantic. He hasn't got his anorak with him. Hopefully he'll be back before the rain comes on. He's almost at the top of the lane when he hears a car crunching towards him. He gets off his bike to let it pass. He recognises its tinny whine before it appears round the corner. It's Mrs Bryce's Imp. She stops and winds down the side window. "What are you doing here?" She sounds quite upset.

"I forgot something yesterday," he says, patting his pocket.

"Is there a car down there?"

She means McLeod's. "No."

She turns her head away and looks down at her hands on the steering-wheel. Harry is afraid she'll burst into tears. He starts to push his bike past the car.

"I'll give you a lift back," she calls. "We have to talk anyway."

If he goes in the car he can make up the lost time and be with Marie at almost the same time as if he had dinner at home. Maybe he'll be able to confine the talk to the weather or something. "That'd be great," he says. "But I'll have to take the bike too."

Mrs Bryce has to get out so the seat can be put forward to get the bike in. The only way it fits in is with its front wheel hanging over the passenger seat, so Harry has to cower down under it.

To look out over the dashboard he has to push against the wheel with the back of his neck.

"Let's be sensible about this," says Mrs Bryce, as they reverse back up the lane. "The best thing we can do about yesterday is forget about it."

"That's just what I was thinking."

"I was in a kind of panic. I couldn't think straight. I think I've messed everything up. You must think I'm an awful woman."

"Not at all."

"So we'll forget all about it?"

If only she would give over. "Fair enough."

"That's settled, then."

They fall into an uneasy silence, and the rain starts, big swollen blotches on the windscreen at first, then a patter that quickly intensifies to a drumming. She turns the car round and starts back towards Dunbreaghy. Muckish appears through the windscreen in wipes that blur over immediately. After a few miles an oncoming car flashes its lights at them. Mrs Bryce stiffens behind the wheel and slows, keeping her eye on the rear-view mirror. She stops the car, reverses into a lane and drives back out in the other direction.

"Is that McLeod?" Harry asks. But Mrs Bryce is watching the car in front with anxious eyes.

"Would you just let me out here?" Harry says. "I'll ride back after all." But they're already bumping down the lane again. The Imp stops bumper to bumper with the other car. McLeod jumps out and runs back to the Imp. Mrs Bryce lowers the side window and his face glowers in. The rain bouncing off his bald head sprays the car's interior. Harry can feel tiny pricks splash his face.

"What's he doing in the car?"

"What business is it of yours?"

"What's going on here?"

"I warned you."

"What are you talking about?"

"I told you two could play at that game."

"I have to be getting back," says Harry.

McLeod's face withdraws from the window and Harry hears his footsteps round the back of the Imp. Harry's door is wrenched open and a hand catches him by the hair, yanking him up. "Come out of it, you little bastard."

The pain is awful. Harry tries to hang on to the arm that's pulling him out of the car. It feels like his hair is going to come out by the roots. He gets one foot on the ground, then the other. Still McLeod doesn't let go. Harry twists his left knee outwards and upwards and rams it as hard as he can between McLeod's legs. The grip on his hair relaxes immediately and McLeod collapses on the bonnet of the Imp, groaning. The next instant blows are raining down on Harry's head and shoulders. "Don't you dare, don't you dare!" Mrs Bryce is shouting. Harry wards off her slaps with his elbows but he loses his balance and falls on his knee and then face down in a muddy puddle. When he gets to his feet again the left knee is out of his trousers and his pullover is a muddy mess. The rain is washing the dirt on his cheek down his neck.

Mrs Bryce is leaning over McLeod, whispering. Harry goes to the Imp and starts tugging at the bike. McLeod limps back to his car, moaning softly, gets in and drives away. Mrs Bryce gets into the Imp and sits staring after him. With her in the car Harry can't get the bike out. She's drumming with her fingertips at the steering-wheel and then suddenly she starts up and drives off so quickly that Harry has to jump back. At the junction to the road she leans across and pulls the door shut. Then the Imp darts off after McLeod's car, with Harry's bike still inside.

"Fuck a brick," says Harry. He limps up the lane to the road. His knee is hurting. It's scraped and bleeding. The rain is running off his face, and plastering his pullover and his trousers to his body, and his guttees are squelching. He takes Marie's passport out of his trouser pocket and sticks it down the waistband of his trousers to try to keep it dry. He starts up the road to Dunbreaghy, half running, half walking. He hears a car behind him and sticks out his thumb. To his surprise it goes down through the gears. He turns round. The incredulous faces of Mr and Mrs McClelland are staring out of their Morris 1300 as it slows down and stops beside him. Harry opens the back door.

"I fell off my bike," he says.

"Put it in the boot," says Mr McClelland.

"It's away down that lane."

"We're in no rush. It'll save your father coming out all this way."

"No, honest. You'd never get the car down."

"Whatever you say."

They drive off.

"This is a stroke of luck," says Harry.

"I don't know," says Mr McClelland. "Half of Harbour Road seems to be gallivanting around here."

"We've already seen the Reverend McLeod and Mrs Bryce," says Mrs McClelland.

"Isn't that your bike?" Mr McClelland asks, and brakes.

Harry's bike is propped up against the stone wall to the left of the road. Mrs Bryce must have dumped it.

"No," says Harry.

"Are you sure? It looks just like it."

"No."

"Fair enough. You should know, shouldn't you?"

"He said it was down the lane," says Mrs McClelland.

"He did, indeed." Mr McClelland's eyes are watching Harry from the rear-view mirror, wrinkling shrewdly. "I don't know what you're up to, Harry. And I'm very glad you're not my son and I don't have to find out."

They drive on in silence to Dunbreaghy, where Harry asks, "Are Brian and Paddy out in the boat?"

"They're going out this afternoon once the tide has changed, as far as I know," says Mr McClelland. "Going with them?"

"I might."

They leave Harry off at the bottom of the lane up to the house. As they drive off Paddy comes cycling down. He stops, and gets off his bike.

"What's happened to you?" he asks. "Where's your bike?"

"Never mind all that. Is this the day you and Brian are going round Horn Head to Falcarragh?"

"Yeah, why?"

"Would you take me and Marie? There's a beach round the far side you could drop us off at."

"And pick you up again?"

"Yes."

"You'll have to ask Brian."

"Wait for us down at the beach. I just need to get changed. Tell you what, lend us your bike, I'll be quicker."

"How am I supposed to get down?"

"Just this one more time. Please, Paddy."

Harry cycles up the drive, and sets the bike against the wall of the house. He looks back down across the fields. Paddy is standing in the cow-path, hands in his pockets, looking down, nudging at something with his foot. Probably looking for a stone. *Go on, throw it, you big wean.* Paddy bends down a bit, hesitates, then straightens up again, and goes on.

Harry is in the bathroom before his mother can react.

"Harry? Your dinner's in the oven," she says, outside the door.

"I'm not hungry, Mum, I'm as good as gone already."

"Is Marie back?"

"Yes."

"Oh dear."

Harry is almost at the hotel when he realises he's left Marie's passport in his other trousers.

20

THEY CHUG OUT of the harbour. Harry and Marie are sitting on the middle seat with their backs to Paddy in the prow, and facing Brian, who's sitting beside the outboard engine. There's a slow but powerful swell, that lifts and drops the boat in great arcs as it moves across the heaving flanks of water in Sheephaven Bay. The wind shears the spume off the backs of the breakers and showers them over the prow, wetting them all. Harry has his arm around Marie, and his free hand cups hers in her lap. Marie passes round a packet of Kent, and tells them about her trip to Galway and Kerry. She's surprised that none of them has ever been down that far. Brian says he's been to Holland, Denmark, and Germany, but no further south than Sligo. To Harry the places she's talking about, Galway Town, Limerick, and Killarney could be Paris, Lyon, or Strasbourg.

"Prods and Micks again?" she asks.

"I suppose so," says Harry.

She tells them about their hotel in Galway, about her father ordering a bottle of wine one evening, and how the whole staff went on a hunt for the corkscrew, about being photographed in Aran sweaters and tweed skirts for a catalogue, and how the photographer drove a potted fuchsia about in the back of his van and set it up as foreground to every photograph, whether it was on a beach or a moor or in front of a farmhouse. She tells them about the argument she had with her father over coming back to Dunbreaghy.

"Port Braddan," Harry says.

"But the hotel's called the Dunbreaghy."

"That's why your letter didn't come." He turns and nods to Paddy. I told you so.

"Speaking of fights," says Brian, "I'd almost forgotten. There was a hell of a row in the Bryces' house earlier on. We were having lunch and he was shouting so loud we could hear every word. My folks were embarrassed, and tried to pretend nothing was happening, and he was shouting away. Bastard this and bitch that. And something about a beach she always goes to. She must be having an affair with somebody, and meeting him on this beach, when she's supposed to be out painting. It was all I could do to keep from laughing. It was like when you're watching TV, and then this great sex scene comes on. Only they couldn't turn it off."

"She was on that beach the other day, where Harry was. But there was nobody with her," says Paddy. "Except Harry, of course. You must have seen her."

"No," says Harry.

They round the rocks of Little Horn, darkly glistening in the wake of the tide, and the rocky maw of Skate Bay opens up before them.

"This is where we nearly capsized that time," says Harry. "It seems ages ago."

"Any idea who the man is?" Marie asks.

"No. A bastard is all I heard," says Brian.

"She was packing her car when we came past. Looked like she was leaving. I spoke to her but she didn't answer. I thought that was funny. Wasn't it, Harry?"

"I had my work cut out to keep us from falling over on the

bike," Harry says. He turns to Paddy. "You should get the brakes on your bike seen to. They screech something awful."

"It wasn't intended to be a tandem," says Paddy.

"What happened to your bike anyway, Harry?" Brian asks. "My dad said it must be an interesting story. Said he was glad it hadn't happened to me, whatever it was."

"Nothing, really. I just fell off it, that's all."

"Wait till you hear this, Paddy," Brian says. "Mum and Dad picked Harry up earlier on round by Falcarragh. They said he looked as if he'd got into a fight with a bear. He says he had an accident with his bike down some lane, wasn't that it?"

"Not quite," says Harry.

"Anyway, they drive on about a mile, and there's his bike, leaning against a wall. He said it wasn't, but it was, because it had that crap sticker on the mudguard. As if it was the one James Bond rides in all the films."

"Today?" Marie asks.

"Yeah, today, earlier on," says Brian. "Didn't Harry tell you about it?"

"It's not that interesting," Harry says.

"How your bike got from down the lane to a mile further up the road, that's interesting enough for a start," says Brian.

"I've been trying to figure that out myself," says Harry. "Somebody must have stolen it."

"From down the lane."

"Yeah."

"Where were you?"

"I was away looking for something I'd left in the dunes yesterday. A book. I fell off the bike first, then I left it and went across the dunes."

"Was this the same beach you were on yesterday?" Paddy asks.

"Yeah."

"And this somebody threw your bike out later," says Brian. "Why would he do that?"

Harry shrugs.

Brian is smiling at Harry, but it's the smile he uses on his parents just before saying something to annoy them. "So why did you tell my parents the bike was down the lane?" he says.

"I didn't."

"They said you did. Both of them."

"Look, Brian, why don't you just mind your own business?"

"Sure."

Nobody speaks for a while.

"I don't understand what you were doing out that road," says Marie.

"I'll tell you later," Harry whispers. "It has to do with your passport."

"Why are you making such a big secret of it?"

Harry smiles, and pats her hand.

Brian keeps watching the Great Horn, and making minor adjustments to their course, not talking, avoiding their eyes, as though the steering is demanding all his concentration. They're keeping fairly close to the cliffs, in the lee of the wind from the Atlantic.

"I suppose you think my business is to take you out in the boat whenever it suits you, to wherever it suits you," he says, still not looking at Harry. "And when it doesn't suit you it's Boy Scout stuff, isn't that right?"

"Just leave us off at the beach, Brian. You don't have to pick us up again. We'll walk back."

"Another thing. About your bike. Dad said there wasn't a thing wrong with it. Whatever accident you had had nothing to do with it."

"Christ, there you go again. I told you already it's none of your business what I do with my bike."

"I suppose it's none of Paddy's business either?"

"Keep Paddy out of it."

"None of his business that you take his bike and he has to walk down."

"Leave off, would you? I can't help it if I had an accident."

"Accident my arse," says Paddy.

Harry turns to look at him. Paddy's face is pale and pinched. "What would you know about it, anyway?" says Harry. "Were you there?"

"I know you, Harry," Paddy says, in a low voice. "I knew you'd forget about Marie."

An inner voice is telling Harry to shut up, but he wants to get Paddy back down to where he belongs first. "Shut up, Paddy," he says, also in a low voice. "You're just in love with Marie yourself."

Paddy jerks as if he's been slapped. It's true, Harry thinks in dull surprise. Why didn't I see that before?

"I'll tell you one thing," says Paddy, "if Marie was my girlfriend I wouldn't be fucking an old hag like Mrs Bryce."

Brian makes a spluttering sound, and then chokes it off, like someone caught laughing at a funeral. "Jesus," he says.

"She was who was with you in the dunes. And Mr Bryce found out and gave you a beating," Paddy goes on. "That must be what happened."

"Balls," says Harry.

"What did happen, then?"

Harry turns back. Marie is trying to smile, shaking her head. Brian is watching him too, smiling his different smile. Harry looks down at the juddering floor. Somewhere there is a sentence that will save the situation. All he has to do is think of it. But his mind is working very slowly. Like trying to run in water. Then the floor of the boat jumps, there's a thud from below it and then the whine of the engine out of water. The boat slews sharply, rocking. Brian reaches for the engine as it hangs askew on one screw for an instant before it falls loose and splashes into the sea. In the sudden silence Harry hears the booming roar of the sea against the cliffs.

"Fuck," says Brian. "We've hit an underwater rock. I wasn't paying attention. It's your bloody fault."

The cliffs are teetering right above them. That saves me from saying anything now, Harry thinks. I can think of something while I'm getting the oars. They're under Marie's seat. He stands up to get at them, but the boat suddenly sways the other way. Christ, Paddy has stood up too. The floor of the boat slips away beneath his feet and the green cheek of a wave comes up to meet him. Coldness encompasses him and he sinks in a cloud of bubbles. *Where's the light?* He swallows a mouthful of water. His hand touches wet fronds of seaweed on a boulder. He pushes away. Now he can see the light spangling the underside of the swell. He surfaces, taking great whoops of breath. Snot splatters out of his nose and down his chin. He coughs the water up; it sears his throat with the bitter taste of gall.

"Harree!" Marie is leaning out of the boat towards him. He swims to her, wiping his face, his guttees walloping about his feet. He's trying to think of something funny to say, something they'll all remember the situation by later, when everything is back to normal. The boat's gunwale is unnaturally high.

"Careful, Paddy's on the other side. He fell in too," says Marie, as Harry reaches up to grab the gunwale. The boat levels out again from Harry's weight and he hangs there for a while, treading water, getting his breath back. Now he feels a pain in his thigh where he must have hit the gunwale going over.

"Are you both all right? Can you get back on board?" asks Marie.

"Are the oars there?" Harry asks.

"Only one. One fell overboard."

"Can you see it anywhere?" Paddy's muffled voice asks from the other side.

"No . . . Yes, that might be it over there. But it's too far away. You're not to try and get it."

"We're moving away from the cliffs," says Brian. "Out to sea. The tide's going out."

"We'll have to leave the boat and swim to the shore before it gets too far," says Harry.

"I can see a place that looks safe," says Marie. "It's a kind of a pebble beach."

"We'd all better take our shoes off, and pullovers," says Harry. He reaches down with one hand and undoes the laces. His guttees bob up to the surface. Then he pulls his soggy pullover over his head and drapes it over the gunwale.

"You do what you like," says Brian. "I'm not leaving the boat."

"We have to," says Harry. "It's being carried out to the open sea."

The boat rocks and there's a splash. "I'm in," calls Marie. "Follow me."

"Come on, Brian," Harry calls.

"I'm staying here," Brian answers.

"For Christ's sake," says Paddy. The boat rocks violently.

"What are you up to?" Brian shouts. "You'll tip the boat over."

"Come out of that, for fuck's sake," says Paddy. "We have to swim in. Now." The boat rocks again.

"All right, all right." There's a splash, and the boat rises in the

water. Harry pushes away and swims round the boat. Ahead of
him he sees two heads dipping in the water, Marie's in front,
Brian's behind her. Harry strikes out after them. They're
swimming parallel to the cliffs. It's very unpleasant swimming in
shirt and trousers, colder somehow, the way the fabric keeps
flattening against your skin. The shock has cleared his mind.
Maybe it's just as well the accident happened when it did. He
was just about to say something stupid. He'll have to admit that
he rode back for Marie's passport. That's a bit strange perhaps,
but it isn't a crime. The only problem is why he said his bike was
down the lane when it was up against the stone wall. All he has
to do is think of an explanation before they reach the beach.

He braked to avoid an oncoming car, and fell off the bike. He
left the bike, and ran on to the nook. When he came back the
bike was gone. The man in the car stole it, had second thoughts,
maybe thought Harry had memorised his licence number or
something, and dumped the bike. *No big deal*. Confidence
returning, he swims on.

There's no sign of a beach where they can land, it seems to be
all sheer cliff to his left. Harry hopes Marie can see where she's
going. He's starting to tire. He can still see the two heads in front
of him. They're turning towards the cliff. Harry swims straight
on for a bit to reach the spot they turned at. It can't be a very
wide beach and if you turn in too soon it will surely bring you
up against the cliffs. Now he can hear the sough of the waves
breaking and the hiss as the water channels back through
pebbles. Marie was right after all. The crest of a wave lifts him
and he sees the place she meant, not much more than a sill of
pebbles at the foot of the sheer cliffs. Such a stroke of luck. It
looks like the only place where it's possible to get ashore in the
whole bay. He sinks back into a trough. The next wave breaks
around him. He cracks his knee on a stone, then he's kneeling

on pebbles, then rolling over as the water pulls him back out to sea. He falls on his back. Torrents of water break on his chest and he swallows some.

Then hands are reaching under his arms, pulling. Marie holds him while he struggles to his feet in the sluicing water. He vomits into the retreating flow, then has to step aside as the gibbets are washed back in again by the next wave.

"Sorry," he says. They limp in towards the cliffs. Their bare feet keep slipping painfully on the rounded, wet stones. Brian is sitting on a rock, coughing. "Fuck you all," he says, half crying. "My dad will go mad."

"Where's Paddy?" Marie asks.

"I don't know," says Harry. "He was behind me. He must be to the right somewhere."

They turn to face the sea again. They should never have gone out in it. *Fuck, fuck, fuck.* The engine is gone, and the boat, too, unless the Stevensons find it with their trawler. There's going to be an awful row. Harry and Paddy will probably have to help to pay for the boat.

"Paddy!" Marie calls.

There's no sign of him. "Paddy!" Harry shouts.

"He should have been in by now," says Marie.

"Unless he turned back for the boat."

"Did you see him turn back?"

"No. I didn't see him after you turned towards the beach."

The boat is bobbing further out, drifting towards the Great Horn, turning slowly round and round. Harry clambers up the big boulders at the back of the beach to get a better view.

"Is he in it?" Marie asks.

"I can't see." Parts of the stretch of water between the shore and the boat are obscured by humps of waves. As he watches a grey veil of rain draws in from the sea towards them, pebble-dashing the swell. They hear the hiss of the drops on the water and feel the first splats on their faces.

"We must do something," says Marie.

Harry turns round to look at the cliffs. They sway above him, dark and glistening. For a moment he thinks they're toppling out towards him and he has to steady himself with both hands. Rain bounces off the sheer walls and soaks them. No way up there. He looks across to where the neck of the Great Horn juts out. The cliffs are actually composed of different layers of rock that dip into the sea at an angle of roughly forty-five degrees. The layers have weathered at different rates; some are worn further back. If you could get up to one of those it looks as though you could follow it easily enough to the top. He sees a narrow chimney of rock winding up the shoulder, leading to a worn-back seam that looks wide enough to crawl up. He looks back at Brian. He's poking disconsolately at the sodden mass of cigarettes in their packet, mumbling and shaking his head.

"There's a way up the cliff over there," Harry says. "You stay here in case Paddy comes in. I'll get help."

Marie only nods, looking out to sea. She's starting to shiver now. She has folded her arms, and the arms of her jumper, elongated in the water, hang down from her hands.

"I'll be as quick as I can. He'll be all right. He's probably out in the boat by now. That was a load of rubbish he was saying. He's just jealous, that's all. Always has been."

"We've other things to worry about now," she says, still looking out to sea.

"OK." He leaves her there, glad to be able to do something, and walks across to the far end of the rocky beach to where he has seen the way up.

Up close the chimney looks even better, not so steep, with plenty of handholds. But the rocks are wet from the rain and he'll have to be careful. He starts up, concentrating on the climbing, thinking only of the next step, the next hold. The chimney narrows as he climbs; he doesn't look down. About half-way up the rain stops.

At the top the chimney closes over his head. He's standing on a ledge. He knows the seam is just above him, even though he can't see it. Once he gets on to that he'll be all right. It's overgrown with heather all the way to the top. He reaches up with his right hand. He can feel the ridge. He flaps his hand about and grasps the root of a heather shrub. It feels a bit skimpy. He gropes further round but there are no others within reach. It will have to support all his weight when he swings out from the chimney to the face of the cliff then pulls himself up.

No point in thinking about it. He changes his grip on the plant from his right hand to his left one, grabs the ledge with his right hand, pushes himself out of the chimney with his feet, scrabbles for a toe-hold on the cliff wall, finds a tiny outcrop and levers himself up sideways. With most of his weight on his left hand the plant suddenly loosens. He flails wildly with his right hand and his fingers tighten round a stout root further in the ledge. He pulls himself on to the seam as the plant in his right hand comes away, scattering little balls of earth down the slope in front of him. He lies on his stomach for a while, trembling, taking deep breaths.

The seam stretches up ahead of him, full of easily accessible heather plants, describing a gradual curve to the top of the cliff. He has done it. He wonders if Marie has been watching. Now all he has to do is scoot up the seam, get to the nearest farmhouse telephone, get Paddy and the boat rescued and have a sensible talk with Marie. The day isn't lost yet. He only has to deny that thing with Mrs Bryce convincingly enough.

He moves quickly up the seam, keeping his eyes on the way

ahead. The sky is blue again and the white clouds are scudding inland past the lip of the cliff. The sight is starting to make him feel dizzy. He stops to get his breath back. The seam's curve has brought him back over the beach again. He looks down and sees Marie and Brian pulling at Paddy in dark fronds of seaweed. What are they doing so far out in the tide? Paddy's arms are going any old way. A wave breaks limply over the three of them and Paddy's head slops in the direction of the beach and then the other way in the backwater.

Paddy is trapped firmly between two boulders and the dark colouring in the water round them isn't seaweed, because it's spreading. It's blood.

21

Try as he may Harry can't get the letters to shape up into words. They fall apart, sprawling across the page like scattered figures. Like small black bodies drowned in a sea of white. He shivers and puts the book away. After a while he sits up in bed again and resumes his watch of the swing doors. They have sheets of metal tacked on to their lower halves, dinged where the nurses push them open with their trolleys. No windows in the doors, so you can't see who's coming. But you can hear the people approach. No sense in getting worked up when you hear the rattle of the trolleys, because that only means the arrival of a meal. And the squeak of rubber shoes only heralds a doctor or a nurse.

It's the tap of high heels Harry is waiting for. She will be wearing them when she comes, people dress up to visit in hospitals. He's glad that he's on his own in the intensive care ward. No other patients to distract him from the outside noises with their empty chatter. He wants to recognise Marie's walk when she comes. He hasn't been fooled by his mother's slow tread, and he heard Mrs McClelland talking to the nurses in the corridor, and Brian's slouch, long before her footsteps were audible.

He has been imagining the quick, determined steps so intensively that when he hears them he isn't sure whether they are real or not. But they get louder and louder. He sits bolt upright, ignoring the sharp pain in his side. Everything depends on what he says. The doors swing open.

"Hello, Harry."

"Hello, Marjorie."

"How's the pneumonia?"

"Fine, thanks." Ironic that he should have the same thing that Paddy had.

"You look like you were expecting somebody. But not me probably." She stands uncertainly by the bed, holding a brown paper bag. "Have you got enough to read? Would you like me to buy you some books in Letterkenny?"

"No, thanks." He has to ask. "How's Auntie Flo?"

Marjorie's mouth puckers and her head jerks. She covers her face with her hands and her shoulders shake. Harry waits, remembering his aunt's demented wail as the Stevensons' boat came into the bay and they saw Paddy, and how she flopped clumsily over the side, got to her feet and stumbled through the shallows towards the body before anybody could stop her, her frock bundled up her fat thighs. Uncle Alec and his dad had to prise her arms off Paddy so they could lift the body from out between the rocks. "He's so cold," she kept moaning. "Why didn't we think to bring warm clothes?"

"If only the funeral was over," Marjorie says, into her hand-kerchief.

"When is it ?"

"Tomorrow afternoon."

"I'll have to see if they'll let me out for it."

Marjorie blows her nose. "Listen, Harry, it would be better if you didn't come. That's really why I'm here. It'll make it easier for my mother."

"I see."

"You know the way you look alike. And there's a kind of a feeling that you and Marie shouldn't have been in the boat, that it was your fault it was overloaded. I know it's not fair but there it is."

"Sure."

"I brought you some grapes." She sits on the chair beside his bed. "I feel so awful, I can't talk to anybody, they've all got their own problems, only . . . I wish I'd been nicer to him, you know? All the time he was just a pest and then this summer I was just starting to like him and now he's gone. I keep thinking, it's so silly, if he came back I'd give him all the cigarettes he wanted. I've even bought a full packet of the ones he liked, Silk Cut, just in case. But he isn't coming back."

"No."

Marjorie cries again. Harry looks away in embarrassment. Sooner or later all his visitors start to cry about Paddy at his bedside, and they seem to expect him to cry too. Even Brian. "Paddy was dead wrong about you and that Bryce woman," he said. "It was McLeod she was having an affair with. He's running around with a great black eye now. It's the talk of Harbour Road. Apart from Paddy, of course. The whole fight was for nothing." Then Brian started sniffling and crying. But Harry can't cry. There's another misery blocking the way to his grief for Paddy. If he knows that Marie still loves him he might be able to mourn for Paddy, but not before.

Marjorie is composing herself again. "Do you think I could have a cigarette?" she asks.

"Smoke away."

"Have one yourself."

"I've given up."

She lights up and goes across to the window.

"I always knew he was Mum's favourite," she says. "I can't comfort her at all. It's as if I'm not there." She stares out at the slate roofs of Letterkenny glistening drably in the rain. "I'm going to England. To Canterbury University. I got the A levels I need. Oh, before I forget, you got your O levels. Your father came down with the letter yesterday."

"Was there anything between you and McLeod?"

She inhales, and blows the smoke out again. "What gives you that idea?"

"Was there?"

"He was having an affair with Mrs Bryce. Everybody knows that."

"So all those times in the church, they were really practices?"

"Yes. There was nothing. Not really. It was only a bit of fun. I was only . . ."

"Stringing him along."

"How do you know about it?"

"Don't ask."

"Christ, Harry."

They are silent for a while, till Marjorie flicks her cigarette out of the window. "I'll have to be getting back," she says. "Dad's waiting in the car."

"He didn't want to come up?"

"No." She comes back to the bed.

"Are the Fischers still here?" Harry asks.

"I think so. They missed their boat because of the police inquiries. They were up at the house yesterday, but I wasn't talking to Marie at all really. She looked awful, like the rest of us, I suppose."

"Was she asking for me?"

"I haven't a clue, Harry, honest."

"Does she know I'm here?"

"I'm sure it was mentioned. Poor Paddy, he was in love with her too, you know."

"How did you know?"

"A blind man could have seen it."

"That's what we fell out about at the end."

"I wondered if something like that had happened. Do you think badly of him?"

"He thought badly of me. He thought I wasn't right for Marie."

"I see. Oh, God. He was in love. You know what that's like. People do anything."

"Yeah." He reaches for her hand. "Would you do me a favour?"

"Go and see Marie?"

"Tell her I've got to see her."

"All right. Have you messed everything up?"

He starts to cry then, the tears he hasn't been able to cry for Paddy.

"I'll see what I can do," Marjorie says, and moves towards the door. "No hard feelings about the funeral?"

"No."

She pushes open the doors. "Looks like I can save myself that visit. Hello, Marie."

"Hello, Marjorie."

Marie comes into the room. Harry feels his heart flip and race and his mouth twist into that horsy smile of his. She's wearing a tweed cape. Her hands reach through it and clasp a handbag. He has never seen her with one before. She's grown up, he thinks. This is what she'll look like from now on.

"It's great to see you, Marie."

She sits on the edge of his bed. "I didn't really want to come," she says. "But I could never have explained it to my parents, after all the fuss I made in Connemara."

"You're here now, that's the main thing."

"Not for long. My parents are waiting outside in the car.

We're on our way to the ferry from Dublin. We've had to take a later boat. The police wanted to ask some questions."

"They were here too. Didn't you catch a cold or anything?"

"No."

Her hand at the edge of the bed is just a few inches away from his. He touches it. She draws it back. "It wasn't true, Marie. That was just a lot of nonsense. I don't want to talk badly of Paddy, but he was out of his mind with jealousy."

She keeps her eyes on the floor. "And you never went for a drive with her or something like that?"

"Never."

She turns to him. "The barman in the hotel saw you when he was driving to work. He told my father. He saw you and her in her car. She's got some kind of funny car and he knows her anyway. You and your bike. He just mentioned it, he didn't think anything strange about it, neither did my father. You think because Paddy's dead you can keep on lying."

"I'll tell you what happened."

"Did you sleep with her?"

"Yes."

"I just don't understand it. How you could do it? What she was thinking of?"

"It wasn't how you think it was."

"It doesn't matter now." She stands up.

"I love you, Marie."

Her face screws up and she shakes her head.

"I'll write and explain everything," Harry says.

"Please don't. There isn't any point." Her voice is thick, as if she has a cold. She moves away, then stops and looks back at Harry as though she's forgotten something. Harry watches her, concentrating on her every movement. But all she says is "Goodbye," and walks towards the door.

"Marie!" Harry calls, but she has already gone out of the door, high heels tapping down the corridor, the doors swinging to and fro in her wake. She'll come back, he thinks. He waits, leaning rigidly out of the bed, watching the door's swing gradually subside, willing them not to stop because it was she who set them in motion, but then he sees that they are still, he must have been imagining their movement for quite some time, and there's no sound in the corridor outside. The hospital has never been so quiet.

22

Harry lowers the blinds, switches out the light, ties a towel round his head so that he can't see a thing and stands at the wash-basin, gripping it with both hands. It's exactly the same make as the one in Donegal, made by Cruikshanks of Belfast some time after the First World War, square with bevelled corners.

"How long are you going to be?" Harry's mother calls up the stairs.

"Can't a body have a bit of peace, even in the toilet?"

He is willing himself to the basin in Donegal on the evening of the first hooley. When I'm sure I'm there, I'll turn around, walk across the bathroom, unlock the door and step out into the wood-panelled hall. Then I can undo the towel. Everybody is ready to go, they're all sitting in the car waiting for me, Paddy's there too. I'll pull the front door shut, get in the car and go down to meet Marie.

The Donegal smells waft in under the door around him, peat, the panelled corridor, the waxed floor, the gas cookers, the musty furniture. *Now, quick. Marie is waiting for me.* He turns and walks in the direction of the bathroom door in the house in Donegal. But he's walking to where the bathtub in Kilmartin is, and its rim will hurt his shins badly. If it's there. He slows down until he's hardly more than shuffling in the darkness and there it is, nudging against his shins. He takes off the towel and makes out the dim outlines of the Kilmartin bathroom. His faith has not been great enough. But it can grow.

Rain gathers on the window-sills, seeps round their sides, and soaks into the walls below in tapering stains. Harry reaches for the big new Larousse dictionary he's bought from his shop money. "Même les murs pleurent," he writes. Even the walls are weeping. Not bad. It has been raining for days now. There's a constant gurgle of water in the drainpipes. As if the house is being given water torture. *La torture de l'eau.* Maybe not so good. He tears the page out of the pad, crumples it up, and throws it into the wastepaper basket.

He has written nine letters to Marie, the first two in English, the others in French. Letters of justification, love letters, letters about her body, letters with news. None of them has been the perfect one he's trying for, but he has sent them off anyway. Sometimes the way to write this perfect letter seems completely obvious to him, the mood comes to him sitting at school or in the bus, where he now sits upstairs, so that he doesn't have to talk to anybody. But by the time he gets to the card table in his bedroom the mood is lost. Sometimes he wakes up in the morning with a memory of having had it word perfect in his mind, but sinking away now, just a few glints getting fainter, and then it's gone.

He has had no replies. He thought it might take a month, and when it passed he gave it an extension. He fights against the insidiously impatient part of himself that expects a letter to be waiting for him every day when he comes home from school. He tells himself, Not today, and not tomorrow, probably not the day after, so that when there is no letter he can say, There, I told you so, I knew it all along.

Sometimes he sees Marie in the crowds in Ballyraine, walking to the shops or sitting at bus-stops. He recognises her in the shake of a head, in a hand brushing back hair or the pull of a mouth before laughter. When he follows her she changes into somebody else.

Sometimes he dreams of Paddy. He's standing silently at the other open window in their attic room in Donegal, waiting for Harry to say something. He is shaken awake from these dreams by his mother or father because they hear him talking in his sleep.

He hears his mother come in from the shop, and go into the living room. When he joins her she's standing behind the armchair in the living room, staring at the TV. The atmosphere radiating off the small screen is electric, like in some huge football stadium. Milling demonstrators with placards, reading ONE MAN ONE VOTE, NOT AN INCH TO THE BIGOTS, SMASH SECTARIANISM-WORKERS' POWER, face policemen with riot shields and batons.

"What's up?" Harry asks. "Is it the Northern Ireland news already? It's only ten to six."

"It's the national news," she says. "There's been trouble in Derry."

Then there's a police baton charge, demonstrators trying to protect their heads, police hitting again and again, water cannons spraying retreating demonstrators. His mother is kneading the headrest and saying, "Dear oh dear oh dear," like a litany. His father has joined them, standing as if he's taken root. They watch in silence as Gerry Fitt is interviewed, his head bleeding.

"There'll be no good come of it," says Harry's dad.

On Friday there's a special David Frost programme from Belfast. They watch the suave international presenter in the thicket of Ulster accents.

"Thank goodness they've got that nice Roy Bradford and not Paisley or some such," Harry's mother says. "Sure he would mortify you."

The audience is soon at fever pitch. Frost is having difficulty in keeping control of the discussion. Everybody in the audience is talking at once, looking as though there's something they have waited all their lives to say. "Looks like Uncle Ludwig and his wife are talking after all," says Harry. His parents give him the perplexed glances they've got into the habit of, and then look back at the screen. Mr Moore settles back in his armchair, folds his arms, and looks at the TV as if he's trying to outstare it.

"I don't see what all the fuss is about," says Mrs Moore. "Why don't they just introduce one man one vote and have done with it?"

"It's the principle of the thing," says Mr Moore.

"What principle is that?"

He switches his glare to her. "It's not what they're really after."

"Well, what's the harm of giving it to them, then?"

"Ach." He turns back to the TV.

23

ONE NOVEMBER AFTERNOON he sees Marie again from the bus in the centre of Ballyraine. She's standing with her back to the street, looking into a shop window. He jumps off the bus, runs across the street, and taps her on the shoulder. The woman who turns round and looks, consternated, into his grinning face is at least forty. After he's apologised the bus has gone. It was the last one to Kilmartin, fifteen miles away. He'll have to thumb.

It's drizzling and he has left his coat on the bus. He starts to walk. By the time he gets to the outskirts of Ballyraine the street-lights are on. Behind the last lamp and the back-lit, slanting rain everything is black. He walks on into it. No cars stop. Gradually his eyes get used to the darkness.

Out by the Cuts he can hear the river Bann flowing to his left. It's a strong, comforting sound. Following an impulse he climbs over the wall at the side of the road and picks his way through a muddy field till he can see the black, flowing mass. It has risen up over the banks and eddied in towards his feet. He stands there breathing in the cooler air that is near the river and watching the swirl of its water. There is something else here, another presence separate from the river but belonging to it, like a friend. "Paddy?" he calls. There's a rustling noise from the reeds on the far side of the river then a heron rises flapping from their midst, flies across to where Harry is standing, cries once, circles, and wings slowly down the river to the bend where it flows on out to the sea and disappears round the corner, its call still echoing in the cool air.

Harry stands there for a long time, taking in the river's quiet. He takes the feeling of peace back with him to the road and resumes his walk. He doesn't try to thumb down the cars that pass him: now he resents their noisy, bright intrusion. When a car finally does stop for him out near the crossroads at Aghadowey he almost doesn't get in, but the man is a customer in the Moores' shop. So unwillingly he exchanges the empty road and the sound of his footsteps for the warm inside of the car and the banality of a conversation. He arrives home at eight o'clock.

He's still carrying the remnants of the feeling of happiness with him like the throbs a deep gong leaves. But when he comes into the kitchen his mum and dad are sitting silently. Relief flits over her pale face and gives way to annoyance.

"Where've you been?" his father asks.

"I missed the bus."

"But that was three hours ago," his mother says.

"I walked most of the way."

"Why didn't you ring? I'd have picked you up. We've been worried sick."

Their fearful, accusing faces irritate him. "Well, I'm here now, amn't I?" he says, and goes upstairs to his room.

"Don't you want any tea?" his mum calls after him.

He's sitting at the card table staring out of the black window, tapping his teeth with his ball-pen when there is a knock at his door. "Harry?" His mother. He hears her come in. He doesn't turn round. She sets a tray with some sandwiches and a glass of milk on his table. He folds up his letter and turns it over. The phrase he's been trying to catch sinks away in the recesses of his mind. Bloody hell. This is the first time she's come into his room since the summer.

"When are you going to give it up?" she asks.

"Give what up?"

"Writing to Marie. She's never going to write back."

He doesn't answer.

"She doesn't even get your letters. Look what I got this morning." She pulls out a letter from her apron pocket and gives it to Harry. Fine blue airmail tissue paper, just like the ones he writes. A stamp with a picture of a jet fighter and 'République Française' on it, dated from six days ago. Just like he's been expecting. He could have been getting one like it every week. But the letter is addressed to 'Mrs Moore' and the handwriting is spidery. He opens it and reads.

Dear Mrs Moore,
You don't know me but I am Marie Fischer's grandmother and as head of the family I feel duty bound to put you in the picture about your son. He has been bombarding this address for months with letters to Marie of a very insalubrious nature which we of course have kept away from her to avoid upsetting her more. I appeal to you as his mother to put a stop to this, seeing as Marie has expressly said that she does not wish to have anything more to do with your son.

Yours sincerely,
Wilhelmina Fischer

The old bag. She's been reading his letters.

"There's no point, Harry. Do you see that now?"

Harry is silent. At last he knows what to do.

"Whatever happened between you and Marie anyway?"

"Nothing."

"You'll just have to give her up, Harry. Let her go. You'd have forgotten all about Marie long since if Paddy hadn't died."

He waits till he hears the door open and close behind him. Then he takes his school atlas down from the shelf.

24

THE NEXT MORNING before he leaves the house for school he asks his mother for the shop key, saying he needs a new Biro. In the shop he walks quickly out to the store, takes the safe key from the inside of the pipe that holds up the shelf construction, opens the safe, takes twenty pounds from the cash-box, replaces everything, takes a fourpenny stamp from the till, locks up the shop, opens it again, fetches a Biro, locks up again, and goes back into the house, holding the Biro. His mother is waiting in the hall.

"Did you think about what I said last night?" she asks. "It's only for your own good."

"You're probably right," says Harry. "See you later."

She smiles and moves towards him, then stops and folds her arms. "I'll make a big fry for tea tonight," she says.

Up at the bus-stop in the middle of Main Street Harry goes into the telephone box and dials the McClellands' number in Belfast. The bus for Ballyraine is already there and he can see the boys inside wiping the windows to watch him as the phone rings.

Mr McClelland answers. "Ah, Harry, right, you'll be wanting to speak to Brian. I'll just go and see if he's up." He clears his throat. "Ah, nice to hear from you."

Harry hears him calling Brian in his deep bass tones. Big

Archy's outline appears outside the telephone box. He taps on the glass and points to the bus. Harry waves him away. Two fingers wag at his face and then disappear. Brian comes on the line. "What is it?" There's an edge to his voice. They haven't spoken since the hospital.

"Brian, I don't want your father to know what we're talking about. Would you keep your answers short without mentioning the thing we're talking about, OK?"

"OK."

"You went to a youth camp in Holland at Easter. Did you get a passport for that?"

"Yeah."

"Is your mouth open or shut on the photograph?"

"Shut, of course. What's that got to do with it?"

"I want you to lend it to me."

"What for?"

"I'm going to France. Can you bring the passport to York Street station?"

Silence.

"Just this one thing, Brian."

"When?"

"This morning. About ten o'clock. You'll have to mooch school. Can you do it?"

"I don't know."

"Please."

"All right."

"Thanks."

When Harry comes out of the telephone box the bus for Ballyraine is disappearing down Main Street. He crosses to the other side and gets into the bus for Ballymoney. The convent girls inside look at him curiously as he sits down in the middle. Shortly afterwards the bus sways off down Bridge Street. The wind throws sheets of rain out of the blackness against its windows.

In Ballymoney the train for Belfast is waiting in the station behind the bus depot. Harry has often made this journey on his way up to stay with Brian. When the train moves out of the station he takes his duffel-bag into the toilet, changes into the green cord jacket and psychedelic tie that are inside, stuffs his school blazer and tie into the bag, and puts his coat on again.

He gets into Belfast at five to ten and goes straight to the ticket office to ask about the boat to Heysham. "You've just missed it," says the ticket seller, his Belfast accent twanging like a sheet of metal.

"When's the next one?"

"Nine thirty tonight."

"Oh." He turns away. What now? He'll have to hang about the shops or something all day.

"Where are you going anyway?" the man asks.

"London."

"Why don't you take the train to Dublin and go across from Dún Laoghaire to Holyhead? If you hurry up you'll catch it. It's leaving from Central Station in ten minutes."

"Which way's that?"

"Left and straight on. The second bridge to your right."

He turns in a hurry and bumps into the person standing behind him. "Sorry."

"Hold your horses." It's Brian.

"Jesus, Brian, I nearly forgot. Have you got it?"

"Yeah." Brian hands him the passport. Harry would like to snatch it and run straight on, but he hangs about, trying to think of something to say.

"I bet Marie doesn't know you're coming," Brian says.

Harry shrugs.

"Your parents are bound to ask if I know anything. What'll I say?"

"I'll ring them tonight from England and tell them myself. What did you tell your dad?"

"That you were inviting me up for the weekend. Like you used to. He was all pleased."

Harry doesn't know what to say to that. It had been another life.

"How long will you be?" Brian asks.

"I don't know."

"Good luck, then."

"Thanks." Harry steps past him and starts to run.

The weather doesn't let up. Before Dublin the train moves through flats that the wind and tide has beaten the sea into, so that it looks as though they're travelling on the surface of the water. When Harry looks out of the carriage window he sees the water sluicing up from the wheels of the locomotive at the front.

He arrives in Dublin at midday. Asking directions at the ticket office in Connolly station he's aware of the contrast between his flat northern vowels and the ticket seller's rounded Dublin accent, and imagines the man is looking strangely at him. They'll all know I'm a Protestant, he thinks, looking anxiously around. He avoids speaking as much as he can after that. He catches the connecting train to Dún Laoghaire with minutes to spare and arrives in time for the one o'clock boat.

The crossing is hell. Harry has only done it once before, from Larne to Stranraer, but it was nothing compared to this. It's far too windy and rainy to stay out on deck, so everybody is inside. It's the first sailing in days because the storm is supposed to be abating and the quarters are packed and steamy, although it's off-season. The ship judders and strains, even the stewards are white-faced, the toilets are overflowing, and the stench of vomit seeps everywhere.

The crossing takes an hour longer than scheduled, which makes it half past five and dark again when they reach Holyhead. There is no time to telephone because the boat train to London is waiting, and the conductor is waving to them to get on board. His mother will be worrying again. Can't be helped.

Harry shares a compartment with a priest he's already seen on the boat, a small, bald man with a friendly smile. "Travelling on your own?" the man asks.

"Yes. Visiting relatives," Harry says.

"From the North, are you?"

"Yeah."

"Terrible, what's going on up there."

"Yeah."

"But sure the problem will sort itself out in ten or twenty years."

"Sooner than that, I hope."

"It's basic arithmetic, isn't it?"

"Arithmetic?"

"Yes. In ten or twenty years, if the birth rate stays the same, our people will outnumber theirs."

"Oh, right."

The priest says something Harry doesn't catch. "Pardon?" He says it again but Harry still doesn't understand. "Don't you have Irish at school?" he asks.

"No."

They look out of the window after that.

The priest gets out at Chester and other passengers get in. A woman with two small boys and a bearded student type who pulls out a rolled-up copy of *Playboy* and starts to read it. The woman has a friendly, tired face and when she talks to the boys her accent is English, but not like the Wallaces' or the Coopers', more like *Coronation Street*.

Harry can't see anything of the countryside, only the towns, Crewe, Stafford, Rugby, names he vaguely knows as he reads them on the station signs as they flash past. The train picks up speed and with it Harry's spirits rise. He feels tired, but with infinite resources, as if he's been storing up all his energy these last months. It's great to be doing something rather than waiting, to be master of his destiny. That's it. Master of his destiny. He'll walk any distance, sleep anywhere, to get to Marie. Hurtling through the dark countryside beside the waxing moon his face grins back at him from the window.

When a man comes round with a trolley Harry realises he hasn't eaten all day and buys some sandwiches. Banana, a good omen.

It takes them ages to get through the outskirts of London. There are built-up business areas that would have been in the middle of a place like Belfast or Dublin, and then they dwindle away into endless housing estates and darkness before building up again. When the railway lines start to squirm away in proliferation like in a snake-pit Harry asks the woman sitting opposite how to get to Dover.

"It's quite easy," she says. "Just take the Underground to Victoria station. That's where the trains go from. I'd show you, only I'm being met." She looks at the student beside Harry but he only settles deeper in his seat, studying what looks like naked women with bull's-eyes painted on them.

Euston station is the biggest place Harry has ever been, and one of the most confusing, with the echoing sounds of the trains and the announcements and the luggage trolleys, but Harry tries not to let it show. He's studying a map of the

Underground when there is a tap on his shoulder. It's the woman from the train.

"My husband says he'll take you to Victoria in the car. It's no bother, it's on our way."

The husband is a small, bandy-legged man with long sideburns who's chewing gum with his mouth open. He doesn't look as if he thinks it's no bother, but Harry is glad of the offer and soon they're zipping through London in a Mini, Harry sitting in front with his duffel-bag on his knees. It's just like in the films, he thinks, trying not to gape like a country yokel at the red buses, black taxis and lights.

"Thanks a lot," says Harry, when they let him out in front of Victoria station.

The woman leans forward from the back seat. "You're not running away from home or anything like that, are you?" she asks.

"No, no," says Harry. Neither is he, surely, if he's going to come back.

A train to Dover is leaving in half an hour. Time to ring up home. He buys a ticket and passes a newspaper shop to get to a telephone box.

"Moore, Kilmartin," he hears his dad say, after the operator has put him through.

"This is Harry."

"Thank God. Are you all right? Wasn't that an English operator?"

"I'm fine. Listen, I'll be away for a couple of days, you're not to worry."

"What do you mean? Where are you?"

"I'm in England. I'm visiting Marjorie."

"Hold on till I get your mother."

"Just tell her not to worry. I'll be back in a day or so." He hangs up and goes back to the newspaper shop. He's seen a postcard stand in it. Everything is going according to plan. Now all he needs is a postcard. But they are all in the seaside kind of humour: girls with their bosoms bursting out of their blouses, huge-arsed women, little red-nosed men. He can't send his mother one of these. He whirls the stand frantically.

> *'I like seeing experienced girls home.'*
> *'But I'm not experienced!'*
> *'You're not home yet!'*

They're all in the same vein. He dashes out of the shop, looking around wildly. He sees a YMCA bookshop and runs into it. At the counter is a stand of normal postcards, animals of London Zoo. He buys one with a lion on it, it seems the most innocuous. Then he gets on the train with ten minutes to spare and writes the postcard.

> I am going to France for a while. Please do not
> worry as everything is all right. Will pay everything
> back. I'll be back in a couple of weeks.
> Love, Harry

By the time he has finished the address and stuck on the stamp he stole from the till he has six minutes to go. Just beyond the gate to the platform there is a letter-box. It would be a relief to have posted the card before the train leaves the station, it would save him looking for a letter-box in Dover. He flaps the postcard between his hands for a while, then jumps up and dashes out of the train and down the platform, out past the gate, posts the card and starts back again. But now there's a hold-up at the gate. The ticket inspector is arguing with a man with a rucksack on his back. It's the student from the other train. "I don't care what your student union says, the train this ticket is for went two hours ago," the inspector is saying. Up on the platform another inspector is looking at his watch. He lifts a whistle to his lips.

"Excuse me," says Harry. "I've got to get on that train. My duffel-bag is on it." The whistle blows. Harry squirms past the rucksack and sprints up the platform as the train starts to move noiselessly away. The inspector turns to him, waving him back, but Harry keeps on running. The whistle blows again and brakes screech. He scrambles aboard, and the train starts off again.

At the queue for passport control in Dover Harry wets his hair and plasters it down to make it look more like Brian's. This is the part he's been dreading, but when it's his turn the official waves him through without any comment.

He arrives in Calais at half past one in the morning. Only a few people descend the gangway with him. He watches the tail-lights of the cars bumping down the ramp to the shore. Maybe he should have asked some of the drivers for a lift, he'd heard that was the thing to do. But what he really wants is a bed. He feels as if he's been stretched in some way.

He walks through the customs shed and follows the signs to Centre Ville, alone by now. He had expected there to be some kind of special feeling about being abroad, but there is none. The streets are empty, apart from a few cars scudding past in the rain. One of the houses has a sign "Hotel du Havre" and when Harry gets nearer he's surprised to see that the "Chambres Libres" light is still on. He might as well ask, he thinks, he's going to have to speak French some time.

The woman at the reception desk seems to understand him all right. Ten francs, she says, for a single room with breakfast. That's surely cheap enough. He has changed all his money on the boat and now has a bit over 250 francs. He pays for the room. She asks him if he's English. No, Irish, he says. British, he corrects himself. English, Irish, British, all the same, she says. He goes upstairs.

It's shabby, with peeling orange wallpaper, and there isn't much room for anything other than the bed, but Harry is feeling elated. I've done it, he thinks, it can't be far now. He sits down on the bed and reaches into his duffel-bag. From the room beyond come the sounds of grunts and creaking bedsprings. He finds the map of western Europe he has ripped out of his school atlas and unfolds it.

"Jesus, I've only come half-way," he says.

25

W^{HEN} H^{ARRY} ^{REACHES} the outskirts of Calais next morning he can make out the landscape, absolutely flat with clumps of woods, criss-crossed by telephone lines. The weather is dry but cold.

He's heard stories of hitch-hikers covering hundreds of miles at incredible speed. Big Archy went through Scotland and England in a day. Like shit through a chicken. And hit London with a bang. That's about the same distance as from Calais to Strasbourg. So, with a bit of luck, he could be there tonight. The trick is to get lifts from long-distance lorry-drivers. He hunkers down at the side of the road, takes out the strip he tore off the paper tablecloth at breakfast and writes BRITISH on it. He checks his map again. The towns are strung out on a line across the north of France: Calais, St Omer, Arras, Cambrai, Charleville, Metz, Strasbourg. Then he gets to his feet and waits for traffic. A fairly steady stream of cars passes him. When he sees an English one coming he holds out the sign. None stops. Jesus, an A01 number-plate on a Riley Sunbeam. A car from home, well, Belfast anyway. He waves and almost runs out into the middle of the road. A gaunt, disapproving Presbyterian face looks back out at him and passes on. But there might be other cars from Northern Ireland. If only the people know he's one of them they're bound to stop. He kneels down again and uncaps the

Biro. Then he sticks it in his mouth. If he writes ULSTER the Catholics won't stop, and if he writes IRISH the Protestants won't. But the Prods will stop for the British one, if they're going to. He writes IRISH on the other side of the paper. The trick will be to know which side to show. Can you really tell by people's looks whether they're Catholic or Protestant?

Three-quarters of an hour later there have been no more cars from Northern Ireland. None of the others has stopped and the lorry drivers don't even look his way. Then a woman in one of those French cars that look like an umbrella on wheels looks at him very carefully while passing and stops a bit up the road. He's off.

There's just about room for Harry between two children and the shopping on the back seat. She saw him on her way into town, the woman says. Her biggest boy went hitch-hiking that summer in England and was treated well, so she decided to give Harry a lift although she wouldn't usually. Unfortunately she's only going as far as the next town but her husband is going to St Omer and will take Harry if they catch him before he leaves. Harry understands most of what she tells him, but talking French himself is a different matter. He stumbles through where he's going and where he comes from all right, but when she starts to ask him about the situation in Northern Ireland all he can say is, "C'est difficile, très difficile." But then he thinks it wouldn't be any easier in English.

They miss the woman's husband and Harry takes up position again. The landscape is more like he expects Holland to be, stretching flatly away to the horizon with canals and steel bridges. At first only drivers who are taking the next turn-off seem inclined to give him a lift. Lorry drivers continue to ignore him. Then he gets a longer lift from a salesman who's often been to the US, is a great fan of Elvis, and seems to think that Harry, by dint of sharing Elvis's language, must also be a fan, and will appreciate his versions. Harry keeps a stiff smile all the way through the man's renditions of the King's hits in a heavy French accent. Now and then he nods appreciatively. It isn't any worse than listening to one of Mr McClelland's stories that he's heard about ten times before. The man has just finished "'Oun' dog" when he has to turn off towards Paris.

He leaves Harry in a small, single-street village with one-storeyed houses. Harry goes into a shop to buy something to eat. The woman tries to fob him off with some very dodgy-looking cheese that looks like she's had it for about a hundred years, with mould in it and everything, but Harry ignores her eulogies and buys a roll of bread and some pre-packed slices of Kraft just like the cheese the Moores have in their shop too. He eats it by the side of the road; it becomes his staple diet.

In the afternoon two girls from Lille university pick him up. He emphasises the romantic aspect of his journey as much as his French allows and they are so impressed by his story that they offer to smuggle him into an empty room in the student quarters of the university at Lille. It's a bit off his route, but worth it for the free kip. He doesn't see anything of the town because it's dark by the time they get there and the girls let the shutters in the room down because it is in the women's residences, so Harry sticks to the room, listening at the door for when nobody is in the toilets on the far side of the corridor to dash across for a pee. He goes to bed at nine o'clock under the coverless quilt and studies Marie's face in her passport for a time, its blue cardboard cover swollen and bent from the Donegal rain, before switching off the light.

He's up and away at six o'clock the next morning before anybody stirs in the residences. It takes him ages to get to the outskirts of Lille, and ages again to get a lift. Nobody wants to stop in the dark. Then the lifts come in fits and starts again. The weather stays the same and the landscape becomes slightly more hilly, but still nothing like the chateau-dotted vineyards sloping steeply up from meandering rivers he has been expecting.

Harry throws away the British and Irish sign. The thing that works best is to get eye contact, to establish some kind of intimacy, without overstepping the mark and staring. Drivers who have no intention of stopping will look away, some of them smiling embarrassedly at nothing at all. Lorry drivers are the only ones who are able to look convincingly as though they don't see him.

The worst drivers are the ones who turn their thumbs down and laugh when passing him. He gives one the fingers and the car instantly brakes and reverses. When Harry overcomes his better judgement and walks up to it the man shows him just one middle finger and drives off again. That's neat, Harry thinks, trying it out. Maybe there's some kind of a future where he can use it on Big Archy.

After a while Harry starts walking between lifts, not even turning round so that passing drivers can see him. Straggling woods nestling in folds of land, a single line of trees on the horizon. Stubby water towers. The occasional Great War cemetery, mostly German. Acres of spindly black crosses on green sward.

Getting into the stride of walking, shifting his duffel-bag every few miles, even resenting the cars that shut him off from the wide landscape, the views unfettered by hedges.

At about five o'clock Harry is walking through gently rolling countryside with hedges, quite like round Kilmartin. It's getting dark. According to his map, which doesn't show most of the places he has come through, the next town to come is Charleville, and it's miles away. Cars are getting fewer and fewer and no longer slowing down to look at him. He isn't going to get another lift tonight.

The barns in this area are solid-looking, red-brick buildings. He picks one that stands a good distance away from the farmhouse and goes up the lane to it. No padlock on the door. The screech of its runners seems to rip across the countryside and Harry waits a bit in case some irate farmer turns up, before slipping inside. He lifts the door while pulling it back and it rolls quietly shut.

In the dim light he sees bales of hay stacked at the back. Just the thing. He can see enough to climb up and crawl into the small space at the very top where a row is missing. He hauls a bale from the back and snuggles down into the space it leaves, resting his head on his duffel-bag. He would like to lie on his coat but he needs it to cover him, so he has to put up with the straw scratching through his clothes. He eats some bread and cheese and then there's only time for a quick look at Marie's passport before it gets quite dark. Then he sleeps.

He wakes as something runs across his leg. He can hear squeaks and munchings. The full moon has come up and a couple of inches away from his head he sees the bobbing backs of mice gnawing at his bread and cheese. There's another sound of rustling through the straw just below his bag. Jesus, that must be a big one. He remembers as a child thinking some animal was trying to chew its way through his pillow to get at him, until his mother told him it was the sound of his own pulse in his ear.

Could there be rats in the bales? Big ones, with naked tails? The straw heaves beneath his bag. He jumps to his feet, grabs the coat and duffel-bag and makes his way back down the bales and out of the shed. Christ, it's cold. He smiles to himself. That'll be something to tell Paddy about.

It's the first time he's forgotten that Paddy is dead. Often, when he used to be doing things he'd be thinking about how he would tell Paddy about them at the same time. You could have double the pleasure that way.

The full moon hangs in the sky, reflected in the sheen of frost on the road. There'll be spring tides in Donegal these days, lapping up the black walls of Horn Head. The cold seeps up his trouser legs, down the back of his neck, and gradually he is completely immersed in it. He puts an inch to his step and tries to imagine that he's swimming in cold water, that he's getting used to it.

He walks through a small place called 'Mon Idée'. It's out for the count, although it isn't even midnight yet. The normal world is behind those lowered shutters lying in its warm bed with its back to him. He feels thin and drawn and cut off, like a ghost.

Marie will be wondering why the stream of his letters has suddenly dried up.

No, she won't, because she never got them. She must think Harry has forgotten all about her, just like Paddy said he would.

A church spire, black against the sky, hills and trees, fog hugging the dells. Like England in the old films. A dog barking. Then a forest looming up around him.

Charleville. Harry isn't feeling his legs any more. Something stirring here, though, although it's only five in the morning. In the market square torch-light beams are darting about; a row of houses jumps out of the blackness, built on the top of arcades, like on a bridge; then the statue of a man in a cape and peaked hat. Murmurs and scrapings, workers emptying vans and setting up fruit and vegetable stalls.

Harry tries to buy some bananas; they give them to him for free and point out the road to Metz. He walks on out of the town.

Traffic starts up but no cars stop. They'll be wondering what I'm doing here at six o'clock in the morning. I swear if I ever have a car I'll give anybody a lift no matter what time it is.

Walking into the sunrise, a hint of red peeking from under the sky and then the greens of the fields emerging from the grey as if somebody is filling them in in a colouring book. The sound of a car slowing and stopping although he hasn't even looked round.

A hand shaking his shoulder. Harry wakes up. The car has stopped and the driver is looking at him with the grim smile of a teacher pitying a stupid pupil. "I drive, you talk," the man is saying. "I take you places, you entertain me. That is the way it works. You don't talk, you go to sleep, I don't drive. Out you get."

Harry stumbles out of the car. He has understood every word, but can't think of any reply. The cold outside brings him round again. Half past nine. He must have been in the car for about half an hour. Where the hell is he now?

Another car pulls up, and the man unwinds the passenger window. "Metz?" Harry says. The man nods and Harry gets in. Keep awake, he tells himself, say interesting things. "It's very cold," he says. "I thought France was a warm country. At home it is not so cold, but wet. I'm Irish."

"Hollandais?" the man says.

"Non, Irlandais."

The man nods. He has slicked-back hair and a moustache so

thin it looks as though it has been done with eyeliner, and a red, puffy nose. The warmth of the car seeps through to Harry's bones. Don't sleep, he tells himself, but his eyes keep falling shut.

Another hand, this time on his thigh. "Now you must do something for me," the man says.

"Fuck off," Harry says in English, and pushes the hand away.

"You are not sympathetic," the man says.

"Fuck off," Harry says again, grabs his duffel-bag and gets out of the car. It's standing in the middle of a copse of poplars at the end of an untarred lane. Harry starts back the other way. When he looks back the man is holding his head in his arms, rocking to and fro.

The road he comes out on to is very minor. What direction should he walk? East. Where's the sun? The sky is a dirty grey quilt that gives no clues. It's eleven o'clock. He could be anywhere. He turns right and starts to walk again.

After a while he hears a car and sticks out his thumb. The man with the slicked-back hair drives past him without looking his way. No other cars come until the road dips into a wooded valley and joins a more major road. On the far side is a canal, beyond that a river and beyond that again a hill that looks like Muckish's sweeter-tempered young brother, with trees right up to the top. The signs point to Mouzay to the right and to Dun-sur-Meuse to the left. He can't find either on his map.

While he's still looking he hears the rumble of an approaching lorry. More from habit than hope, Harry sticks out his thumb without looking up from his map. There's a squeal of brakes, a bronchial snort and a dragon's hiss. It's a French army lorry. But where is Harry to say he's going? He hasn't a clue where he is. He walks up to the driver's window.

"À Strasbourg?" he says, on the off-chance. The man nods and jerks his thumb towards the back.

Harry wakes at three o'clock in the afternoon from the pressure of the soldier's body next to him. A steep incline is rolling it against him and squeezing him up against the backboard. The soldiers lying in the back with him are still comatose and snoring on their kit-bags, as they had been when he climbed in. They must have been marching all night, just like him. There is a constant crash and shudder of gear-changes and the grind of the engine labouring as the lorry sways around bends. The air that is wafting through the tarpaulin flaps has got very chilly. Harry sits up and shakes his head. He has a crick in his neck from lying on his duffel-bag and a taste in his mouth like old mackerel from the lorry's diesel fumes. He sticks his head out of the flaps to get some fresh air.

A stone wall is snaking under the backboard and on its other side the snow-covered slopes of a wooded gorge plummet down into fog. The road they are ascending winds back down behind them, also covered in snow, clinging to the side of a mountain, appearing and disappearing as it negotiates the snowy wooded outcrops, till it too disappears into the fog. Occasionally the top of the lorry brushes against the lower branches of the trees that hang out over the road, dislodging loads of snow that thump on to the tarpaulin and slither down the sides.

Jesus Christ. The fucking Alps. Harry rifles through his duffel-bag till he finds his scrap of a map. The Alps are away down at the bottom. Could they have got that far in the time? Maybe he has been asleep for a day. He shakes the soldier next to him till he groans, stirs, and opens his eyes. "Les Alpes?" says Harry, pointing out the back.

"Non, les Vosges," the soldier says. He takes Harry's map and taps his finger at the place. Vosges, right enough, in capital letters curving round Strasbourg. Never heard of them, but what odds. He's nearly there.

"Merci," he says, but the soldier is already snoring again.

26

Two HOURS LATER the lorry stops with a shudder and a jolt, and there's a bang from the driver's cabin. They have been driving through Strasbourg for about half an hour and Harry has been wondering where to get out. He gathers up his duffel-bag, jumps out, and walks to the front of the lorry. The driver points behind Harry, gives him the thumbs-up sign and the lorry rumbles off. Harry turns round. A cathedral, this must be the centre. It looks very old, but not finished for all that; there's scaffolding all up it and it has only one spire where there was obviously intended to be two. The street leading up to it is lined with shops. An old man is selling roasted chestnuts from a model locomotive. Harry asks him where the station is, and he gives Harry a whole string of directions, then, seeing his bewildered face, asks him where he wants to go. "No trains to Obernai," he says. "Buses. But no more tonight. Tomorrow morning." He tells Harry how to find the bus station, it's just round the corner. Harry thanks him, and then asks him if he knows where Fischer's clothes shop is. Marie sometimes helps out in the shop. Maybe she's in today.

"Fischer. Fischer." The man puts his forefinger on the tip of his nose and closes his eyes. Then he takes Harry by the shoulders and points him down the street. "Straight ahead.

Across that square. Down the street in the middle. Five minutes' walk."

The shop is still open when Harry finds it. It's dark again, so he can look inside from a few steps back without anybody seeing him. There's no doubt about it, there are even tweed jackets hanging in the window. Marie isn't in the shop, but he can see Monsieur Fischer fussing around. He doesn't want to declare himself in the shop, old man Fischer would probably put a spanner in his works before he could get to see Marie.

The best thing to do would be to get Marie on her own. He reads the opening times on the door: 8 a.m. to 6 p.m. Marie starts school at nine o'clock. He'll try to be at the house at around eight. He walks back in the direction of the cathedral. It's floodlit by now and hovers above the steep-roofed houses like a vision. The skeleton of some huge sea monster that has rotted away to its feathery bones, its joints encrusted with coral. This part of the town is ancient, older than any towns Harry knows, like something out of a fairy-tale, with its half-timbered houses that burgeon crazily outwards from their upper floors.

He's feeling at peace. He will see Marie tomorrow and explain everything. He tries to imagine her face when she sees him. He stops and looks at his reflection in a shop window, then pulls at a straw that is hanging out of his back pocket. He hasn't had a bath since leaving Kilmartin. How many days ago was that? Only four, incredible. Still, he hasn't even washed since the morning before yesterday. He really needs to clean up some-where.

People are overtaking him with eager steps, on their way to spend the evening somewhere. He strolls on through the narrow streets that surround the cathedral. Couples are reading and discussing the menus that hang outside the restaurants. They look so carefree. Harry senses their anticipation and excitement with a feeling of envy.

A large group of young people a few years older than Harry swing arm in arm into the street, chattering and laughing. They're wearing fleecy coats and scarves, but the girls have miniskirts on in spite of the cold. They move quickly towards a restaurant and go in. From across the street Harry watches them sit down at a big table in the centre of the room, their figures distorted by the green, bottle-glass windows. Obviously they're students and this is their local. It would be nice to be one of them. Harry hasn't felt the need for company since Paddy's death. He crosses the street to look at the menu and his eyes are caught by a small sign hanging in the doorway to the side. "Hôtel Michelet".

Half an hour later, showered and shaved, Harry slips into the restaurant and sits down at a table next to the student group. The hotel room had been surprisingly cheap, fifteen francs – besides, he's counting on only needing it for one night.

The students pay no attention to him until he orders a beer. Then one of them with a Che Guevara beard and beret turns to him. "You are English?"

"No, Irish."

"And what brings you to Strasbourg?"

Harry shrugs. "Love."

"All the way from Ireland to Strasbourg for love," says the girl on Che's far side. "That is a big love." She points to the boy sitting beside her. "My boyfriend don't even walk me home in Strasbourg last night."

The boyfriend scowls. "I tell her already. That was football on TV. Anyway, why are you all alone if your love is so big?"

"Come and join us," says Che.

Harry moves in between Che and the girl.

"Where is your love?" she asks, leaning towards him. She looks like Cleopatra, with her heavily underlined eyes and dark, bobbed hair, but more like the one in *Carry on Cleo* than Elizabeth Taylor.

"In Obernai," Harry says.

"But surely this little distance cannot keep you from her if you have come all the way from Ireland."

"I'm going tomorrow."

"She will be very happy."

"I hope so. She doesn't know."

"Doesn't she love you too?"

"Maybe she has stopped."

"Why?"

"I loved someone else."

The girl looks perplexed. "You said you love this girl in Obernai."

"It wasn't love with the other one, it was . . ."

"Sex," says Che, nodding sagely.

"Yes."

"Aha," says the girl's boyfriend. "At least I only watch football."

"Your girlfriend is too bourgeois," says Che.

Steaming platters of sauerkraut spiked by sausages and strewn with boiled meat arrive and the group's attention turns to the food. It looks like something Desperate Dan would eat. Harry is handed a plate. From all sides strips of pork and sausages are heaped on to it and their finer qualities explained. Conversation concentrates on comparison of sausages here and in other places. Harry can't understand what they're on about, after all, it's only food. Then he realises that he's ravenous and starts to tuck into his meal.

★

Hours later Harry and Che are crossing the square in front of the cathedral. Everybody else has disappeared.

"You see the cathedral?" says Che, grabbing Harry by the shoulder.

"Yes."

"When I walk here in daytime and look up I am coward." He mimes a trembling fit.

"Dizzy," says Harry.

"Yes. I think the cathedral wait for me to come round the corner so it can fall on me. *Pouf.* But when I drink wine I am a hero. I can walk up and down and look all the time." He demonstrates, cocking his nose at the cathedral. The third time he comes past Harry stops him. "There is a tower missing on the cathedral," he says.

Che rolls his large eyeballs at him and then at the cathedral. "Police!" he shouts.

They're in another place. Che says it's called the Holy Grave.

"Should have a roll-away stone for a door," says Harry. They're drinking Alsatian red wine.

"The girls are all gone," says Che, looking unsteadily round him. "Good. So we talk about love. You come to Strasbourg for love. That is good because . . ." He raises a finger and looks at Harry. "Because love is . . ." His eyeballs roll up beneath his flickering lids, showing only the whites, and his chin hangs down as if he's had an attack of lockjaw. Then his jaw snaps shut and his eyes open. "I know. We say what love is not. That is easier. You start."

27

Sᴏᴍᴇʙᴏᴅʏ ɪs ᴛʜᴜᴍᴘɪɴɢ at Harry's door. He's lying fully dressed on his bed and the lights are on. "It is ten o'clock, Monsieur. You must come down to breakfast. It is your last chance because I must go out."

Harry struggles to a sitting position. "OK. In a minute." His head feels like one huge, throbbing nerve, and his throat as if somebody has been scrubbing it out in the night with a toilet brush and scouring powder. He can't remember how he got back to the hotel.

They spent hours looking for it, he remembers the latter part of that. They were down at some river, little Venice or something. A huge roundabout with fountains.

"The name, the name, you must remember the name," Che extolled him.

"I can't remember, wait a minute, it's like a tyre." Che didn't understand, and Harry didn't know the French word. He staggered to a car and grabbed one.

"Pneu?"

"Yeah."

"Pirelli?"

"No."

"Dunlop?"

"A French tyre."

"Michelin."

"That's it!"

"I hope you do not mean the Hôtel Michelet?"

"*Exactement!*"

"But that is right beside the first restaurant!"

"That's right."

Remembering Che's face on hearing this Harry laughs out loud, but stops immediately because of the way it presses his brain matter against his skull. He closes his eyes and lets air out slowly between his teeth. When he opens them again they're focused on the list of room prices on the door. Fifteen francs. Christ almighty. He fishes in his pockets. No notes. He counts the coins. Five francs forty. Fuck, fuck, fuck. He has a vague memory of the red wine being very expensive. How many bottles had they drunk?

What odds.

"Can I stay another night?" he asks at breakfast.

The manager lowers his newspaper. "You are leaving your luggage here?"

"Yes."

"Good."

So that's that. Harry puts on his last change of underwear and his school uniform again. He leaves the green cord blazer and the tie he's worn the whole journey in the duffel-bag. He buttons up his coat so that the school blazer can't be seen, checks that he has both passports, and leaves the hotel. After he's bought the bus ticket he has three francs twenty. So be it, he thinks. He'll come to Marie like a pilgrim of old, penniless, and throw himself on her mercy.

In Obernai people direct him to the terraced wine hills at the far end of the village, to the right after the market square, past the church and the graveyard. A red-brick wall marks the zigzag climb of the road up the side of the hill. On the longest stretch of the wall a head with a halo within another outer circle is painted and beside it the words 'Clos Sainte Odile'. Just as Marie described it. Harry slowly climbs the rise, his head clearing in the cool air. It's a fine day. The slant of the sun's rays in the morning lights the autumn leaves in the vineyards from behind so that they look as though they're shining from within. The noises from the village seem very far away.

At the right side of the haloed head, cast-iron gates are let into the red-brick wall. A small metal plate is soldered to the bars of the gate. It says "Fischer". Harry opens the gates and steps inside. The house that stands at the end of the gravel drive looks more like the ones he's seen on his journey here rather than the half-timbered kind that predominate in the village and in Strasbourg. The windows on the upper floor are of equal proportions to the ground-floor ones, giving the house a watchful aspect. The gravel crunches under his feet. The lawn is streaked with hoar frost, leaves have been swept together in glistening piles. It's very quiet.

As he approaches the house the door opens. Harry slows down. At first he can't see anything but then he makes out a glint of spectacles at about waist level and then a figure sitting in a wheelchair.

"Are you the Irish boy?" the figure addresses him in English. Marie's grandmother.

"Yes."

"Thought so. I've already rung the police."

"Why?"

"Well may you ask. We been expecting you. Your mum rang up, didn't she?" She speaks like the people on the train in England had spoken, not upper class, as Harry had expected.

He mounts the steps and looks down at the old woman. She looks back, her gums working. She's holding a cane across her knees.

"I just want to see Marie."

"Well, you can't. She doesn't want to see you."

"Is she in?"

"Are you hard of hearing? I've just told you you can't see her."

He makes to push past her but she turns her wheelchair so that it's blocking the doorway. "Leave my granddaughter alone! Don't you think you've done enough harm?"

"Sorry about this," says Harry. He grabs the wheels and tries to turn the chair round so he can push it back. She holds firmly on to the wheels but when Harry succeeds in pushing it back a bit she lets go to rap at his hands with the silver head of her cane. The wheelchair becomes unbalanced suddenly and starts to teeter on two wheels. Harry has to lunge at its back to prevent it toppling over and spilling her out across the hall. Her bewhiskered jowls wobble impotently right up near to his face and her lips are making wet tutting noises. He gets the wheelchair straightened up and pushes it back far enough to get past.

"I'm only going to talk to her," he says, his voice trembling with exertion. She shakes her cane at him. He opens the first door on the left, only poking his head in to look. He doesn't want Grandma jamming him inside with her wheelchair. A sitting room, nobody in it. He dashes across the corridor and looks in the room opposite. Some kind of study, empty too. The door at the end of the corridor opens into the kitchen. Nobody there either.

"She's not in anyway," says the old woman.

"I don't believe you." Then he hears the car crunching up the drive. He runs up the stairs and tries the doors on the first floor. Bathroom. Bedroom. Bedroom. Locked. He pulls at the door. "Marie!"

He hears footsteps inside.

"Don't you dare open that door, girl!" comes the old woman's voice from downstairs.

"Harry?"

"Open the door, please, Marie. I've got to talk to you."

"There's nothing to say. You shouldn't have come." Her voice is just at the other side of the door.

"Please, Marie. I've been writing to you, but they don't give you my letters." He can hear her breathe. "Please, Marie."

"There's nothing you could write that would change anything."

His face is right up against the door and he can feel the wood of the door panel vibrate against his cheek with the sound of her voice, and that's why he doesn't notice the policemen moving quietly up behind him until his wrists are grabbed and hand-cuffed.

The old woman watches them march him down the stairs and out past her.

"You had no business keeping my letters from her," Harry says. "I love Marie."

"Och, love."

Outside he cranes his neck back towards the house as they push him towards the car. In the front room on the first floor the shutter is closed but the slats are slightly open and as he watches a shadow falls across them, outlined by the light behind. It stays there as he is bundled into the car. He watches it for as long as he can through the rear window until the car swings on to the road.

★

"God, as if you people weren't giving us enough bother as it is."
The young man from the British Consular Office in Strasbourg
shakes his head, sighs, and jiggles his foot. His hair is carefully
Brylcreemed to one side and he's wearing a dark blue jacket
with some kind of badge on it, a white shirt, striped tie, grey
flannels and black shoes: a prefect to Harry's junior pupil. "You
come here with a false passport and no money, break into a
house, assault a helpless old woman and then expect us to get
you out of all the mess. It's asking a bit much, I'm afraid." He
jiggles his foot again. "I suppose you're playing truant from
school too. Maybe you could just tell me what the point of it all
is?"

"Love," says Harry.

"Oh, right." The man fishes out a cigarette from a packet of
Benson & Hedges and lights it. He then studiously ignores Harry
as he smokes it, making trumpet noises with his lips between
drags and tapping out some rhythm on the cigarette packet.

The police sergeant comes back and sits down at his desk with
some ceremony. He's a small, well-built man with long hair
carefully combed from his nape up and across a bald patch. He
speaks English quite well. He unwinds the report he's typed
from the typewriter, lays it on his desk, studies it briefly, then
looks up. "Monsieur Fischer has just been here," he says. "He
wishes there to be no . . ."

"Charges," says the man from the consulate.

"Charges, yes. It seems it is all a mistake and you are a . . . not-
quite-friend of the family. You are free to go."

"Well, that's one thing anyway," says the man from the
consulate. "Now all we have to do is get you home."

"That is also arranged. By Monsieur Fischer. He has booked
a seat for you on the plane from Strasbourg to London tonight.
And he gives you this." The sergeant puts an English twenty-

pound note on the desk. "That is for the flight to Belfast."

Harry reaches for the note but the sergeant keeps his hand on it. "Monsieur Fischer does not wish for the money back because he wishes never to see you again."

"A not–quite–friend indeed," says the English official.

"And it also seems you have some papers belonging to the young girl," says the sergeant.

Harry digs into his pocket and takes out Marie's passport. Then he starts to cry suddenly.

"For God's sake," says the man from the consulate and grabs for the passport.

"Piss off." Harry sniffs, snatching it away. He lays the passport on the desk. The policeman takes it and relinquishes the note.

"That just leaves the tiny matter of your own passport," says the Englishman.

"What is the matter with the passport?" asks the sergeant. "It is valid, we checked. Unless this is not Brian McClelland, as we have entered in the record."

Harry and the official look at each other. The official takes another pull from his cigarette, jiggles his foot and looks out of the window. The sergeant looks from one to the other.

"So, then, there is no problem," he says. "You must only see the young man on to the plane at the airport on your way back to the city. You will please inform us that you have done this." He takes the report from his desk, tears it into two halves and throws it into the wastepaper bin.

"It is not always so easy to start again, young man," he says.

28

Harry throws his schoolbag into a corner of the kitchen, pours himself a cup of tea from the kettle on the range and picks up the *Newsletter*. He goes into the sitting room, where his mum has put on a fire and sits down to read. After a while she comes in from the shop.

"Looks like O'Neill's done it," Harry says. "Listen to this: 'Flood of Congratulations', 'Civil Rights replies – primarily appeal to good sense and Christian spirit of the Unionists', 'We back O'Neill'. Have you seen all these pages of letters of support?"

"They're telling a different story on the radio," she says. "Craig is up to something. And there's a lot of bad feeling about. I hear it in the shop. The folk are going on about O'Neill selling us down the river. Your father even agrees with them if he's in the mood."

"Och, Dad."

"He's not a bad man, your father, but people like him have to be brought round slowly, or they just go stubborn. And these Civil Rights people aren't interested in that. All they want to do is confront and provoke. They don't want their demands given in to at all. And our side don't want to give in to them anyway – they'd be losing face."

"The whole thing will blow over once we have one man, one vote."

"I've been thinking about a story I read when I was a girl, up in Ardbane. It was about a boat that got caught in the outer swirls of the maelstrom. You hardly notice it at first, you can't see the spout in the middle, but there's no getting away from it. That's what it feels like now."

Harry doesn't like to hear his mother talk like this. It irritates him that he should be the one to say the cheering-up things. "Since when have you been so pessimistic?" he says.

"I've just been seeing things more clearly lately. That reminds me, it's time we had a talk about your future. How did you get on in your Christmas exams?"

"Not too bad. History was a bit worse than O levels but still a pass, and the teacher says I can catch up all right. English Lit is the same and we got the French results today, they're even a bit better."

His mother is leaning against the door, arms folded. "So, what are your plans?"

"I was thinking of leaving school and working in the shop, seeing as you're always going on about how you need some-body."

"You can put that out of your head."

There's a beep outside. Mrs Cooper.

"You owe me." Her eyes are boring into his. Not a word has ever been said about the money from the safe.

"I haven't been taking any money from Dad for working in the shop. I'm paying it all back."

Another beep from outside. Harry wishes his mother would go out to Mrs Cooper.

"I'm not talking about money," she goes on. "I'm talking about me. Did you ever stop to think what the holiday in Donegal meant to me all the time you were feeling sorry for yourself? I felt like somebody up there, like my parents were. Do you think the Bryces and the McClellands and all the rest of them would give us the time of day in Kilmartin? People like us go to Portrush for our holidays. And stay in a caravan. Last summer was the end of a dream for me. Sooner or later we all have to live without our dreams. I can't go there again, and that's all right, but I want it to be on my terms. That way I can manage."

Three long furious beeps from outside.

"I'll get it," says Harry. He walks out to the pavement. As he approaches the Rover Mrs Cooper swivels her head to glare at him. But just before he reaches the window his mother cuts in in front of him and bends down to speak through the side window.

"Mrs Cooper, we'd be very glad to have your custom but I must ask you to come into the shop personally in the future, like everybody else. Your legs are just as good as mine."

She straightens up and moves away, revealing Mrs Cooper's stricken face as she fumbles at the gear-stick and drives the car off in leaps and starts, like a beginner.

When Harry goes back into the sitting room his mother is sitting in the armchair, waiting for him. "McAtamney's hardware up the street is closing down and we're leasing the premises. Opening one of those self-service supermarkets."

"I didn't know we had the money."

"That's what banks are for. 'You needn't act as if you're doing us a favour, Mr Kerr,' I said to the manager. 'If you don't lend us the money I'll just go to the others.' You couldn't have seen him getting the papers to sign for dust."

"You'll be needing help, then."

"But not yours. We've advertised for an assistant. I want you to go on and do your A levels and go to university. To an English university. I want you to get out of here, for a while at least." She starts to cry then.

Harry can't go to her, he's watching the small, weeping figure in the armchair from far inside himself. And gradually the tears dry up and she dabs at her eyes with a handkerchief. "Foolishness, foolishness. What would your father say if he saw me? Is that agreed, then?"

"Yes."

"Right. I'd better get back into the shop. We were just putting up the Christmas decorations. You can come in and give us a hand when you're ready."

Strasbourg – All Saints' Day

HARRY HAS ANSWERED the phone already in his dream, but it keeps on ringing, hauling him up from sleep. When he lifts the handset it's Monsieur Bruckmann speaking French on the other end, and it takes Harry some time to adjust to what he is saying.

After lengthy consideration, the Frenchman says, and due consultation with his headmaster, it has been decided not to go ahead with the school partnership in the light of recent events. Mr Moore will understand. But that is no reason why their programme of sightseeing should be cancelled. He will pick Harry up at half past eight for the nine o'clock session in the Council of Europe.

Oh, no, says Harry, he would prefer to spend the day just looking around on his own, he has some shopping to do.

Shopping, says Monsieur Bruckmann, has he forgotten the shops are all shut today? It is All Saints', a national holiday, when all Alsatians tend their family graves and put lights on them. The only thing Harry can buy today is flowers. Perhaps Harry would prefer to see his model of the Snowdonia railway, complete with mountains and bad visibility, Monsieur Bruckmann suggests brightly, reverting to English.

Bad visibility? Harry queries.

Gauze in the valleys, Monsieur Bruckmann explains, and a

film of glue on the inside of the carriage windows, for the steamed-up effect.

The next time perhaps, says Harry, forgetting that there isn't going to be a next time. He wishes Monsieur Bruckmann well, and hangs up. He sits up at the edge of the bed, yawns, rubs his eyes. So that's where Marie's going today. To the family grave in Obernai. So what was all the fuss about? Is she scared her grandma will rise from the grave if I go with her? What was that other thing Bruckmann said?

He rings up Monsieur Bruckmann again.

"What do you mean, in the light of recent events?" he asks.

"Haven't you heard?"

"No."

"There was a big bomb in Ballyraine yesterday. It was on all the news. The town centre has been destroyed."

"Was anybody hurt?"

"Nobody was killed. But some people were taken to hospital."

"Thank you."

Harry rings off and dials his home number.

"Yes?" Jenny's sleepy voice.

"Are you all right?"

"Do you know what time it is?"

"Seven o'clock. The time you get up at anyway."

"Not on Hallowe'en I don't."

"OK. Sorry I rang up. And I don't want to know if you're all right or not."

"Christ, Harry. Are you talking about the bomb, or what?"

"Yes."

"Well, then, I'm all right."

"And otherwise?"

"All right, too."

"Anybody we know hurt?"

"No. But the windows are out. All over the estate. And the glaziers can't come until tomorrow. And it's raining, as usual. The council has dumped a load of plywood down at the corner for people to board up with in the meantime. But it's too heavy for me."

"And you can't think of anybody to help you?"

"Bastard."

"Maybe I could take an earlier plane."

No answer. *Come on, now it's your move.*

"Can you get away earlier?" she says finally.

"I'm finished here, more or less. Well, less."

"Didn't any of your plans work out?"

"The exchange has fallen through. Because of the bloody bomb."

"And what about your old girlfriend, did you see her?"

"I did happen to call in on her, yes. I thought I might as well. On the off-chance. How do you know about her?"

"You told me, of course. The very first time you took me home at Canterbury. It must have been just after we met. Don't you remember? After the Lindisfarne concert."

"No."

"You came up to my room and told me all about her. For hours on end. And I had a paper to write on *Germinal* for the next day."

"Was I drunk?"

"Oh, probably. How did it go?"

"We talked about old times."

Silence.

"Have you heard from William?"

"No."

"Jenny?"

"What?"

"Will we give it another try?"

"What do you think?"

"I think we should."

"Maybe we should."

"'Bye."

"'Bye."

Harry rings up Air France at Strasbourg airport. Yes, the girl says, there is a seat on the flight at 7 p.m. to London that evening, and they can change the booking at no extra cost. No, she is desolated, she can only reserve the booking till midday for him, he must finalise it within that time in person, here in Strasbourg airport, of course. Buses leave from the Place Kléber.

Fuck. Now he'll have to spend the morning making the booking, and there's no point in ringing Marie until he's sure he's got it.

The bus takes an interminably long time to get through Strasbourg. From his vantage-point above the crowded streets Harry looks down on carloads of bored-looking, sombrely dressed people in the front and bouquets of flowers in the back. As the journey drags on Harry is more and more tempted to jump off the bus at traffic-lights, but he doesn't have a clue where he is, and he keeps hoping the airport isn't much further away, and he sits on, watching the minutes tick by. It'll all work out. It just needs a bit of replanning. When things have quietened down at home on all fronts I'll get in touch with Monsieur Bruckmann again. Or with some other school in Strasbourg. The school Marie's daughter goes to, for example. They're all dead keen to have British partner schools. They always need accompanying persons on the exchange visits too. Marie could stay with me. With us?

Am I gone in the head completely?

But by the time Harry is back at the Place Kléber it's after two o'clock, and it takes him another quarter of an hour to get to her shop. He finds the name "Bonnardot" on a bell in the doorway at the side of the shop, but no one answers it. *Fuck, fuck, fuck.* He's missed her. He'll have to wait until she comes back. But what if she comes back too late? She might think six o'clock is plenty of time to be back for, if they're going out that evening, but Harry will have to be at the airport by that time. What if she goes to the old house in the Rue de la Paix to check up on things, or to tidy up? He stands looking into the window of the shop beside Marie's in indecision. A boutique with expensive, third-world handicrafts. African hunters in gangly ebony. China rhinos and crocodiles. What in the name of God were those huge knobbly things that looked like potatoes or sea-washed boulders? Ah, Buddhas bending over, burying their faces in anguish. Or bursting their guts laughing.

He sees the reflection of a taxi, and turns just in time to hail it. Three-quarters of an hour later they're inching their way through the streets of Obernai, which are clogged with tourists. Nothing seems familiar to Harry. It looks like the other villages he drove through yesterday with Marie. But today it all sets his teeth on edge: the neat houses with their abundant flowers, the roofs like witches' hats, something out of a Walt Disney cartoon. What kind of a fusspot would you have to be to keep your house looking like that? The tourists get on his nerves, too, stumbling off the pavement and into the taxi's way like blundering cows.

"Blow your horn," he says to the driver.

"Will you pay the fine?"

"Yes."

"What's the hurry? We'll get there. Everybody gets to the graveyard in the end."

Then Harry sees a sight he remembers at the far end of the village, the nun's head painted on the wall up the hill, and directs the driver up past the graveyard to the road to the house. He has imagined an old, empty, boarded-up house, with a rusty lock on the gates, and Marie's Twingo parked in the drive, but there's quite a bustle in the lane outside, with cars being parked, and people, carrying flowers again, coming and going. In the well-kept grounds inside Harry can see benches set out across the lawn. He has a moment of doubt whether this is the place at all, but there is no other house in the vicinity, and then he recognises the shutters on the upstairs windows, and sees the sign on the gate, *Maison de Retraite*. It's an old people's home. *Fuck, fuck, fuck*. Harry curses the impulse that made him take the taxi to Obernai. If he doesn't catch Marie at the graveyard at the bottom of the hill now the whole outing will be in vain.

The cemetery straggles round the red-brick church on three sides, dotted with huddles of people, mostly old women, bustling about the graves with an air of ownership. The light is failing now, too weak to recognise anybody except from close up, so he starts to move along the rows, looking for the name Fischer on the headstones. Some graves, of the recently deceased, presumably, are bathed in a sea of light from a host of candles, solitary flames burn on others, some are wells of darkness. The only sound is the crunch of gravel and the raucous squirts of water into cans. There is peace here, Harry can sense it at a remove from his own turmoil, like looking down at night from a plane at the lights in the countryside. He finds one older inscription, but it's for a Ludwig Fischer, and his wife Else; both died at the end of the last century. Maybe Marie's parents aren't buried here at all.

"Excuse me, I'm looking for the Fischer grave," he says to an old woman, who is working intently at a grave, bent over like a waitress setting an elaborate table.

She straightens up, clutching her back. "There are many Fischers here," she says.

"Marie Fischer's family. They lived up that hill."

"Ah, Maurice Fischer. The old people or the son?"

"The old people, I suppose. Actually I'm looking for Marie herself. I thought she might have come here today. Have you seen her?"

"They were here, but they might have gone." She looks past him. "The grave is over there, by the wall. Right in front of the tap."

Harry moves quickly in the direction she has shown him. He can see the tap, but there's nobody near it. *Damn.* He looks back at the gate. Nobody is moving towards it. He's probably just missed her. The taxi outside has gone, too. Harry has told the driver to come back in half an hour, and he's probably in some café. He feels like having a shouting fit. Since getting up he's been pushing the day in front of him rather than moving through it, and now it seems to have compacted into an impenetrable mass. *Not just the day, my whole life.* He walks quickly on to the grave. A black headstone, engraved with straightforward golden letters.

> Gustav Fischer   1885–1960
> Wilhelmina Fischer   1892–1982

That would be the English grandma.

> Maurice Fischer   1919–1984
> Johanna Fischer   1921–1985

There is a photograph of Marie's parents, framed below their names, younger than Harry remembers them. Mrs Fischer looks attractive, as if she is trying not to smile, her husband has that slightly forbidding look Harry recalls. They were probably younger then than I am now.

The only thing for it now is to get back to Strasbourg as quickly as possible. He nods to the photograph, and walks back towards the gates. The old woman is still poking and patting at the grave. She looks up as he passes. "Nobody there?" she asks.

"No."

She straightens up again with a sigh and looks at the far end of the cemetery. "No," she says. "They aren't down at the child's grave either."

"What child's grave?"

"Marie's child. The son. Down there at the side, where the children all are."

Harry starts off in that direction. He can see the graves are more makeshift here, wooden crosses mostly. But looming out of the darkness there's one made of the same black marble as the Fischer family grave. He slows down and then stops. *You can still get out of this, Harry Moore. You don't have to go down there. Go now, get in the taxi, go back to Strasbourg, nobody will ever be any the wiser, least of all you.* But he's walking again, moving faster, and then suddenly he breaks into a run. He has to know that it isn't true, and he's saying it, "It isn't true," again and again, even long after he can read the inscription:

Lucien Bonnardot 1969–1975

The taxi moves through the rolling fields at the foot of the Vosges mountains, the driver glancing wide-eyed from the rear-view mirror at Harry's face, racing as Harry has bidden him do.

But at each bend the road unfolds another stretch, expanding as though feeding on his multiplying thoughts.

Nobody's fault, the old woman at the graveyard had said. Tragedies happen. The cleaning-woman from the village coming in too late in the morning, in a hurry, leaving the gates open. The boy wobbling out on his tricycle, the postman in his van, driving too fast to be sure, like all the young ones, but not deserving of this.

The whole family heartbroken, they'd all doted on young Lucien, even the old witch of an English grandmother. For all the cursing she'd done that time with Marie being pregnant, and nobody knowing who the father was.

Terrible how Marie had blamed herself. All that time in the nerve clinic on Mont Sainte Odile with the nuns. But it is all so long ago, time cures all ills. Marie has got over it now. She comes every year, with her daughter and her former husband, such a nice man, they are separated now, such a pity, he was so good to her when she had her troubles, he married her when the boy was still alive although he wasn't the boy's father, everybody knew that, he was heartbroken, too, and he stayed with her when she was in the clinic, and then later, well, who knows what happens to marriages, it isn't like in my day, but they still make this family outing every year, the girl, too, always hanging on to her father.

A photograph of Lucien on the gravestone, enclosed in glass, flickering in the red light of the graveyard candle Harry held up to it. Hands are clasped around the boy's middle, holding him. Marie's. He's smiling up into the camera, to a trusted face. He's got Marie's dimples in his cheeks. And he's got the Moore eyes. Mine. Paddy's. For a moment I thought I was standing at Paddy's grave, where I've never stood. His arms are spread wide. He's going to be lifted up, to be cuddled. Marie is about to hand him over to the photographer. To her husband.

Harry sees Marie sitting over a photo album, picking the one for the grave. *How would you do that?* And then it's as if he's two persons, the one is sitting slumped forward in the back seat of the taxi now, hands over his face, sobbing, and the other is watching, and something inside him is numb and stale as old bread. That's right, Harry Moore, this other is saying. Do it now, and later, after you've seen Marie. Because when you say goodbye to her she's not to notice a thing. Because she's got most of hers done. She's through to the other side. And you didn't help her. And one thing is sure. She didn't want you to know about Lucien then, and she doesn't now.

"*Pardon*, Monsieur?"

Harry has said this last thing out loud.

"Nothing."

He sees them out of the taxi window before he's ready. They're crossing the square, heading towards the house where the shop and the flat are. A man in the middle, with a hint of an important, middle-aged swank to his walk, his daughter holding his arm and laughing at something he's said. At his far side, a bit apart but not much, Marie, in a black coat and hat, smiling across at the other two, breathtakingly beautiful.

A family, coming home from a day out.

He tells the driver to wait for him, gets out behind the three, and calls Marie. She turns, makes a few uncertain steps, then says something to the other two. The man has turned, too, his smile frozen on his face. He makes to move on, but the girl remains standing, looking back, still holding her father's arm. Marie walks on towards Harry, a hesitant smile on her face, and he moves towards her.

"I wasn't expecting you yet, Harry," she says, as she draws close and stops. "I was going to ring you later. My former husband is going to come up for a bit. It's a thing we do every year. It doesn't mean . . ."

"It's all right, Marie. I have to go earlier. I have to go very soon, as a matter of fact."

Her eyes are searching his face. "What's the matter, Harry? Something has happened, hasn't it?"

"A bomb at home."

"Oh, no."

"My wife isn't hurt, but still . . ."

"How soon do you have to go?"

"Now, more or less."

"Oh, God."

Suddenly they're caught up in the flotsam of a disbanded Hallowe'en parade, small vampires, devils, ghosts and Frankensteins straggling homeward. A boy, dressed in a white sheet, his face also made up white with black rings under the eyes, stretches out his hand towards Harry. "On veut . . ." Before he can finish he's yanked away by a bigger girl in a witch's costume. Keeping hold of his hand she crosses the street with him.

"Faites attention au trafic," Marie says to them, and the girl nods without turning round.

"And the other thing is," Harry says, "the exchange has fallen through."

"What about all your plans?"

"I don't know."

"I see. This is all very sudden. So you won't be coming back to Strasbourg."

"I don't know what to say. The whole thing has been such a mess-up. I feel like an absolute fool. I am an absolute fool."

"For going back to your wife? I don't think so."

"For coming to Strasbourg."

"For that, yes, maybe." She smiles at him. "A nice fool."

Up ahead the man says something to Marie's daughter, and she turns and walks on with him.

Marie turns to watch them, then turns back and says, in a low voice, "Well, do you see now that it was better for me to go home last night?"

"No."

"Oh, Harry. So how did you think it was going to end? When you were doing all your plotting and planning."

Harry shakes his head. "I'll write."

She smiles again. "Better not. You wrote me enough letters that time. Oh, that reminds me."

She opens her handbag, searches through it, and hands him an envelope.

"What's this?" Harry asks.

"You were saying yesterday how you never got a letter from me, and when I was back home I thought, that one I wrote came back to me after about half a year. I'd written my home address on the back, and I knew it had to be somewhere and I turned the place upside down looking for it until I found it. That's it. I was going to give it to you later."

"A letter from you. Oh, God."

"Well, it's not from me, exactly," Marie says. She shuts her handbag and shoulders it again. "It's from the girl I was then. To the boy you were. Care of Harry Moore. I take no responsibility for whatever's in it." It's addressed in girlish handwriting to 'Harry Moore, The House on the Hill, Dunbreaghy, Co. Donegal'. It should have been Port Braddan. The stamp says Arthur Guinness, 3d, and the postmark is Gaillimh. It's still sealed.

"It's ancient," Harry says.

"Just like us," says Marie.

They embrace then. One of them is trembling, or they both are.

"I was thinking of him today," she says then, when he can no longer see her face.

"Who?"

"Paddy. Do you think we could have saved him? If we'd paid more attention?"

"It wasn't anybody's fault." And Harry knows that's not what she's asked, and that she's not talking about Paddy, but there's no answer to her question for him to give. And she's pushing him gently away as if she realises that too. She's gone all quivery like an image in a breeze-rippled tarn, he's smiling and hoping she won't notice, and she reaches out and touches his arm, and then, just in time, she turns away, and walks quickly towards the man and the girl up ahead.

"There's a reading-lamp in the back of the seat if you want to open that," says the taxi driver. They're almost at the airport. Harry has been holding the envelope in the palm of his hand the whole time, looking at it.

"It's the only one I'm ever going to get," he says. "She wrote it thirty years ago."

The taxi driver shakes his head. "That's the post for you."

Harry switches the light on, opens the envelope, and reads.

> *Guess who!*
> *Pity this letter can't creep up behind you and cover your eyes with its hands. I'm missing you like mad, desperately, isn't that what you say? I feel it in my stomach, it's like being hungry all the time, only I'm not, I'm off my food completely. Is it the same with you?*

The only thing that makes this trip bearable is when I'm sitting in the back of the car and have peace to think about you. And make plans. Here's the latest: we both go to England to study in two years' time. Brilliant, don't you think? Even if we don't get to the same university we'll be able to see each other at weekends. And the best thing about it is it was my father's idea. He came up with it a couple of months ago, said it would improve my English and broaden my outlook. And Grandma, of course, was all for it.

Christmas should be OK, I just can't talk to my father at the minute because he's mad at me about my passport. I'll tell you all about it, it was a close thing!

1. You're not allowed to go to any hooleys until I come back.

2. You're especially not allowed to dance with that girl Foster who follows you with her calf-like eyes.

I'll have to stop soon. I want to get this letter to the letter-box without my father noticing, and they're still in the dining room downstairs while I'm writing this upstairs in this horrible hotel, looking out on a square. I can see the letter-box, it's beside a bus shelter where a couple are kissing. I wish it was us.

Every time we pass a boy on a bike when we're driving I pretend it's you. Sometimes I even think it is, that you've followed us down here, but of course it never is. I think of your face, when you're riding in front and you turn to see if I'm there and you smile.

Tomorrow we're starting back to Dunbreaghy. I'll probably be there before this letter is!

Love and kisses

Marie